Summer of

Summer of Enlightenment

CHERYL MILDENHALL

Black Lace novels are sexual fantasies.
In real life, make sure you practise safe sex.

First published in 1994 by
Black Lace
332 Ladbroke Grove
London
W10 5AH

Typeset by TW Typesetting, Plymouth, Devon
Printed and bound by
Cox & Wyman Ltd, Reading, Berks

ISBN 0 352 32937 8

Chapter One

She noticed him as soon as she entered the small café. A silky, dark head bent in studious concentration; strong, perfectly manicured hands lightly gripping the crisp pink paper of *The Financial Times*. He looked as though he was enjoying whatever it was he was reading, as though share prices and business take-overs were a language that he understood perfectly, one he was born to speak. Karin always admired that in a man.

It wasn't as though she lacked intelligence, far from it, always near the top of the class at school she had succeeded in shocking everyone who knew her by refusing a place at Oxford in favour of marrying the man of her dreams. At least she had thought he was at the time. She sighed inwardly, if only she'd known then what she knew now.

The man with the newspaper looked up, possibly feeling her eyes upon him, although now she was concentrating on her own inner thoughts not the delectable hunk of manhood her sparkling green eyes perceived. Coming back to the present she blushed, he certainly was attractive and it seemed the only free seat was at his table, what a promising day this was turning out to be!

'May I?'

She stood directly in front of him, her hand upon the

back of the empty chair. His voice in reply was like rich, dark honey tinged with an accent of indeterminable origin.

'Of course, feel free.'

The way he said the words, with an expansive wave of his hand but without even a hint of a smile, seemed to her like an open invitation to take much more than an empty seat at his table. Or perhaps that was her own wishful thinking. She glanced covertly at him over the top of the heavy card which bore the scant menu, noticing his attention had returned to his newspaper. He was definitely foreign, she decided, probably from the Mediterranean. His accent was definitely not French or Spanish but then perhaps he had lived in England for a long time. She loved the colour of his skin, lightly toasted yet creamy, similar to the colour of the milky coffee the waitress placed in front of her.

'Would you like anything to eat with that madam?' The unsmiling woman, pencil poised expectantly over her order pad, nodded curtly at the cup of coffee.

Hastily Karin returned her attention to the menu, a tight knot in the pit of her stomach seemed to have obliterated the hunger pangs she was feeling when she first entered the café. Still, she would regret it later if she didn't eat something now.

'I think I'll have a croissant with salmon and cream cheese.'

Her voice sounded strange to her own ears, dull and distorted as though she were swimming underwater. The man looked up, his deep blue eyes staring directly at her. Instantly she blushed again, making her feel so embarrassed that she reddened even more. His gaze was very unnerving, making her feel as gauche as a teenager. No, that was an unfair comparison, her own almost-teenage daughter Natalie would never behave so naïvely. It was a testament to her upbringing, Karin supposed, that her daughter was brimming over with self-confidence.

Not even the recent split between Karin and her errant

husband had fazed Natalie for very long, she soon stopped shadowing her mother's every move out of concern for her sanity and finally asked, glibly, if Karin minded if she spent the summer holiday in France with her ex-husband Colin's parents. Stunned and relieved all at the same time, Karin agreed, although she felt a little less pleased when her son, Chris, asked to spend the summer at his father's new home. Despite her anger with Colin she couldn't deny her son his request, particularly as at sixteen he had reached an exceptionally vulnerable age – no longer a child but not yet a man, he needed a father's influence, even if his father was an adulterous swine.

This left Karin alone for the first time in her adult life. Alone or free, depending on which way you looked at it. Being an optimist, Karin preferred to think of herself as being completely and utterly footloose and fancy-free, without a care in the world and a lot of lost time to make up for: especially in the sex department.

Thinking of sex automatically led her eyes back to the man seated opposite. With a jolt she realised that he had not stopped staring at her, the warmth of his steady gaze encompassing her like a lover's embrace. As she felt herself drowning in the shimmering blue pools of his irises, invisible fingers plucked at her nipples causing them to harden and swell beneath the thin fabric of her summer blouse, the tingling of her clitoris heralding an involuntary rush of warm moisture between her tightly crossed legs.

Too embarrassed to meet his eyes any longer, as though he could see the effect he was having on her body, she shifted uncomfortably on the hard, wooden seat and re-crossed her legs, momentarily enjoying the friction this caused to her sex-starved body parts and noticing the look of appreciation on his face as he glanced downward at her slim, lightly tanned limbs.

He made no move towards her, nor did he speak, yet she felt as though she were imprisoned by him. His contemplation of her pinning her to the chair so firmly that she was powerless to resist, her body glowing warmly under his visual caress. Not only was she unable to move, she couldn't even find her voice, all efforts to speak thwarted by a constriction in her throat that continued down the length of her body to the pit of her belly. Everything around them, the sights, sounds and smells of the café and its trade, melted into an indistinct blur of background noise. The two of them were all that existed, he tall, dark, sinister; she much smaller, blonde and open to a fault.

There was no way of knowing how long they remained like that, captor and captive, as silent and unmoving as the broken clock on the wall above the counter, yet in a split second the spell was broken. Shattered by the arrival of a harassed waitress at their table, anxious to clear their debris and they themselves out of the way to make room for the growing throng of weary shoppers and hungry office workers who crowded the small waiting area by the door. In a flash he had folded up his newspaper, picked up his briefcase and was on his feet, treating her to a curt nod before turning on his heel, heading for the door and out of her life, perhaps forever.

She felt like crying and cursed her stupidity and inexperience. She should have spoken, exchanged names, telephone numbers, something. Now their meeting would be consigned, like so many others, to her memory banks – at best as possible fantasy fodder for a later date. She stared hard at the table, willing away the actual tears which threatened to spill down her cheeks. Her croissant lay untouched upon the plate, the dregs of her coffee suddenly smelling foul. With a loud sniff she stood up and pushed back her chair, her legs feeling slightly unsteady as she made for the door. Suddenly she felt a hand upon her arm and turned quickly, hoping that somehow he had returned without her noticing, realising perhaps that he desperately needed to know who she was.

'We prefer it if our customers pay before they leave madam.'

It was her waitress. Even less friendly than before, her face bore a mixed expression of outrage and determination. Karin suddenly realised her mistake and, blushing yet again, scrabbled about in her purse for the right money, she was damned if she was going to give this harridan of a woman a tip.

She knew he would be long gone by the time she reached the street, yet it didn't stop her anxiously scanning the waves of people that surged past her in both directions. Straining her eyes to look further into the distance, she could not see a single tall, dark man. If only she had thought to look inside the numerous cars which edged the kerb despite the unspoken threat of double yellow lines, she would have realised that he had not lost sight of her. In fact, from behind the wheel of an ice-white BMW, his unblinking stare followed her every move.

Reluctantly she gave up any thoughts of pursuing him, common sense telling her there was nothing else to do but continue with her day as though nothing out of the ordinary had happened. Next on her agenda was a visit to the beauty salon for a sunbed session to top up her tan and perhaps, afterwards, an invigorating soak in the Jacuzzi. With a bit of luck her new friend, Rosalinde, would be there and they could enjoy another no-holds-barred heart to heart talk. It was only a few weeks earlier that she had first met Rosalinde at the salon but they had both shared so many intimate thoughts and feelings that Karin felt they were true kindred spirits, enjoying a much closer rapport than she experienced with her other older friends.

A quick glance around the bustling salon revealed no sign of Rosalinde. Karin wasn't unduly concerned, there was still plenty of time for her to put in an appearance before lunch, hardly a day went by when her friend didn't visit the salon for one treatment or another. With a shrug, Karin turned and announced her arrival with a careless wave to the receptionist who nodded and indicated that Karin should proceed straight up the stairs to the solarium. Once inside the stark little room she undressed quickly, pausing momentarily before stripping off her panties as well: no harm in displaying an all-over tan to any new lover who might happen along she reasoned.

The glass base of the sunbed felt cold and uncomfortably hard at first, prompting Karin to wonder, not for the first time, why she bothered to put herself through such agonies. It wasn't just the solarium sessions, or the leg waxing, or the eyebrow plucking and hair streaking sessions which she endured for the sake of vanity. Having recently been thrown, unceremoniously and against her will, back in the embarrasingly ageing mêlée of the dating pool she had embarked on a programme of exercise and general self-improvement, determined that in a few years hence she would greet her forties with a new body and a new life. Preferably one that included a lusty, tireless man who demonstrated his appreciation by providing her with plenty of great, multiple-orgasmic sex.

She hugged the fantasy to herself, her body growing instantly warm despite the fact that she had not yet switched on the sunbed. Almost without realising where her thoughts were leading she found her mind filled with the memory of the man in the café, now there was a man she could happily spend the rest of her life with. Handsome, virile, definitely sexy, with a gorgeously seductive voice, she didn't have to try too hard to imagine what it might be like to wake up and see his head on the pillow next to hers. With a wistful sigh she pulled the canopy over her, adjusted her goggles and set the timer. Immediately the fluorescent tubes came to life, suffusing her naked body with artificial sunlight and transporting her feverish imagination to golden Mediterranean beaches, populated by dozens of dark-haired, coffee-skinned men all eager to attend to her every physical need.

Absent-mindedly she allowed her hands to drift across her body, her fingers lightly brushed her pink tipped breasts, stimulating nipples which needed little encouragement to spring to life, provoking tantalising sensations to stir in the pit of her belly. Moaning slightly, she parted her legs, sweat mingling with her own juices to form a steady stream which trickled teasingly between her buttocks, moistening her vulva in readiness for the probing and caressing of her own fingers. Only half aware of her surroundings she concentrated on the image of the man in the café, now transported to lie beside her on hot sand and anoint her desperate, yearning body with oil, her flesh searing under the heat of his magic touch.

Totally at the mercy of her own feverish imagination, Karin experienced the very real sensation of burning granules of sand invading every crevice as she opened herself up to the lure of his probing gaze. Floundering helplessly in the depths of his azure eyes, she gave herself up to the exquisite torment of his hands upon her naked flesh as, slowly, deliberately, he touched her everywhere, no part of her remaining sacred or secret to the stimulating power of his caress. The fantasy continued unabated, growing in its intensity in tandem with the strength of sensation she felt within herself until she came upon a stumbling block. Frustratingly she found that she couldn't envisage him naked, couldn't imagine the appearance or dimensions of his penis.

True, she didn't have much to go on in that department but she had seen countless images of naked men, on television and in magazines, and she was renowned for her creativity and highly fertile imagination. Surely she could conjure up a cock?

Despite her best efforts, Karin was forced to concede defeat or lose the fantasy entirely. The man would have to remain cockless for now, his crotch a blurred territory full of promise but little else. Strangely she felt as though he had let her down when she most needed him and, as a result, her orgasm was merely inevitable rather than wonderful.

Eventually she drifted off into a contented sleep that,

fortunately, filled her head with positive dreams full of hope and men and sex, although not necessarily in that order. Fragments of the dreams remained with her as she slowly awoke, re-entering reality within minutes of the sunbed reaching the end of its allotted time, and they succeeded in invigorating her, leaving her feeling refreshed and eager to embrace the rest of the day.

Downstairs in the main salon Rosalinde was waiting for her and smiled knowingly as Karin approached, her face glowing and content – Karin had already admitted to her friend that she particularly enjoyed a solitary session of self-gratification as she toasted herself on the sunbed, believing it was something to do with the irresistible combination of nakedness and heat.

'Rosalinde, hi, have you got time for coffee and a chat?'

Tucking a dark strand of silken, newly washed hair behind her ear the older woman looked at her watch and smiled apologetically.

'I'm sorry Karin, I'm running late today, Nicolai woke with a raging erection and his secretary's on maternity leave.'

'Nothing to do with Nicolai I hope,' Karin responded drily, wondering how this otherwise intelligent woman could cope with a husband who paraded his affairs in front of all and sundry.

At least she had sent Colin packing the moment he finally broke down and confessed that he'd been seeing another woman. At the time she had pretended to be shocked and amazed, although in reality she had known for months. Some of her friends thought she had been too harsh, or to hasty, asserting self-righteously that she should have at least given Colin a second chance. But, as far as she was concerned, the adultery was not his first transgression, merely the final straw in a marriage that had been long dead. It was kill or be killed and she had no intention of laying down and playing dead, there was too much life still to live and far too much spark left within her for that.

Now Rosalinde was looking at her with a questioning look in her eyes, 'Is there anything the matter, did you want to discuss something important?'

'Oh, sorry Rosalinde I was miles away, thinking about Colin.'

The older woman was immediately contrite, feeling guilty at the way she'd raved on about Nicolai's sexual appetites when Karin was obviously missing having a man in her bed. She checked her watch again.

'Look I can call and say I'll be a little late if you need to talk.'

Karin shook her head, smiling, she longed to tell her friend about the man she had met in the café but could see she was anxious to be off.

'No, really Rosalinde, it's very kind of you to offer but it'll keep.'

Rosalinde was intrigued and obviously torn between not wishing to be late for her appointment and wanting to hear her friend's news, they hadn't had the opportunity to talk properly for almost a whole week.

'Look, call me at home later, if I'm not there leave a message and I'll call you,' snapping shut her Gucci bag Rosalinde added, 'I could do with a good gossip.'

Despite her insistence that she leave, Karin couldn't help feeling deflated and more than a little envious as she watched Rosalinde climb into her dark green Jaguar convertible. Her friend was so *together*, she mused. Although Rosalinde was several years older than herself she couldn't help admiring the woman's elegant beauty and her innate good taste, from the tips of her perfectly manicured fingers to the toes of her immaculately shod feet she was the image of refined perfection and, despite plenty of probing, Karin had still not managed to uncover a single blot on her impeccable psyche.

Okay, perhaps she wasn't exactly happily married but she was content and her husband was rich and undemanding enough for Rosalinde to live the kind of semi-independent life she clearly enjoyed. In the few weeks that Karin had come to know her, she had become increasingly intrigued by Rosalinde's references to her husband. It seemed he was a wolf in wolf's clothing and that no woman was safe when he was around. She shivered, repelled yet excited at the prospect of perhaps meeting him one day. Of course, she would support her friend and hate him on sight, such an outright louse deserved to be shunned by any woman who had her wits about her.

Smiling to herself at the thought of teaching Rosalinde's mysterious husband a lesson Karin made her way to the Jacuzzi, determined to spend the rest of the day pampering herself just as she had planned. First a soak, then a little lunch followed by some shopping. Perhaps she would treat herself to some new underwear to show off her newly tightened, tanned and streamlined body.

The water was warm and inviting, its invigorating bubbles agitating around her like champagne. She lay back, luxuriating in the pleasurable sensations that the foaming water created upon her sex-conscious body. In a few short weeks she had turned her back on wifedom and motherhood, becoming instead a voluptuous, desirable woman, in her prime and ready to satisfy and be satisfied by as many men as she could handle. A teenage virgin when she had first met Colin, she found herself longing to re-lose her cherry, preferably to someone handsome and exciting. Unfortunately, aside from being propositioned by a couple of Colin's leery, well-married and less than attractive *friends* she had not met a single man with whom she could contemplate having a sexual relationship.

Suddenly she sat upright, realisation bringing her to her senses at long last. That was it, her problem was that she kept thinking in terms of a relationship when she should be concentrating on SEX! Physical encounters were what she needed, not another husband or even a lover, just downright dirty, unfettered, roll in the hay type sex. It seemed obvious now she had thought it but up until this moment her life had felt empty, directionless; now she felt like a woman with a purpose.

With a whoop of delight she ducked under the water then rose like a dripping siren, voluptuous and alive to the possibilities of life. The noise attracted the attention of one of the salon's assistants, a nice girl in her early twenties and Karin smiled as she popped her heard around the door.

'Are you all right madam?' Her fresh, lively face was muted with genuine concern.

'I'm fine, really, I was just having a funny moment.'

The girl looked uncertain but, satisfied that there was nothing seriously wrong with Karin, apologised for disturbing her and closed the door again. Once she was certain that the girl had gone, Karin climbed out of the Jacuzzi and padded over to the door. As quietly as she could she pushed the bolt into its keeper. There was something about the irresistible combination of nakedness and warm, bubbling water . . .

Karin always found it much easier to achieve a self-induced orgasm in a Jacuzzi than almost anywhere else. Apart from the fact that the warmth and the motion of the water was extremely relaxing, she had discovered that by sitting directly on top of one of the many water-jets she could achieve a staggering climax in a matter of seconds without having to lift a finger, so to speak.

This time she found the image of the man in the café had already receded in her memory and decided that she should concentrate on a few 'old favourites' from her extensive collection of private fantasies – mainly erotic snippets gleaned from literature and films. Easing herself into an arousing position she closed her eyes, allowing herself to wallow in the silence and the warmth until eventually the first of her fantasies began to unfold:

She was at a party, a very select party of very important men. Clad only in a white lace basque and stockings she was serving them with food and drink. Some of the guests appeared not to notice her, others eyed her appreciatively, touching her whenever she came near them. Each time she bent over the table to refresh a glass of wine one of them would snake a hand between her legs, rubbing and probing her as she stretched further across the table top. At the same time someone on the other side of the table would reach out to grab her breasts as they emerged from the ineffective constraints of the delicate lace. Their manipulations were all very different, some gentle, some more determined, yet each a fraction more exciting, more stimulating than before.

She frowned slightly, it was a good fantasy but not the one she really wanted to use today. Shifting slightly so that her vagina was directly over the water-jet she let her mind change channel.

In this scene she was seated on a sofa, fully clothed. In front of her stood a young woman holding a riding-crop. In low, controlled tones she spoke.

'I know you've been sleeping with my boyfriend you bitch,' she moved closer. 'Don't try to deny it, he's already admitted it, he said you have a great body.' The woman waved the crop around agitatedly, 'Take off your clothes.'

Karin squirmed excitedly as the water pulsated against her aroused flesh but from the depths of her fantasy she spoke quietly, hesitatingly, 'Please . . . I . . .'

'Don't bother to argue with me, bitch. Just do it!'

Conscious of the woman's eyes upon her and with mounting excitement, she rose and stripped off her clothes. The woman nodded approvingly.

'He was right, you do have a fantastic body.' She reached with the tip of the crop and stroked it across Karin's naked breasts, 'Great tits.'

As a real-life response, Karin used her free hand to stroke her nipples as they swelled and hardened under the fantasy sensation of hardened leather, sending tantalising thrills of excitement coursing down her body to meet and expand within the pulsating nub of her clitoris. Such exquisite pleasure was almost unbearable, in a matter of minutes she had reached the point of no return.

Using the leather-tipped end of the whip, the young woman traced a meandering course from Karin's breasts, across her stomach and thighs to the silken vee of her pubis. Nudging her legs apart, the tip of it slid between her labia, the loop of cold leather creating an explosive combination of fear and lust that almost drove her to the edge of insanity. Her climax was instantaneous.

Gradually the waves of pleasure ebbed away, leaving her floating limply in the water, her limbs and lower body feeling leaden yet totally relaxed. A contented smile drifted across her face, it was the strangest of fantasies but one that was guaranteed to work every time. For a while she lay in the water, her mind almost devoid of thought. She didn't have a bad life at all, she had a comfortable home, friends, family and enough money to make the prospect of embarking on a career outside the home one of choice rather than necessity.

No doubt she would start to think about earning her own living in a few months' time but for the remainder of the summer she intended to concentrate on finding out a bit more about herself – particularly where her physical self was concerned, there was such a lot she still had to learn. Karin grinned to herself, reminded of a particular slogan that girls had proudly sported on T-shirts and bumper stickers about ten years earlier, 'So Many Men – So Little Time', it just about summed up the way she was feeling. With renewed determination she climbed out of the water, if she was going to start learning all she could about grown-up sex she'd better get started right away.

Chapter Two

As soon as she arrived home, laden with carrier bags of new clothes and underwear, Karin made a pot of tea and settled down in an armchair with the telephone, preparing to call Rosalinde and share the deliciousness of her recent encounter with the man in the café and her subsequent decision to totally gratify her sexual self. Disappointingly, the telephone simply rang and rang, the monotonous tone gradually dissolving her enthusiasm. She was just about to hang up when her call was finally answered by the surly voice of a man who introduced himself as the gardener. Sullenly refusing to take a message, he told Karin that Rosalinde had gone away for a couple of days.

'Madam will be back on Friday, around three. Why don't you try her then?'

Karin, who couldn't help noticing a distinct trace of sarcasm in his voice as he uttered the word 'madam', reluctantly agreed. It was frustrating that there was nothing else she could do for the time being, the intensity of her recent experience was already beginning to fade and, as it was only Monday, she felt it would be a strain to try and maintain the freshness of her news for four more days. And who the hell did that gardener think he was, there was no need for him to be so offensive? Next time she saw her friend she would suggest that she have a harsh word with the 'hired help'.

Slightly miffed, she sipped her tea and turned her mind inward once more to the subject that occupied most of her thoughts and dreams at the moment. Tame though it may have been by the standards of a lot of women her age, as far as Karin was concerned her encounter with the handsome man in the café was a turning point. Not only had his interest made her feel desirable but it had succeeded in opening her eyes to the reality of being a single woman once again. She felt reborn, on the brink of self-knowledge. Suddenly, she had discovered that there were a thousand new experiences out there in the big wide world just waiting for her to grasp them with both hands, and she intended to try them all.

It was frustrating that Rosalinde had gone away so unexpectedly. She wanted to tell the world of her newly discovered liberation, to tear off her clothes and run down the street laughing like a madwoman, then shout it from the rooftops. She yearned to share the thoughts and feelings swirling around inside her with someone who would truly appreciate the aesthetics of such a realisation, who would understand the significance of being liberated in this way. But who else could she talk to who was that laid back? It was a real quandary and it made her realise how much she had already changed.

She was no longer the old Karin, devoted wife and mother of two. Almost overnight, it seemed, she had evolved into footloose and fancy-free Karin, woman of the world. She giggled to herself at the thought, perhaps that was a bit of an exaggeration but there was no doubt she was fast leaving her old life behind. The old Karin could have called any number of girlfriends, knowing each of them would revel in such soul-baring conversation. But she also recognised that her old friendships were basically shallow and therefore their camaraderie would surely be short-lived. A fundamental lack of real understanding, or simply blatant jealousy, would doubtless compel them to denigrate he as soon as her back was turned.

She thought hard. A close relative should have been an obvious choice of confidante but, as far as this particular situation was concerned, her sister and mother were right out. Knowing them as she did, they would probably rush to call Colin as soon as they could and he, being typically male and therefore trapped securely in the vice of double standards, would automatically resort to branding her a whore and an unfit mother. She considered her dilemma carefully, always returning to the same conclusion. Although the length of their friendship could be counted in weeks rather than years, the only person she could really trust and who would understand totally without judging her, was Rosalinde.

The week dragged by interminably, broken only by her visits to the salon for her tanning sessions and various other treatments so that, by the time she finally spoke to Rosalinde, Karin had managed to work herself into a dreadful state of feverish excitement. Her sexual self had lain dormant for too long and now she was just starting to appreciate the potential experiences that lay ahead of her. Thank God she hadn't left it too late, sleeping with Colin for all those years had not taught her that much she now realised.

There was so much to be enjoyed, so many possibilities, such a varied choice of men. She was like a kid let loose in a sweet shop and she intended to gorge herself until fully satiated, then glut herself some more. Her encounter in the café had been a mere appetiser, albeit a very tasty one, and for now the fantasy of that particular man would have to suffice until a real sexual encounter took its place.

When Karin finally managed to speak to Rosalinde, her friend's immediate response was to invite Karin to her home.

'The garden's looking so lovely, we must have a proper old-fashioned high tea on the lawn. You can bare all as soon as you get here,' Rosalinde added enthusiastically, not knowing she had inadvertently employed a particularly prophetic turn of phrase.

From the address Rosalinde gave her, Karin had been able to tell immediately that she lived in a fairly exclusive area but had not expected it to be a property which was little short of a stately home. Lost in awe, Karin stared at the building before her, like a golden monolith, its broad, Costwold stone façade seemed to absorb the penetrating rays of the hot sun. She imagined the interior to be airy and cool, warmed only by Rosalinde's innate good taste in furnishings and a roaring log fire on winters' evenings. Briefly, she contemplated what it would be like to make love in front of an open fire. It was a symptom of her current state, it seemed, to find her thoughts veering automatically to the sexual possibilities of every situation. Rosalinde's voice interrupted her train of thought.

'The estate agent described it as a "gentleman's residence" when we bought it, I didn't want to disappoint them by telling them Nicolai's no gentleman.'

She guided Karin to a gate between the house and the garage block, the narrow path meandered through a substantial herb garden at the side of the house, finally ending at a wide expanse of lawn.

'I am right in thinking only you and Nicolai live here aren't I?' Karin asked, feeling slightly shocked that just two people should occupy so much space.

Rosalinde nodded, 'That's right, although the apartment over the garage is occupied by Madge and Bert,' she led the way across the lawn to a broad patio, spanning the width of the house.

'Madge is a treasure, she cooks and manages the house while Bert keeps Nicolai's car well tuned and helps out with odd jobs.'

Under a gaily striped canopy a table was laid for tea, it all looked too perfect to be true.

Rosalinde invited Karin to sit down, 'They're a nice couple, middle-aged and very sensible. Even Nicolai is forced to mind his manners when Madge is around.'

At the mention of good manners, Karin was reminded

of her abortive telephone call to Rosalinde earlier in the week.

'That obviously wasn't Bert who answered the phone the other day when I rang,' said Karin grimly. 'Whoever he was, he was very rude, said he was the gardener.'

'Oh yes,' Rosalinde coloured slightly, 'that would be Jon, he does tend to the gardens several times a week and sometimes acts as Nicolai's chauffeur.'

She looked thoughtful, 'I apologise if he upset you Karin, he's rude all right but not usually in the way you mean.'

Before Karin had the opportunity to ask Rosalinde what she meant by that remark, they were interrupted by a pleasant-looking older woman pushing a heavily laden tea trolley. No doubt this is the remarkable Madge, thought Karin, admiring anyone who had the ability to make the infamous Nicolai toe the line.

'Tea's all ready to be served madam, would you like anything else before I go home and start on me soaps.'

'No, that's fine, thank you Madge.'

Rosalinde turned to Karin and spoke under her breath, 'She's mad about soap operas, watches them all. She even tapes the daytime ones and then spends most of the evening catching up.'

'I used to like *Dallas*,' Karin admitted.

'Shh,' Rosalinde looked at her in mock horror. 'Whatever you do don't let Madge hear you, she'll start reminiscing over every episode from day one,' she warned, laughing. 'Myself, I prefer something a little more romantic, like *9 ½ Weeks*!'

The spread that Madge had prepared was delicious and the two women sat for well over an hour, eating thinly cut cucumber sandwiches and three different kinds of cake, drinking iced tea and relishing every detail of Karin's liberation of mind and body. There was certainly a close association between food and sex. At first Karin felt hesitant about describing her more intimate thoughts and feelings but after a little while she began to relax considerably, finding it remarkably easy to open up to Rosalinde who proved to be an excellent and appreciative listener.

Eventually, there was a lull in the conversation, both women lapsing into silence, staring out across the lush sun-drenched gardens, each lost in their own private thoughts. Karin noticed how warm the day still was despite the fact that soon it would be edging its way gradually into evening. Satisfied by an excellent meal, she began to feel pleasantly drowsy and was only roused from her brief siesta by the muted but insistent ringing of the telephone. As soon as she heard it, Rosalinde immediately jumped up. Going inside the house to answer it, she returned a few minutes later, frowning.

'That was Nicolai,' she explained. 'Apparently he's left some important papers on his desk and wants me to run them over to his office.

Karin started to rise from her chair but Rosalinde put out her hand as if to stop her.

'If you don't mind waiting I'll only be about twenty minutes, please feel free to have a look around the place while I'm gone.'

Karin was more than happy to wait, she wasn't in any particular hurry to go home to an empty house and was dying to explore Rosalinde's *mansion*.

'Don't worry about me, Rosalinde, I'll be fine, take as long as you need.'

As soon as her friend had left she stood up slowly and stretched, glancing briefly around her before stepping hesitantly inside the cool hallway. The interior of the house was everything she had expected and more besides. A comfortable looking sitting room and dining room were visible to her left and right and a narrow passage with more doors off led to the kitchen. An imposing staircase beckoned and she climbed, hesitantly at first, then more purposefully. It was immediately apparent that Rosalinde and Nicolai had separate bedrooms. Of all the closed door off the landing his was behind the first door she tried.

Typically masculine, the main bedroom and attached

dressing room were decorated throughout with wood panelling, the soft furnishings in sombre colours, predominantly navy and burgundy. Surprisingly, compared with the almost unnatural neatness of the rest of the house, the bed was still unmade and some magazines littered the floor. Automatically, she bent to pick them up, turning the pages she saw they were business journals. She felt strangely surprised by this, for some reason she had expected the pages to be filled with pictures of nude models, posing provocatively with pursed lips and wide-open legs. The only thing crude about these publications were the oil prices. Dropping the magazines onto the bed, she decided to continue with her exploration. Pausing to peer around the next door she encountered a luxurious bathroom in deep blue, complete with double-sized bath, separate shower, basin, lavatory and bidet. The bathroom also obviously doubled as a gym, as it was equipped with a stationary cycle and a rowing machine as well as a selection of dumb-bells and an exercise bench.

She was beginning to formulate a picture of Nicolai in her mind and found herself intrigued by this mysterious character. From all Rosalinde had said about him, she had initially envisaged him as a sad old man in the midst of a mid-life crisis, his days spent chasing young women around his office as though in a cheap blue movie. Now she had been given the opportunity to glimpse other facets of his character, for instance, the rich, successful business man who took great care of his body and his appearance.

Thoughtfully retracing her steps back to his bedroom, she stepped into the vast dressing room. Her new perception of him was totally vindicated by the contents of the room which boasted rack upon rack of stylish Italian suits and shirts, lining three of the four walls. The other was given to floor to ceiling shelving stocked with hundreds of pairs of shoes. She had built up a pretty concise image of the man in her head, now she was desperate to know what he actually looked like. Retracing her steps into the bedroom she hunted around for a photograph of him but to no avail. Perhaps, despite everything she said about him, Rosalinde kept one of him in her room?

If she had been impressed with Nicolai's suite of rooms, then Rosalinde's was pure heaven. The bedroom itself was huge, bright and airy, complete with *en suite* bathroom. A vast range of closets lined one whole wall and, on the opposite wall, two sets of sliding glass doors opened out onto a wide balcony which ran the full length of the room. Stepping right inside, Karin immediately noticed that the bedroom was similar to Nicolai's in size and layout but without the separate dressing room. This time the room was dominated by a huge, pale cream satin-covered bed, about eight feet square, above which was a mirrored ceiling. It was pure Hollywood and strangely at odds with Rosalinde's usual air of understated elegance. Karin felt a slight tremor of unease, there were a few things about Rosalinde and Nicolai Andreas that definitely didn't add up.

Pausing only to glance around for the elusive photograph of Nicolai, she crossed the room and stepped outside onto the balcony. Below her, almost as far as the eye could see, stretched well-tended lawns and flower borders. She inhaled deeply, the rich scent of early summer blooms mingling seductively with the sweetness of freshly cut grass. She was just about to turn around and go back inside the bedroom when, out of the corner of her eye, she caught a glimpse of the most beautiful man she had ever seen.

If she had simply been shown a photograph of him she would have stated, quite categorically, that he was not her type but, standing there on the balcony in such fairytale surroundings, he seemed to her to be perfection in male form. From her vantage point she watched intently as he came back into full view. Striding across the lawn towards the house, she saw quite clearly he was in his mid to late twenties, about five feet ten, brown as a berry and very well built. As he turned to tend to a perfectly box-cut privet hedge which ran around the perimeter of a small rose garden she noticed, with a gasp of surprise, that his untamed mane of tawny hair streaked with sun-bleached blond, fell well below his shoulders. All he wore was a pair of frayed denim shorts, white sneakers and baseball cap to match.

He must have felt her eyes upon him as, at that moment, he turned around, looked upward in her direction and waved. She started to raise her hand in reply, then stopped, realising that this *person* was probably the ignorant oaf who had answered Rosalinde's telephone the other day when she had called. With a toss of her head she turned on her heel and returned to the bedroom. Back inside the house she realised how stifling the air had become and was relieved to see a small electric fan by the bedside. Reaching out to switch it on, she was suddenly startled by the sound of the telephone. Immediately she noticed an extension phone on the table right next to her, it jangled insistently. Hesitating at first until it became apparent that no one else was going to answer it, she cautiously picked up the receiver.

'Hello, the Andreas residence.'

She spoke hesitantly and it was a relief to hear Rosalinde's voice on the other end of the line.

'Karin, hi, you're going to hate me but I'm going to be held up.'

She thought Rosalinde sounded out of breath.

'The damn car's overheated and I just about made it to Nicolai's office before the bloody thing conked out. Bert is going to come out and have a look at it but I don't know how long it will take. Can you wait at the house for me, watch TV or something, then we can have supper together when I get back?'

Relieved at not having to cut her visit short and spend the evening alone, Karin readily agreed.

'No problem, I'll wait.' Then a thought occurred to her, 'Do you mind if I have a little nap though, I feel absolutely exhausted.'

'No, feel free, use my room, do what you like, I'll be back as soon as I can.'

As soon as she replaced the receiver, Karin switched

on the electric fan then lay down on the bed. Although the coverlet was cool her clothes felt sticky and rumpled, hesitating for just a second she shrugged and stripped off her dress. Underneath she wore peach satin cami-knickers. They were the result of a promise she had made to herself the day of her revelation in the Jacuzzi, namely that from that day forth she would always wear attractive underwear.

'At least this way I'll still look sexy if I get knocked down by a bus,' she laughed to her reflection as she lay down on the bed.

In no time at all she relaxed into a dreamy state, her subconscious enjoying a series of erotic images which flickered back and forth from the subtle to the more explicit. From under the filmy cover of sleep her body responded to the sexual nuances of each scene, stimulated beyond the limits of her wakeful experiences. Blissfully unaware of her own reactions, she rolled onto her stomach, writhing against the cool satin coverlet, moaning incoherently. Making love to a shadowy figure, she spread her legs wide, grinding her hips into the bed. This was how Jon found her when he climbed up the ladder to the balcony to water the pot plants.

Naturally, being his master's eyes when he wasn't present, Jon hadn't missed her arrival at the house. Overawed by the surroundings at first she had later relaxed and allowed herself to sprawl unselfconsciously in a chair on the patio, looking blonde and beautiful in a hot and rumpled sort of way. He realised that she was past the first flush of youth, but then he prefered *real* women, not silly young girls who worried about spots. Thankfully, older women didn't act like that. Instead of viewing him as a potential husband and father of their children they enjoyed sex for sex's sake, there were no ulterior motives, no deals being struck – 'I'll let you do this if you promise to love me forever' – and once they had stopped panicking about silly, inconsequential things like imaginary lumps and bumps, cellulite and stretch marks, they would give themselves wantonly, abandoning themselves to him and his ability to give them pleasure.

Unbeknown to the two women, he had overheard a good part of their conversation and had almost climaxed there and then as Karin described to Rosalinde, in graphic detail, her physical frustration and newly discovered desires. So engrossed in Karin's revelations they hadn't noticed him eavesdropping behind the hedge at the side of the house but he had not missed a thing. Enthralled, he had watched the way Karin's eyes had widened and sparkled as she described her meeting with the man in the café. And, with an urgent stirring in his loins he had witnessed how, through the thin material of her dress, her breasts swelled and her nipples hardened as she reached the climax, so to speak, of her disclosures.

And now, here in Rosalinde's bedroom, he again felt privileged to watch her enacting a private fantasy. Drenched in perspiration, the peach material clung wetly to her body, working its way into every crevice as she thrashed and squirmed upon the bed. Jon walked over to where she lay. Tentatively, he reached out his right hand, stroking the smooth, taut mounds of her buttocks, the material slipped easily into the cleft between them but still she did not awaken, continuing to toss her head from side to side, mouthing indistinguishable words.

Suddenly, without warning, she shouted out and turned over completely, staring right at him. In panic, his first instinct was to dart out of the room but it soon became apparent, to his intense relief, that she was still dreaming. Clamping her eyes shut once more, she started to moan. He let out an almost imperceptible sigh of elation, it was okay, he could breathe again. Despite his nervousness at being caught out he couldn't resist the opportunity to inspect her at close quarters, sweeping his eyes over her body he was incredibly aroused by what he saw. Her long blonde hair was tousled, curling damply around her face and neck and, although silent now, her lips pouted slightly as though she was annoyed about something. Moving his eyes further downwards he noticed that her nipples, which had almost managed to escape the confines of her underwear, were hard and deeply pink, like raspberries. Arching her back now, her full breasts thrust against the thin fabric pulling it taut against her crotch, clearly outlining her labia and mound of pubic hair.

Feeling bolder but not wishing to wake her just yet, Jon let his fingers drift gently over her breasts, encircling each nipple slowly. Using the thumb and forefinger of each hand he tugged slightly on them, rubbing them gently, stimulating the tight buds until they swelled to twice their previous size. Then his fingers continued their journey south, smoothing the silky material over her ribcage, the gentle swell of her belly, then down still further to linger on the mound of her pubis, feeling the moist heat emanating from her womanhood. Carefully, stealthily, he unhooked the crotch of her camiknickers, breathing in sharply as his fingers grazed her labia. Tentatively he peeled back the peachsilk to reveal his prize, silk upon silk, the pink satin skin oozed a glorious muskiness that made him long to slake his thirst with her juices.

Languidly, she awoke, floating between her dream-state and reality, yet barely able to distinguish between the two. Carelessly, she acknowledged the sensation of an unfamiliar touch upon her skin. Aware that she had awoken, yet not daring to look at her face, he concentrated all his attention on her body, moving the fingers of his left hand frustratingly slowly across her breasts whilst insinuating his right hand into the hot, moist crevice between her legs. Lost in the hypnotic trance of fantasy, she ground her hips, writhing against his expert fingers. Her eyes drifted open, slowly, recognising the tawny hair which brushed her face as he bent his head to lick her nipples but not recalling exactly who owned such a fine mane. Then, suddenly, she exploded, not with passion but with fury as she realised who he was.

'You,' she spluttered, 'how dare you.'

'Don't give me that,' his hazy sea-green eyes held hers disconcertingly, 'you were loving every minute of it.'

She tried, unsuccessfully, to glare at him. He was right of course, she had been lost in the very depths of pleasure. In close-up he was even more good-looking, with high cheekbones and a wide, generous mouth that twitched endearingly at the corners as he stifled a grin. Which was what he was trying to do now.

'You were very rude on the 'phone the other day,' she countered, realising she sounded petulant, but not wishing to let him off that lightly.

'Shut up and take that thing off.'

He ran his eyes slowly down her body and, ignoring her protestations, pulled down the straps of her camisole in one swift movement, exposing her breasts completely to his insolent gaze. There was a simultaneous sharp intake of breath from both of them, then in one deft movement he ripped the flimsy material from her body. The very act itself made her come instantly and she felt the wetness of her own orgasm flow down her legs. Pausing only for a brief moment to remove his own clothes, Jon ordered her to spread her legs. Without considering the possibility of refusing, Karin did as he asked, flinching under his probing stare. Her clitoris throbbed agonisingly as she opened her legs wider still, anxious now to feel his hands upon her burning skin. Using the fingers of both hands he gently parted her labia, the coolness of his touch being immediately replaced by the heat of his tongue as he teased her to the point of a second climax. At the last moment he moved his head, skilfully stimulating her with his fingers instead, so that he could watch the expression on her face as she came.

From that point on he never took his eyes from hers as he probed her with his fingers until he was satisfied that she was thoroughly satiated. Rolling over her onto his back, he took her hands, placing them firmly around his cock.

'My turn now,' he grinned at her, putting his hands

behind his head and making himself more comfortable on the bed.

Karin felt awkward, she had always felt less than expert at stimulating Colin and he had never let her forget it. Tentatively, she moved her hands up and down this unfamiliar shaft, instinctively tightening her grip as he began to moan. Emboldened, she positioned herself over his groin, her hair fanning out over his thighs and stomach as she bent her head and touched the end of his throbbing penis with her lips.

'Aahh,' Jon wound his fingers through her hair, trying to force her mouth over his glans.

Recognising that she was the one calling the shots now, she resisted, instead using her tongue around the side and base to tease and stimulate him to the point of climax. A small trickle of semen was her cue to stop what she was doing, she wasn't brave enough yet to swallow another man's come.

She had had enough of foreplay. Raising her head she stared him straight in the eye, 'Take me.'

He needed no further invitation, in a split second he had flung her onto her back and straddled her. Eager for him, she wrapped her legs around his waist, pulling him into her. He thrust deeply, rhythmically, stimulating a place deep within her that she never knew existed before. Urging her hips higher, her legs wider, she gazed at him, spellbound with lust. He truly was a magnificent specimen, totally without pretence or artifice. With Jon what you saw was what you got, and she was getting it all. Oooh, she was going to come. Twice more he slammed into her, a look of intense concentration on his face. He felt her vaginal muscles contract forcefully, she was about to come, now so could he.

When Rosalinde finally returned home several hours later she found her new friend and her gardener soaping each other down in the shower. Making a tactical and somewhat hasty retreat, she couldn't help envying Karin her new-found freedom. For all her insistence to the contrary, life with Nicolai was empty and shallow. She had it all, except the one thing she craved the most, a real relationship.

'Well, at least you didn't allow boredom to creep in while I was out,' mused Rosalinde sardonically when Karin, looking totally wanton, finally put in an appearance downstairs.

She had the grace to blush, 'No, just the gardener.'

Gratefully, she took a long draught from the white wine spritzer that Rosalinde had thoughtfully prepared for her and then, in gales of laughter, added, 'And about five times altogether!'

Chapter Three

By the time she finally left Rosalinde's house the sun was beginning to go down and a slight chill had crept into the evening air. Night fell quickly in the country and, uneasy about driving down unfamiliar lanes in the dark, she headed straight for the bright lights of the motorway, opting to take the less scenic but more direct route home. Feeling satisfied, she smiled at her reflection in the rear-view mirror, noting with pleasure how her skin glowed and her eyes sparkled. This was, without doubt, the best she'd felt in a long, long time and there were no two ways about it, Jon's performance that afternoon had been truly impressive, most men would think themselves lucky to have half his stamina.

But that was the key difference, or so it seemed to her. Jon was substantially younger than her ex-husband, was it possible to find the same enjoyment and tirelessness in someone her own age? The last thing she wanted was to live out her days as a pitiful old hag chasing around after young gigolos. Despite her real concern she chuckled at the thought, enjoying the picture her overactive imagination had instantly conjured up.

A blur of flashing lights appearing behind her reflection caught Karin off guard, jolting her out of her dreamy state. Hastily, she readjusted her mirror, a quick glance revealing the image of a bright yellow Porsche being pursued by the motorway police. Feeling the first stirrings of panic, she forced herself to concentrate on the road ahead, fortunately it was pretty clear. Indicating, she pulled over to the left-hand lane, flicking her eyes up to the mirror as she did so. Less than a few car lengths behind her the Porsche was weaving dangerously from side to side, obviously trying to force a clear path through the traffic, the insistent wail of the police siren now so close it drowned out the silken tones of the soul singer who had been successfully recreating an Al Green classic on her car radio.

Hating motorway driving at the best of times, Karin gripped the steering wheel and forced herself to remain calm despite the mounting anxiety that clenched at her stomach and forced the blood to pound in her head. The Porsche was just behind her now, the driver obviously intending to overtake her car on the inside, down the hard shoulder. As it drew alongside there was a sudden roar from the engine as the driver floored the accelerator. Failing to secure a grip on the loose surface, the sports car seemed to go out of control for no apparent reason and in a split second had plunged straight into the grassy embankment.

As it did so, the rear of the Porsche swung out wildly, grazing the side of Karin's car. Taking huge gulps of air in an effort to temper the shuddering panic that had overwhelmed her, she immediately slowed down and eased her car over to the left until it came to a smooth halt on the hard shoulder. Winding down her window, she shakily breathed in the cool night air, taking huge gulps until, after what seemed like an age, her heart-rate steadied leaving her sufficiently calm to switch off the engine and get out of her car. As she walked back down the hard shoulder in the direction of the accident scene, she noticed a police car had pulled in behind the Porsche which, in its current sorry state, was now no longer a threat to anybody. Two police officers were on the scene, their hats laying on the ground having been knocked off, or fallen off. Each held on to a struggling youth as they tried, in vain it seemed, to handcuff the two boys together whilst valiantly trying to ignore the abuse and threats being hurled at them. At that moment another set of blue flashing lights appeared on the horizon.

'That'll be the inspector,' said one of the police officers to no one in particular.

Karin thought she detected a note of apprehension in his voice and wondered who would end up being in the most trouble over this incident, the driver of the Porsche and his equally manic passenger, or the police themselves.

She stood watching as the harassed looking police officers forced their captives into the empty patrol car. One climbed into the car with the two youths whilst the other did his best to appear casual as he sauntered over to the Range Rover that had now come to a halt some distance behind the scene of the accident, blue lights still revolving. Ignoring their waiting colleague, the two occupants of the Range Rover strode towards her.

Even from a distance it was obvious that the shorter of the two uniformed men was someone important. An unmistakable aura of authority surrounded him and, although dressed in standard police uniform, he nevertheless appeared more well groomed and a good deal more sophisticated than his much younger companion.

'Excuse me madam, did you actually witness the accident?'

She didn't need to look up to know which of the two officers had spoken, from the commanding tone it was obvious that it was the one who had captured her interest from afar. She mumbled something about it all happening too quickly and finally looked up, only to see him striding resolutely away from her, heading in the direction of the patrol car officer who was still hovering uncertainly in front of the Range Rover.

'That's the duty officer, Inspector Maddison,' speaking in almost reverential tones the taller policeman nodded in the direction of his retreating colleague.

With difficulty Karin tore her eyes away from the man who had captured her interest, forcing herself instead to concentrate on the other police officer who stood by her side. In her estimation he only appeared to be in his late teens. A real rookie, she thought, smiling in spite of her shaken state. Encouraged by her smile, the young officer introduced himself as P.C. Baker and asked her, solicitously, if she felt up to making a statement about what she'd seen.

'I really didn't see much,' explained Karin, 'it all . . .'

'. . . happened so quickly,' P.C. Baker finished for her. 'I know, it always does. But, if we go over the whole incident carefully, from start to finish, you may be able to shed some light on what happened here. So far all we seem to have are wildly conflicting accounts.'

He glanced in the direction of the patrol car, where the two police officers were obviously having trouble agreeing on the circumstances of the accident now that the duty officer was on the scene.

'It wasn't really their fault you know,' she offered, smiling at the constable.

He merely nodded, making it clear he had to at least look as though he had no opinion of his own. Karin fell silent, she didn't really want to discuss it now, she was just anxious to go home, have a stiff drink and go to bed . . . alone. Feeling slightly woozy all of a sudden she put out a hand to steady herself. Straight away her fingers came into contact with thick blue serge. Bewildered, she looked at her hand as though it belonged to someone else, she was gripping P.C. Baker's sleeve, too terrified to let go in case she fell to the floor in a dead faint. The young P.C. looked concerned, she really did seem to be looking a little green.

'You're probably suffering from delayed shock, why don't I help you back to your car so that you can at least sit down?' His tone was gentle, full of compassion.

Nodding gratefully, she allowed him to escort her as he had suggested. In her disturbed state it seemed they had a great distance to cover until they reached the security of her car. Unsteadily, she sank into the driver's seat, closing her eyes against the glare of the police strobe lights reflected against the backdrop of pitch-black sky, almost immediately she felt hot tears rolling down her cheeks. Unused to such an overt display of vulnerability, P.C. Baker was hesitant about disturbing her and just stood quietly watching as Karin sobbed for several minutes. As her tears began to subside he reached out and touched her shoulder gently.

'The inspector said that, provided you leave your name and address with me first, you can go home. As long as you feel up to it of course,' he added quickly.

Seeing her glance behind her left shoulder, at the damage to the side of her car, he did his best to reassure her, 'It's only a scratch, but if you'd prefer not to drive yourself . . .'

Karin shook her head, 'No, no that's okay, I'll be all right now,' adding, 'really, I will.'

When she saw the doubtful look on his face she burrowed in her handbag and pulled out a leather wallet, extracting her driver's licence she handed it to him so that he could note down her name and address.

'My telephone's not working at the moment I'm afraid, but I'm home most days.'

What she didn't tell P.C. Baker was that she had actually ripped the telephone cable out of the wall herself the day before. It was during a fit of rage brought on by a particularly vitriolic telephone call from her ex-husband and she still hadn't got around to getting it repaired. He told her not to worry and that they would be in touch. Karin couldn't help wondering if the young constable was this nice to everybody or, as she suspected, he fancied her a little. Too bad, but he really was a bit too wet behind the ears for her liking. But the inspector . . . now he would be a different matter altogether.

As soon as she got home she closed the curtains and made her way wearily up the staircase. Pausing only to strip off her clothes, which were now creased and grubby, and dump them in the laundry hamper, she stepped into the shower. The sharp jets of hot water revived her almost immediately and she marvelled, not for the first time, at her amazing recuperative powers. Closing her eyes, she turned this way and that allowing the steaming spray to work its magic on her exhausted body.

It was actually a relief not to have anything planned for the weekend and, for the first time since her split with Colin, she positively enjoyed the solitude, using the time simply to lounge around reading, eating, sleeping and generally recouping her strength. By the time Sunday evening arrived she found that she felt totally restored and was genuinely looking forward to the coming week with a tingle of anticipation.

She awoke bright and early the following morning, more than a little surprised to find herself really keyed up at the prospect of meeting Rosalinde after her exercise class. Breakfasting on a handful of dried apricots and figs she flicked through her morning mail, thank goodness there were no bills, just a couple of circulars and a letter from an old schoolfriend, Carla. What a surprise, she hadn't heard from Carla in ages, shame there wasn't time to read it now. Feeling as though the day had already got off to a good start, she looked forward with optimism to the rest of it. Even sitting behind the wheel of her car for the first time since the incident on the motorway didn't dent her high spirits. It was only when she arrived at the salon for her rendezvous with Rosalinde that she found not everyone felt they were destined to enjoy a perfect day.

As she stepped through the door and glanced toward Rosalinde's usual chair she was surprised to see it was occupied by an elderly lady, her blue-rinsed hair wound into dozens of tight little coils.

If I ever start looking like that I think I'll get someone to shoot me, Karin thought to herself uncharitably.

She couldn't imagine being that old and didn't want to, particularly when she was feeling so vibrant and alive. Her good mood had been boosted even higher by the glow she always felt when exercising. Feeling as light as air she had revelled in each movement, enjoying the way her body acted and reacted to the physical demands made upon it and, thanks to the regular and frequent exercise sessions, she was now looking and feeling as taut and as lithe as the other women she had envied so much when she first started. She never tired of the low whistles and admiring looks she received as she bounced along to the music in an aerobics class, or stretched and sweated her way through her twice-weekly body conditioning sessions.

Just then she noticed Rosalinde emerging from a door at the back of the salon and raised her hand in a silent greeting. Her friend nodded and mouthed something unintelligible before turning around to speak to her usual 'girl'. While she waited Karin glanced at herself in the mirror, she was still dressed in her exercise gear – a high cut leotard worn over contrasting exercise shorts in a stretch fabric. The outfit was one of her new purchases, she loved the way the thong-style bottoms disappeared right into the cleft of her buttocks making them look even more shapely. Smiling briefly at her reflection she bent over to search for her purse amongst the tangle of things in her sports bag, suddenly she felt a sharp pinch on her right buttock and a hand snake its way between her legs. Jerking her head up she noticed Rosalinde making her way across the room, her face like thunder.

Karin stopped dead, waiting for the hand to move or the owner to introduce himself, but neither happened. The hand stayed where it was, rubbing gently backwards and forwards, her sexual parts automatically stirring and preparing for action. Cursing the weakness of her own flesh, she made no effort to remove the hand herself, instead she glanced downward just in time to catch sight of the fingers as they enfolded her pubic mound. With relief she saw that it was quite darkly tanned, automatically assuming that it belonged to one of the trainee stylists, a normally shy young man of indeterminate Mediterranean origin. She smiled to herself, young lover number two, this situation could have possibilities? The hand had left her crotch and was now making a slow climb up between her buttocks. That was it, she thought, time to teach young Mr Octopus a lesson. Slowly, she straightened up, using her recently developed gluteus muscles to trap a couple of his fingers with a vice-like grip. Glancing provocatively over her shoulder her expression froze, the hand belonged to the man she had fallen in lust with the previous week, the one she had met in the café.

Immediately, she relaxed her buttocks, allowing the almost-stranger to repossess his hand. In complete contrast to her earlier expression Rosalinde was now smiling broadly as he grimaced in an exaggerated fashion, putting on an overt display of massaging his digits as though they were broken. Despite her acute embarrassment Karin couldn't resist appraising him anew. He was tall, much taller than she remembered, and slim, dressed in an immaculate and stylishly cut, grey pinstripe business suit. Her memory banks updated themselves as she surveyed his lightly tanned face which was composed of classical lines, making it difficult for her to assess his age. At a rough guess she would say he was in his mid to late forties.

Beneath thick, dark brows and lashes his unforgettable blue eyes crinkled at the corners into deeply etched laughter lines. She hadn't seen him smile before and had to admit his expression was very endearing, so much so that she couldn't help smiling back at him, simultaneously thanking God for creating such a gorgeous looking man and placing him between her legs. He opened his mouth slightly, as though he was just about to say something to her, when Rosalinde's clipped tones cut through the air of sexual tension between them.

'Nicolai, what brings you here, I thought you had no interest in my activities?'

Rosalinde's voice brought Karin back to reality with a sickening jolt and, disappointed at the interruption, she swivelled around to catch her first glimpse of the infamous Nicolai. With overwhelming dismay it quickly dawned on her that the dreaded Nicolai and the man she had just fallen deeply in lust with all over again were one and the same.

Oh my God, she thought, immediately recognising a severely tricky situation on the horizon.

Desperately, she tried to regain her composure, she wanted to be able to stand firm in support of her friend, not fall weakly at the feet of her confirmed Casanova of a husband. Her first impulse was to get away from Rosalinde and Nicolai as fast as possible, there was no way her friend could have avoided seeing what had happened and she was desperate to save any further embarrassment. Against her better judgement she fancied the guy like crazy on sight, if she left now she would avoid the risk of upsetting Rosalinde any further. She turned to the older woman, ready to make her excuses. But, far from appearing affronted, Rosalinde was smiling indulgently at Nicolai.

'Don't mind my husband Karin, he's not used to simply shaking women by the *hand*.'

She patted him affectionately on the cheek, whilst Nicolai had the effrontery to wink. Karin found their behaviour totally bewildering, she had always firmly believed in the sanctity of marriage, at least until Colin had shattered her illusions. Obviously she had a lot to learn, she thought to herself grimly. Before Karin had time to protest otherwise, Rosalinde ordered cappuccino for the three of them and she found herself seated next to Nicolai on one of the squashy, grey leather sofas that furnished the salon's reception area. She was uncomfortably aware of the heat and overtly masculine scent emanating from the body only centimetres away from her own and felt as gauche as a young schoolgirl who had just discovered boys for the very first time.

She groaned inwardly when a nerve started to twitch in her right thigh, she and Nicolai both noticing it at the same time. Heedless of her possible rebuff, he unthinkingly put out his hand massaging the quivering limb with firm, deft strokes. It was pure bliss and she longed for Rosalinde, the salon and everyone in it to melt away into oblivion, all she wanted was to be alone with him, now.

Unbidden, their eyes met and held together for an indecent length of time, Karin being the first to tear her gaze away from his, remembering, with an overwhelming feeling of guilt and self-reproach, that they were seated opposite the woman who was both his wife and her best friend. It was an impossible situation, with Karin trying desperately to rekindle the feelings of loathing that she had developed for Nicolai in his absence, as an antidote to her desire for him. Nothing on earth could have prepared her for this encounter, she had been so firmly convinced that, if and when she finally met the infamous Nicolai, she would instantly recognise him as the hateful, unscrupulous bastard Rosalinde had painted him to be. Damn it! Originally she had every intention of standing firm alongside her friend in opposition to this unrepentant, unfailing womaniser of a husband. Instead, she was trembling violently inside, every nerve-ending alive to the possibility of this man's caress, her right thigh on fire under his assured manipulations.

If Rosalinde noticed anything amiss she certainly didn't show it. Totally oblivious to the torment that Karin was suffering at her husband's hands, she chattered away nineteen to the dozen about the salon, the treatment that she had just had, a mutual friend of theirs, and a newspaper article about a woman in her mid-fifties who had just given birth to her first child. It was an unremitting monologue and quite uncharacteristic of Rosalinde who was normally economical with her words. Unable to concentrate on anything she was saying, Karin merely nodded every now and then and sipped her coffee in guilty silence.

Eventually, she realised Nicolai and Rosalinde were preparing to leave together. As he rose to his feet, Karin was embarrassed to find her face directly in line with his crotch, it bulged with such intriguing fullness that she had to fight hard against an almost primitive urge to reach out and stroke it. She inhaled the musky scent of him, desire forcing her insides to turn to water. A voice broke through the haze of lust that enveloped her, Rosalinde was inviting her to have lunch with herself and Nicolai. What a predicament. Karin wanted more than anything to accept their invitation, yet she knew if she did so all would be lost, there was no way she could spend another moment in their company without disclosing the feelings bubbling up within her, dangerously close to the surface. It took all her strength of will to refuse the invitation. But Rosalinde insisted.

'Oh Karin you must, there's a perfect little place I've been dying to show you for ages, it's just around the corner,' she wheedled convincingly as she saw Karin's resolve weakening.

Automatically, Karin's eyes flicked to Nicolai, silently questioning. Nicolai said nothing, his face was closed. Seeing him like that almost made Karin crumble, she desperately wished she had the strength of will to refuse, to walk out of the salon with her head held high and to forget she'd ever heard of Nicolai Andreas. But she couldn't do it. Was she weak, or merely human? She was still too inexperienced to tell the difference.

'Okay,' she conceded, 'but there's no room in these clothes for food, I'd better shower and change first.' She pulled at the restrictive leotard, wincing as it automatically sprang back to mould itself to her body.

Rosalinde laughed, paused to whisper in Nicolai's ear, then took Karin by the arm.

'What are you waiting for? I'm sure they'll let you grab a quick shower here if I threaten to faint with hunger otherwise.'

Through sheer force of will Karin made it to the spiral staircase without looking back to see if Nicolai was watching them, or rather her. Then she weakened, turning her head ever so slightly so that she could catch a glimpse of him, with a pang she noticed Nicolai's eyes were already otherwise engaged, wandering up the legs of a group of giggling secretaries who had just arrived for a lunchtime treatment. Whether she cared to admit it or not it looked as though his diversion with her had merely been momentary, as far as he was concerned she was already past history.

Rosalinde had been right about the restaurant, it was absolutely perfect; but for lovers' romantic tête á têtes, not unfortunate threesomes. Intimate would be the kindest way to describe the tiny, Italian bistro. No matter how hard she tried, Karin could not avoid coming into contact with Nicolai. Their knees collided under the table, fingers brushing as they reached for the condiments, the grissini, or their wine glasses and each time it happened it was as though an electric shock passed between them.

After a while Karin gave up all attempts at trying to make polite conversation, concentrating instead on her meal, which was delicious, and avoiding Nicolai's probing stare. Still Rosalinde chattered on. It seemed she was totally oblivious to Karin's uncomfortable silence, or the atmosphere which draped itself around them like a thick curtain. Finally, feeling that she needed some relief from the charade being enacted at their table, Karin made her excuses and edged her way through the narrow restaurant to the ladies' room. Naturally, it was located at the back of the overstuffed restaurant and this time she was only too aware of Nicolai's eyes following her movements. Once inside the cubicle she sank weakly against the wall, allowing herself to breathe for the first time, it seemed, since they had arrived. Taking several huge gulps of air she straightened up and turned to the basin to splash cold water on her wrists and temples. Feeling revived by the icy droplets of moisture on her skin she looked up slowly to regard her reflection in the mirror. To her surprise, hers was not the only face she saw, smiling at her from over her shoulder was Nicolai.

'Wha . . .' she started, wondering how on earth he could have entered the small room without her noticing.

Turning her around he pressed his body firmly against hers, forcing her buttocks over the edge of the basin. Lifting her hair from the back of her neck, he began to kiss her throat, slowly, deliberately, allowing his tongue to drift across her burning flesh, upward to tease the lobes of her ears, then south towards her cleavage, stopping just short of the outermost swell of her full breasts which now heaved violently with pent up desire. Deliberately forcing all thoughts of Rosalinde from her mind, she allowed herself the luxury of indulgence in his caresses.

He refused to allow her to touch him, stepping backwards or to the side to avoid her blindly groping hands. He could possess her but she would never hold him, he wanted her to know that beyond a shadow of a doubt. And for now it was enough. For now she relished his attention and demanded nothing more. To her increasing frustration he didn't touch any other part of her body. Frantically, she ground herself against him realising that they could not remain where they were indefinitely. Soon someone else would demand to avail themselves of the facilities. As though he could read her mind Nicolai ran his hands over her breasts and buttocks, pulling her hips towards him.

'Shame I can't have you here and now,' he murmured against her neck, adding so quietly she wondered for a moment if she had heard him correctly, 'I'll just have to continue to enjoy my video of you instead.'

'Mmm,' she arched her back, then, 'what did you just say?'

Nicolai looked at her, his expression deadpan, inscrutable, 'I said I have a video film of you.'

She was totally baffled now and tried to take a step backwards but, with the basin and wall behind her there was no room for manoeuvre. Her voice faltered when she spoke.

'You must be confusing me with someone else, I've never been filmed on video.'

As though her words had not registered with him he

toyed with a tendril of her hair, rolling it between the thumb and forefinger of his left hand, then in measured tones he replied, 'Surely you can't have forgotten Jon already?' His voice dripped with amused sarcasm, 'Was it four times or five, I can't quite remember?'

Karin was horrified, she knew Jon was young and relatively crude but she still would have credited him with more sensitivity than to brag about his sexual exploits to his employer. But even so, that didn't answer her question about the supposed video of her.

'Oh, don't worry,' he hastened to assure her, 'Jon didn't tell me, he didn't have to.'

Karin was really confused now and close to tears.

'I don't know what you mean,' she said in a small voice.

Nicolai dropped the tendril of hair and stood back, regarding her cowed expression with cool disdain.

'My dear, I thought you realised, our house is equipped with closed-circuit TV, there are cameras in every room. Nothing goes on in that house that I don't know about and it's all stored on tape for future reference.'

Apparently oblivious to her stunned expression, he peered over her shoulder at his reflection in the mirror, straightening his tie and smoothing back his hair. He had such an air of smug, self-satisfaction that Karin had an overwhelming urge to lash out at him, to physically remove the supercilious smile that touched the corners of his mouth. But she was immobile, shocked into inactivity. Eventually she would figure out a way to get her hands on that video tape and destroy it for ever but for now she was powerless to do anything other than stare at him, aghast at his calculating insensitivity.

'I'll tell Rosalinde that you had to leave, shall I?'

He leaned forward, smoothing his thick, dark eyebrows with a dampened finger and forcing her to shrink further back to avoid touching him, heaven forbid she should be contaminated by this loathsome creature. She stared after him miserably as he walked out of the door without even a backward glance. The problem was, although at this moment she hated him with every fibre of her being, she also wanted him desperately. Somehow she would make him pay for this. She would not be satisfied until she had him exactly where she wanted him, on his hands and knees begging to be allowed to make love to her.

Chapter Four

It was almost a week later when the Range Rover unexpectedly pulled up outside her house. Irritated, she looked up, her mind had been so full of Nicolai and the damn video tape of herself and Jon that she had completely forgotten about the accident on the motorway. For the past few days she had tormented herself with the dilemma of how she should attempt to retrieve the tape and, today for the first time, had managed to concentrate her mind on something else for a few hours.

The object of her attention was one of a series of erotic novels which had just been published. This particular volume was about a woman stranded on a desert island with a tribe of especially well endowed, sex-starved natives and, although the plot was totally improbable, it had nevertheless succeeded in making her feel very aroused. The chapter she was just enjoying had completely captured her feverish imagination and the last thing she felt like thinking about was a car accident. With a sigh of resignation she shoved the book under the nearest cushion and walked out into the hallway.

The police officers were only half-way down her driveway by the time she opened the front door, giving her a good opportunity to study Inspector Maddison as they approached the house. She certainly liked what she saw and felt her stomach tighten in response. Although he had sounded thoroughly English when he spoke to her at the scene of the accident, he looked more than a little foreign. With his olive skin, dark hair and thick dark brows he could easily pass for a Greek, or an Arab perhaps, but it was his eyes that spoke volumes about his exotic parentage. Heavy lidded, like deep black pools, they stared implacably at her until, unnerved she glanced away, stepping back so that the two men could enter the narrow hallway. Surprisingly, it still hadn't occured to her by now that she had a natural predisposition towards foreign-looking men, particularly those who were tall, dark and handsome. A psychiatrist might well have suggested to her that she was deliberately choosing men who were the complete opposite of her ex-husband, at least in appearance.

Whatever mental reasoning stimulated her subconscious to desire such men, she couldn't fight the physical arousal they induced within her. On weak legs, she led the way through the cluttered living room guiding them into her favourite room in the house, a bright, airy conservatory filled with comfortable cane furniture and overflowing with pots of herbs, cacti and flowering plants of all kinds. Until that point no one had spoken and she felt strangely unwilling to be the first to break the pervasive silence. Eventually, out of politeness if nothing else, she felt compelled to speak.

'Can I get you something to drink, I . . . I mean, a cup of tea or something?'

She felt extremely uncomfortable, sensing the inspector's eyes upon her the whole time. A furtive glance at him showed her he still wore the same blank expression, although his grave eyes seemed to be boring into her very soul. She shivered involuntarily, who could tell what thoughts lurked behind such an emotionless façade?

In contrast, his mouth was soft and seductive with very full red lips and, now that she was standing close to him, she saw his swarthy skin appeared baby soft, like velvet, even where the blue-grey tinge of five o'clock shadow showed through. And the length of flesh at the nape of his neck, from the hairline down to the place where it disappeared into his collar, was covered with a downy layer of fine, dark hair. Fighting the urge to reach out and stroke her finger down his cheek, she turned instead to face the younger officer, P.C. Baker. He responded instantly by accepting her offer of tea, even volunteering to help her make it, whilst Inspector Maddison merely shook his head, his lips forming an insolent smile.

It was a relief to be in another room, away from the Inspector's penetrating gaze. P.C. Baker chattered incessantly, appearing totally at ease as he pottered around her kitchen, arranging cups on a tray, finding milk and sugar and, eventually, carrying the tea tray into the conservatory where he set it down on a low table. Karin wondered why she wasn't at all surprised when he offered to be 'mother'.

Once the tea had been poured and they were all settled comfortably on the cane furniture Inspector Maddison finally found his voice which, much to Karin's surprise, wasn't even slightly tinged with a foreign accent. Slowly, methodically, he began asking her very simple, direct questions about the motorway accident which only required a yes or no answer. Despite his forbidding air his tone was gentle, lapsing every now and then into a slightly cockney brogue. After about half an hour he began to probe more deeply, his expression appearing to soften as Karin struggled to remember the more minute details of the incident. This time P.C. Baker was the silent one, scribbling away furiously in his notebook as Karin spoke. Another twenty minutes or so elapsed by which time Karin had begun to notice a subtle change in the atmosphere. P.C. Baker's existence appeared to be receding whilst she was becoming increasingly conscious of Inspector Maddison's presence and of her own physical state.

For some strange reason she felt as though he, Maddison, was touching each part of her body in turn, as though his words were really caresses, and her arms, breasts, buttocks and thighs thrilled to each imaginary touch. She was staring directly at him now, aware only of her rapid breathing. Her blood pounded in her ears and she swallowed deeply as she followed his gaze southward, slowly down her throat until finally coming to rest on her heaving chest. Her breasts swelled fit to burst, her nipples hardening perceptibly beneath the thin cream silk of her blouse. Unable to tell whether her voice still sounded normal she fell silent, concentrating instead on trying to regulate her laboured breathing. Struggling for composure, Karin stood up abruptly and walked over to the full-length, sliding glass window on the opposite side of the conservatory. She needed to put some distance between herself and the inspector otherwise she was in danger of giving in to an overwhelming urge to touch him. All too soon she realised her mistake, now two pairs of eyes were upon her and she was aghast to realise that the light from the window behind her made her thin, crêpe skirt almost transparent.

All at once she felt ridiculous, these two men were there for one reason and one reason only, they weren't interested in her, they were just doing their job. Anything else was purely the result of her overactive imagination, fuelled by the erotic content of the book she had been reading when they arrived. Resolutely regaining her composure, she turned to face them.

'I really don't think there's anything else I can tell you about the accident.'

Inspector Maddison immediately picked up her cue, 'Of course, we're sorry to have troubled you ma'am.'

The two men rose to leave, insisting that they could find their own way out. Feeling drained by their visit, Karin nodded weakly and gave a half-wave, only waiting to hear the 'click' of the front door latch before allowing herself to collapse into the nearest chair. She seriously wondered if she was going mad from spending so much time alone. For as long as she could remember she had always had people around her, firstly her parents and family members, then a husband and her own children. Was it her own feeling of insecurity that led her to believe, without reservation, that those to whom she was physically attracted would automatically reciprocate her desire? With a heavy heart she forced herself to climb the stairs to her bedroom. The letter from her friend Carla had contained a suggestion that they meet, 'for old times' sake', and tonight they had a supper date. If she didn't get a move on she would be late.

The restorative spray of the shower came to her rescue once again, dispelling the shame she had been feeling and making her feel thankful that she was, by nature, a born optimist. To lift her mood still further she decided to wear her very best underwear. Black and silky, it still lay nestled in the gift box, lined with layers of tissue paper, that had lain under last year's Christmas tree. A cruel gift for a straying husband to give his unsuspecting, ever faithful wife. Fearing that she might become maudlin again, Karin resolutely pushed all thoughts of Colin to the back of her mind, he had already ruined enough years of her life, she wasn't about to let him spoil what promised to be an extremely pleasant evening.

Her thoughts returned to the two policemen or, more precisely, Inspector Maddison. Delicious new fantasies began to formulate as she lathered and rinsed her body again and again. Now that she accepted the situation, as she perceived it was nothing more than a fantasy, she allowed her mind to dwell on the rough blue uniforms with their cold, hard silver buttons and peaked caps – the whole ensemble staid and serviceable, yet commanding instant respect and obedience. Definitely an exciting combination, she thought, one could almost call it irresistible . . .

As she soaped herself feverishly between her legs she allowed her mind to drift, abstract words floating in and out of her tormented subconscious.

'Dominate . . . obey. Do it . . . obey . . .'

Writhing against the pressure of her own palm the words became a mantra in her head. Soon she was going to come, she could feel it building, growing within her until she almost reached the point of no return. The words gave way to a cacophony of jangling bells.

'Aaah, noooo . . .'

Reality hit her like a bucket of ice-cold water. The doorbell was ringing. Oh God, what now? Quickly, descending back into reality, she stepped out of the shower, pulling on her bathrobe. Taking the stairs two at a time she flung open the front door, no one was there. Gingerly, she stepped out of the door onto the path, craning her neck to see as far as she could both up and down the street. Apart from a white BMW parked near the corner there was no sign of anyone or anything. Annoyed at the pointless interruption she stepped back inside, shut the front door and made her way back upstairs to her bedroom.

Through her bedroom window she was surprised to see the Inspector's Range Rover parked outside her house once again, yet it hadn't been there when she went to answer the front door. Could it have been the pair of them ringing her doorbell? Despite her attraction to Inspector Maddison she couldn't help feeling a little annoyed, after all she was trying to get ready to go out and she felt as though she'd answered enough questions for one day. With the front of the vehicle almost entirely obscured by a large conifer which stood at the entrance to her driveway it was impossible to see the occupants, but she didn't miss the twitching of her neighbours' curtains.

'If I was my mother I'd be worried about what they were thinking right now,' Karin grumbled to herself, as she started to dress.

Whatever their reason for being there it obviously wasn't to see her, as they made no attempt to call on her again, or even leave the vehicle as far as she could tell. Shrugging off her apprehension she concentrated on her make-up. Far from feeling tired following her solitary session in the shower, Karin felt so invigorated that she wished she was going dancing, or to the theatre, rather than simply meeting a friend for a 'cosy heart to heart'. With an overwhelming feeling of acute restlessness, Karin cursed the fact that her telephone was still not working. Damn it, she couldn't even call Carla and cancel. By way of consolation she poured herself a large, straight vodka from the bottle she kept by her bed. She justified its presence there as an occasional aid to relaxation, just in case she had difficulty sleeping. On her way back to the dressing table she paused to admire her reflection in the cheval mirror. There was no doubt about it, the agony she put herself through in her exercise classes was certainly beginning to pay off.

She had put on the black silk underwear of course, a figure hugging bustier top and tiny panties edged in lace which moulded her taut body into an extremely pleasing hour-glass shape. For her outer-wear she had wriggled into a clinging, strapless dress, also in black silk, complete with very sheer, black hold-up stockings and a pair of black suede stiletto shoes. To complete her outfit, she wore a modest pair of gold ear-rings, whilst another new purchase, a pillarbox red, quilted leather Chanel handbag added a vibrant splash of colour to an otherwise sombre ensemble. She felt chic yet at the same time decadent, like a high-class hooker who wouldn't consider removing even her coat for less than a couple of thousand. Once again an erotic fantasy began to unfold in her mind and, in an exact repeat of her previous disturbance, she was jolted out of her reverie by the insistent ringing of the front door bell. Even before she reached the bottom of the stairs, she could see the outline of a uniformed figure through the obscure glass of the front door. Sighing, she opened it, raising her eyes angrily to clash against the impassive gaze of Inspector Maddision.

'Yes?' She deliberately allowed the irritation she felt to show in her voice.

Inspector Maddison appeared totally unconcerned.

'I apologise for the intrusion, madam,' he said, looking anything but apologetic, 'but I wonder if you would mind accompanying me to the station?'

'Are you serious, I was just about to go out?' Now she really did feel annoyed.

'It won't take long, I assure you, but there are one or two matters which we must settle between us.'

She looked closely at him, the way he said those words, almost intimately, rekindled her desire.

'Very well.'

The evening was far too warm for a coat but, feeling distinctly under-dressed in his presence, she grabbed a shawl from the coat-stand by the door. Trying desperately to appear nonchalant, she smiled at him.

'Okay, what are we waiting for, let's go?'

The drive to the station was uneventful, although she was surprised to note that P.C. Baker had not been waiting in the Range Rover. Inspector Maddison drove quickly and expertly, his strong hands holding the steering wheel lightly as he weaved the spacious vehicle through the heavy evening traffic.

Later, she wondered why she hadn't been surprised to see him standing on her doorstep, or at the events that had taken place at the station. Perhaps she wasn't so much self-obsessed as intuitive. Was it possible that she was more attuned to the thoughts and feelings of others than either she, or they, realised? If it were not for the soreness of her breasts and the pulsating sensation between her legs, she could almost believe that what had taken place between herself and the Inspector had not been real at all but merely an extension of her earlier fantasies.

Upon their arrival at the local police station he had led her down a long corridor to a small, dismal room, empty apart from a simple wooden table and two chairs. Locking the door behind them, he'd turned around and stared at her, failing to invite her to be seated. Neither had spoken at first. Oblivious to the shouts and sounds of doors banging elsewhere in the building they simply continued to stare at each other, each second of time magnifying the overwhelming sexual tension between them. Later, when she went over the events in her mind, she decided it had been almost like making love without touching. Virtually against her will, she had felt her body stirring sensuously beneath the black silk garments. Like a corset, they compressed her flesh as the heat of desire caused her curves to swell, her nipples and clitoris throbbing so agonisingly that she longed to simply burst through the material, to feel the cool air waft over her, to expose herself totally and utterly to his penetrating stare and, most of all, to make him respond to her as she did to him.

As if he could read her mind, he suddenly took charge of the situation. Crossing the room purposefully in a couple of strides, he lifted her several inches from the ground and carried her backwards, using his body to pin her against the wall. She felt the hardness of his body through his uniform, the heat of his passion making her feel faint. His fingers sought hers as he kissed her, neither gently nor passionately but with an air of authority that was almost cruel. Automatically, she forced her tongue against his teeth but he resisted even this small attempt by her to assume some vestige of control. Their fingers still entwined, he raised her hands above her head. Aghast, she felt the sudden chill of cold steel about her wrists and found that in one swift movement he had handcuffed her to a small shelf bracket jutting from the wall at exactly the right height. As she stood rigidly, arms aloft, her body and lips still trapped by his, she felt the urge to laugh at the ridiculousness of the situation. It seemed preposterous, yet he was not laughing, nor did he even smile. Eventually she broke free of his lips.

'Let me go.'

She tried in vain to sound commanding. His eyes bored into hers relentlessly. For God's sake what was he thinking? Her nostrils filled with the different scents of this man, citrus and spice aftershave and the comforting aroma of starched clothing mixing incongruously with the more threatening scent of sweat and the subtle muskiness of his own arousal.

'Of course,' she laughed to herself at her sudden burst of knowledge.

This one particular physical reaction gave him away, forcing him to be betrayed by his own body. Karin recognised that he was human after all and she found her new-found power over him strangely arousing. True, he had physical power over her, not to mention the handcuffs and a position of authority. She shivered momentarily, excited at the mere thought. But what she really found stimulating was the certain knowledge that she could reduce this man to nothing, solely through the power of her own physical allure and the helplessness of his desire to possess her body, if not her soul.

The effect of this realisation was cataclysmic: it was true, power was the ultimate aphrodisiac. Simultaneously she experienced a sudden rush of wetness between her legs as he released the zipper on her dress, allowing the fluid material to slither to the floor like a pool of black oil. Staring boldly back at him, Karin couldn't help noticing the sharp intake of breath, a slightly twitching nerve in his cheek the only movement in an otherwise deadpan expression. Glancing down her own body and then back at him, if she'd had any lingering doubts about the way she looked she certainly didn't have them now, his eyes said it all. Hungrily they roamed freely over her body, causing random sparks to ignite within her and making her stomach flutter and contract. Resuming his composure, he allowed his gaze to travel slowly to meet hers. From the tips of her stiletto-clad feet, up and down each shapely black stockinged leg, lingering for a second on the black satin mound of her pussy before continuing its agonisingly slow journey over her belly. Eventually his eyes alighted on the smooth, full globes of her breasts which, thanks to her arms being raised aloft, had almost broken free of the confines of the bustier top.

Long, interminable moments passed yet he made no further move towards her. She began to feel a little uncomfortable under his supercilious stare. Not a word was spoken and, bound as she was by the handcuffs, there was not a damn thing she could do about it. As he turned away and walked out of the door her disappointment was almost tangible, she couldn't bear if he left now, particularly if he planned to leave her like this. Perhaps it was a favourite game of his, or maybe it was a cruel joke. Helplessly, her mind began to ponder all sorts of terrible possibilities, the worst being that her husband could be behind it, trying to set her up, to get his own back on her in the cruellest of ways. If she had been thinking rationally she would have realised straight away that Colin didn't have the imaginative capabilities for arranging something like this. Although, if she had been thinking rationally, she would have been more concerned about being discovered handcuffed and half-naked in a police interview room than the possibility that the inspector might not, after all, come back to screw her.

She almost cried with relief when he did return. Without any word of explanation for his brief absence he dragged the table across the room then pushed it into the corner, picking up one of the wooden chairs he placed it a few feet in front of her but did not sit down. Walking over to her, he kissed her briefly on the throat, allowing his tongue to travel slowly down the moist crevice of her cleavage. Deftly, he unhooked the bustier and tossed it to one side, his large hands moulding themselves completely around her breasts. As he kissed and licked each nipple in turn, Karin felt the ebbing sparks of desire flicker into life, ultimately bursting into flame. Moaning and writhing in tormented provocation, she could hardly tolerate the exquisite agony of his assured manipulation of her body. Every lick or nibble of her highly sensitised flesh, each time he brushed against her stomach or thighs, or sucked upon her swollen nipples, sent shock waves spiralling down her body, causing her vagina to moisten and her clitoris to swell and throb unbearably. With every fibre of her being she willed him to touch her there, to gratify her intoxicated flesh with his assured dexterity.

Infuriatingly, he continued to stimulate her breasts, resolutely ignoring the rest of her body until she almost screamed aloud for his touch. Yet all the time she did not utter a word, not willing to give him that satisfaction. That was until the moment when, from somewhere deep within her, a low guttural moan broke free, a primitive response sounding almost inhuman. Eventually he stopped caressing her, kneeling down instead to raise each of her feet in turn so that she could step out of the discarded dress. She felt totally powerless, as though it was the most natural thing in the world for him to operate her limbs. As he bent his head, she longed with every fibre of her being to run her fingers through the thick dark hair and force his head between her legs. Feeling another surge of wetness soak into her panties she wriggled her hips tantalisingly, and thrust her pelvis foward slightly, hoping to urge him to respond to her bidding. If he noticed her predicament he gave no indication of it, steadfastly ignoring her frantic bumps and grinds of encouragement.

Slowly, deliberately, he rose to his feet once more. Taking a few paces backwards he sat down on the chair in front of her. Once again her explored her thoroughly with his eyes, taking his time, missing nothing. On this occasion she felt more vulnerable, more exposed. Clad only in black panties, stockings and shoes, the sight of her was a feast for any man's eyes. His insolent gaze alternated between her body and her eyes, as though he wanted to see the mixture of discomfort and excitement manifest itself on her face. When he finally spoke, his voice came as a shock, a laser beam of sound cutting a clear path through the haze of her desire.

'Turn around.'

The simple command caused new ripples of excitement to course through her body. Being handcuffed, it took some time for her to comply with his order, yet he waited, still appearing impassive, apparently confident that she would eventually obey him. And she did. Turning slowly, fully aware that her recompense for the arduous workouts at the gym were deliciously taut buttocks, she was rewarded by another sharp intake of breath. Such reactions were her only indication that she was having any effect on him at all. It suddenly occurred to her that she hadn't noticed if he had an erection. She turned her head as far as she could and glanced between his legs but the combination of his being seated and still dressed in full uniform made it impossible for her to tell if he was physically aroused or not.

His eyes held hers for a split second, then he uttered a second command.

'Face the wall and bend forward as far as you can.'

Again, the handcuffs made this manoeuvre a little difficult but by arching her back she managed to make her bottom jut out further. It was a particularly uncomfortable position, although none the less arousing and, after what seemed like an age, she finally felt the pressure of his hands upon her body. The crotch of her panties was now saturated with her own juices, lubricating the silk so that it slid easily into the cleft of her buttocks as he began to knead each luscious mound firmly and rhythmically. Still he took his time, continuing the kneading process, fully aware that her panties were rubbing tantalisingly against her clitoris, the friction inducing sensations that roused her almost to distraction.

Almost imperceptibly, she felt his fingers creeping under the elastic of her panties, moving the sodden material to one side before plunging deep into her vagina. Pressing her aching breasts against the cool wall she ground herself against his hands, feeling him probe and knead and rub until she exploded in a rush of exhilarated ecstasy. Almost roughly he turned her around to face him, she could see by his expression that he too had almost reached the point of no return. He kissed her hard at first, like the first time, then more gently, almost reverently, releasing the handcuffs as he did so.

Tentatively, she touched his hair, sliding her hands possessively around his shoulders, feeling the stiff blue serge and cold silver buttons of his uniform rubbing against her naked flesh. In return he ran his hands over the contours of her body, sliding her panties downward in one fluid movement. Kneeling before her he began to kiss her belly, slowly, languorously, his tongue encircling her navel whilst his hands gripped and kneaded her buttocks once again. This time Karin had the freedom to use her hands to guide him, quickly parting her labia with one hand she gently urged his head forward with the other. Thankfully, he didn't attempt to resist her. The moment she felt his breath on the red-hot, pulsating bud of her clitoris she thought she would scream aloud from her pent up frustration.

Now she was totally at his mercy and she could care less, she wanted him to look at her and touch her, every part of her. To probe and explore each tiny morsel of her quivering, fervid flesh. When she eventually felt the cool touch of his lips as they pressed against the core of her desire her climax was almost instantaneous, triumphantly riding the crest of myriad waves of indescribable pleasure. She was totally lost now, hurtling along on a roller coaster of sensation. Dimly aware of his tongue and lips upon her, his fingers deep within her she continued to ride until, finally, she opened herself up to him as wide as she could, urging him to enter her completely.

In one swift movement he stopped, picked her up and carried her across the room, laying her unceremoniously upon the bare wooded table and positioning her feet, one on each chair, so that her legs were spread wide at the edge of the table ready to receive him. Without preamble he unzipped his fly and entered her, using deep, penetrative strokes. Yet despite his passion it did not end quickly, his execution as slow and deliberate as the build up, unremittingly he thrust hard and deep into her for a long, long time until they were both completely spent.

No words were exchanged between them during the short drive to her home and, when he left her at her own front door, his face bore no trace of either emotion or exhaustion. In total contrast, Karin felt completely drained of energy and could do nothing more than lay on her bed for ages afterwards, too spent to move and completely oblivious to Carla's persistent knocking on the front door.

Chapter Five

Although she was never again 'taken in for questioning', for several weeks Inspector Maddison was a frequent visitor to her home. Despite the fact that each time he arrived unannounced, Karin, through some sixth sense (or sex-sense as she described it to Rosalinde) was ready for him, almost panting aloud in her desire to be possessed totally by this unyielding mortal. In all that time he never revealed himself to her. Although they occasionally socialised, their relationship never progressed into anything more than a series of highly charged sexual encounters, each one as stimulating and ultimately satisfying as its predecessor.

Despite the strangeness of their relationship they had an unspoken understanding, each of them equally enjoying their 'roles'. She, stripped of her clothes and her dignity, available to his every whim. He, stiff, unyielding in his uniform, never dropping his pseudo sadistic persona. It was totally unlike anything she had ever experienced before and Karin never yearned for them to indulge in 'normal sex'.

Two days after their first meeting, the inspector took her to a dinner party held by his chief superintendent.

'Don't bother with any underwear,' he instructed her on the telephone, adding, 'and make sure you wear something *easy*.'

Karin understood only too well what he meant by that remark. She knew he would want to fondle her discretely throughout the evening and perhaps take her quickly at the earliest opportunity. She wasn't wrong. Although a late starter as far as experimental sex was concerned, she was learning fast.

Not surprisingly, it was with more than a little sorrow and regret that she learned he would be going away for a couple of months, 'on special duties'. At the time she was stark naked and handcuffed, at wrists and ankles, to a dining chair. The inspector was seated a few feet from her in an armchair, reading through some notes he had made on his latest arrest. Every so often he would glance up and stare mercilessly at her until she was forced to turn her head away, her face flushing hotly, her whole body on fire, yearning for him to touch her.

Their encounters were often like this and she could never be sure how long he would keep her captive, or if he would even touch her at all, sometimes all he wanted was to look at her and no amount of pleading on her part would induce him to satisfy her mounting desire. Fortunately, their last time together was oustandingly physical.

'I took it really hard,' she tried to joke with Rosalinde a few days later, 'although it certainly wasn't on the chin.'

Wincing at the memory of that final night's antics, she realised the soreness was only just easing, more fool her for letting him try to penetrate her with his police truncheon. Rosalinde listened to Karin's graphic descriptions with a mixture of horror and undisguised envy.

'It's not so bad,' Karin said, more to convince herself than anything else and, comforting herself with the knowledge that before he left he had given her the truncheon, not to mention the most monumental orgasm she'd ever had, as a going away present.

Just looking at the truncheon reminded her of what she was missing and, try as she might, her own hands were no replacement for the real thing. She was also a little sorrowful to realise that the finer details of her last time with him were beginning to fade around the edges a little. What she needed were a few new diversions to fill the gaps that had opened up in her life. She was missing the kids like crazy now and, although she'd had several long telephone conversations with both of them, like her gift from Inspector Maddison, they were not satisfactory substitutes.

Since she'd had her phone fixed she'd become quite close to Rosalinde, hardly a day went by when they didn't speak to each other. Usually it was late at night when one telephoned the other and Karin soon learned that Nicolai's philandering lifestyle left Rosalinde feeling almost as lonely as she, as he was rarely home before three or four in the morning. Despite the intimacy of their conversations, Karin deliberately avoided mentioning the existence of the video tape of her and Jon, not knowing for sure how her friend would react. She could not be certain but she felt, almost instinctively, that Rosalinde was unaware of the fact that Nicolai oversaw and recorded everything that happened in the house. If she ever found out there was bound to be trouble and Karin didn't want to be the one to cause it.

Aside from their intimate telephone discussions they still met several times a week, both at the salon and at Karin's exercise class – after some initial resistance she had finally persuaded Rosalinde to join. The only drawback to their regular exercise sessions, as far as Karin was concerned, was that each one left her feeling more energised and aware of her body than ever before, and it was such a shame not to be able to make the most of the potency she was experiencing.

All in all, it was certainly turning out to be an interesting summer, and hot in more ways than one, each day dawning brighter and even warmer than the one before. Leaning out of her bedroom window, inhaling the sultry, heavily scented air, she decided this was the best summer she had ever known and there and then resolved anew to make the most of every day. On the spur of the moment she decided to start right away and cheer herself up by taking a drive out into the country, where she'd look for an idyllic spot to stop for a picnic.

Resolutely pushing all memories of previous 'happy-family' picnics to the back of her mind, she grabbed her keys and jumped into the car, simultaneously winding down the driver's window and opening the sun-roof to let in as much cool air as possible. She quickly reached the centre of the village where she paused at the local delicatessen to stock up on cheese, bread, fruit and, as an afterthought, a bottle of crisp, dry white wine – perfect picnic fare. As she left the shop she caught sight of her reflection in the shop window. Mindful of where she was, she avoided the temptation to pose and admire herself, although she felt particularly pleased with her choice of outfit: the stark white button-through cheesecloth skirt and lace, waistcoat-style blouse contrasting nicely against her lightly tanned skin, making her at least appear to be cool, calm and collected. When it came to her choice of underwear she had decided to dispense with unnecessary garments, merely slipping on a skimpy pair of white lace panties.

The sun blazed directly overhead, boosting the temperature into the upper eighties. And the clear blue sky, the caress of a slight breeze ruffling her hair as she drove and the sound of Prince blaring from her stereo, all conspired to enhance her 'glad to be alive' feeling. Although she'd already driven some distance she had hardly seen a soul, the arrow-straight road ahead was clear as far as the eye could see and a quick glance in her rear-view mirror confirmed that the road behind her was also deserted. Not suprisingly, she wasn't prepared for the insistent blast of a car horn when it happened, causing her to jump visibly. Angrily, she turned to glare as a white AC Cobra convertible overtook her at a dangerously high speed.

Although she only caught a glimpse of them as they hurtled past, she could see the driver and passenger were both male, their contrasting very dark and very blond hair streaking out behind them in the rush of air. Both wore sunglasses which glinted as they simultaneously turned to wave cheekily at her as she was left, fuming, in their wake.

'People like that shouldn't be allowed on the road,' she muttered furiously to herself, refusing to admit that her anger was grounded in envy. If she was being honest with herself, she would admit to feeling more than a little desirous of their car and that she had a sneaking admiration for their devil-may-care attitude.

She tried to quell the smug feeling of satisfaction that overcame her as she noticed the sleek lines of the convertible just ahead of her, they were obviously having problems with the car as it was belching out smoke from the exhaust pipe, its speed gradually becoming slower and slower. Eventually, they pulled it onto the grass verge just in time for it to grind to a complete halt.

'Serves them right,' Karin smirked, despite herself. This time is was she who waved gaily as she sped past them.

She had driven less than half a mile when feelings of guilt began to assail her. She had seen no other traffic on that particular road during her drive and no sign of habitation or a telephone box, in all likelihood they could be stranded on the roadside for hours. Wrestling with her conscience and her common sense, she finally conceded, using the next field gate she came to as a suitable place to turn her car around. Within minutes the Cobra was in her sights once more and she fought against a slight feeling of annoyance that the occupants, far from being distressed, appeared totally relaxed and completely unperturbed by their plight.

Lounging slightly backwards against the bonnet, hands deep in pockets, they remained composed, faces turned up like hedonists to the fierce rays of the sun. Their identical outfits of tight, white denim jeans and emerald green pique shirts contrasted superbly against their bronzed throats and muscular arms. An expensive-looking gold wrist-watch and designer sunglasses completed each immaculate ensemble. Karin felt her breath catch in her throat, despite her earlier annoyance with them the scene really was a superb display of man and machine in perfect harmony.

They didn't seem surprised to see her, although she was pleased to notice how they both immediately glanced appreciatively at her legs as she stepped out of her car and crossed the road. Karin found herself idly wondering if they always did *everything* together, she fervently hoped they weren't gay, it would be such a waste! The dark-haired one stepped forward, removing his sunglasses to reveal deep green eyes that matched his shirt, they were edged with thick, dark lashes that Karin would have killed to have been born with herself.

'Hi, I'm Karl,' his voice was pure velvet.

He proffered a hand and she took it, immediately feeling extremely vulnerable as her small hand was crushed by his strong handshake. Inexperienced as she was in such matters, she didn't think it likely that *he* was gay.

'Karin,' she replied shyly, her nervous smile taking in both men.

Karl too glanced at the other man who made no effort to join them. When he did finally move he took his time, stretching slowly as he straightened up, pausing to smooth his hair and glance at his watch.

'That's my partner, Dominic,' Karl explained.

Despite the introduction Dominic still did not walk over to them but stared at Karin with an intensity that made her feel extremely uncomfortable. She couldn't see his face properly because of the sunglasses he wore but she could feel his eyes roaming all over her. Her clothes were sticking to her perspiration-drenched body, outlining every curve. She was totally unnerved by him, feeling naked under his steady gaze. Embarrassed, she fought the urge to cover herself, deciding instead to stare back at him equally intently, albeit with false boldness.

She had to admit that, although he wasn't really her type, particular with his fair colouring, he was still very attractive. His confident, overtly sexual aura certainly helped, as did his physique. Not too tall for her liking, only about five feet nine or ten, he was perfectly in proportion. His broad, only slightly muscular shoulders tapering to a neat waist and hips. Under the close-fitting material of his shirt, she could see his stomach was ironing-board flat and she was sure that, if he turned around, his buttocks would be firm and enticingly 'grabbable'.

Eventually, Dominic strolled lazily across the road, unlike Karl he didn't remove his sunglasses but she could see that his features were every bit as pleasing as his body. The first thing she noticed was his hair, from a distance it had appeared completely blond but now he was closer she saw that it was, in fact, quite dark although streaked heavily with bleached highlights. And what she had taken to be a beard was merely a few days' deliberately unshaven growth. On anyone else such efforts would have looked totally contrived but on him the effect was devastating, making him look like a rich Californian beach bum.

Standing very close so that his body almost grazed hers, he took both her hands, turned them over and kissed each palm, slowly and deliberately.

'Thank you for coming back to rescue us lovely lady.'

Scarlet with embarrassment, Karin had to struggle to find her voice. 'The road's deserted and there's no phone for miles as far as I know.' As soon as she said them, Karin cursed the stupidity of her words. If the men were rapists or murderers, or both, then she had just given them *carte blanche* to do their worst.

Oh well, in for a penny ... she thought, adding, 'Would you like a lift to the nearest garage?'

She was surprised that the two men hesitated over her offer, surely they didn't want to be stuck here indefinitely? They couldn't help but notice her look of confusion.

'It's very kind of you to offer, but . . . well, we're worried about leaving the car here unattended, it's extremely valuable.' It was Karl who spoke, sounding apologetic. Then Dominic whispered something to him, and he nodded, turning immediately back to Karin.

'Would you have any objections if just Dominic went with you to get help while I stay here with the car?'

Karin considered her response very carefully, of the two men it was Dominic who made her feel most ill at ease. Then she came up with a solution.

'Look,' she tried to speak casually, 'I was planning to stop and have a picnic anyway, so why don't I stay here, have my picnic and watch your car, while you two borrow my car and go and get help?'

Karl looked doubtful, 'One of us really should stay with the car.'

Again the two men went into private conference. Karin's stomach was in knots, what if they decided it should be Dominic who stayed behind? She needn't have worried, Karl was quick to volunteer, standing a little closer to Karin as though to confirm the arrangement. Dominic nodded his agreement and, although he wasn't a lot taller than Karin, made a great show of adjusting the driver's seat in her car. Karl took the bag of picnic things from her and walked across the road to the Cobra, opening the boot and removing a thick, chequered car rug.

Dominic turned Karin's car around easily in the narrow lane, then saluted cheerily as he sped off in a cloud of dust.

As though he read her thoughts, Karl said, 'It's okay, he won't wreck it.'

Karin smiled back at him, feeling herself start to relax for the first time since she had stopped to help them. Opting for the field next to the car as a picnic spot, Karl helped her over the wooden fence. There was no stile, making it awkward to climb and Karin had no choice but to unbutton her skirt practically all the way to the waistband, bunching the voluminous material in one hand as she used the other to steady herself. Gallantly, Karl averted his gaze but looked back just in time to see Karin fall from the fence, her legs splaying wide as she did so.

He said nothing but the mood between them had

changed considerably, the friendly atmosphere now charged with sexual tension as the possibilities of their unusual situation crowded in on both their thoughts. She wondered if it was just the shock of the fall which had left her feeling slightly shaky. With trembling fingers she tried to button her skirt, eventually giving up when she reached mid-thigh. Looking around she realised how isolated they were, with not even a crow or a sheep in sight, let alone another human being.

Carefully, he laid the rug under the shade of a clump of tall bushes which edged the field, in her fevered imagination it looked as though he were preparing an altar for human sacrifice – her body being the sacramental object. Although they were some distance from the road the Cobra was still clearly visible, which for some reason Karin found strangely comforting. The hammering in her heart slowed to a fast but rhythmic throb and she started to set the picnic out on the rug. Unexpectedly, Karl caught her by the wrist.

'Take off your panties,' he murmured.

Karin was dumbfounded, thinking the heat must be playing tricks on her.

Karl repeated his request but made no further move towards her. His tone, although commanding, was calm and unthreatening. After a few seconds, when she realised he was deadly serious, she looked him straight in the eye trying to sound a lot more resolute than she actually felt.

'I'll do no such thing.' With bated breath she looked down at her hands, waiting for his reaction.

Eventually, when he made no move towards her, she raised her head again, at least expecting to see him glaring at her. Instead he was busy uncorking the bottle of wine she had brought, although she had not remembered to bring anything to drink from. He patted the rug beside him.

'Drink?' It was as though nothing had happened and she started to wonder if she had imagined it or that perhaps, deep in her subconscious, she was trying to enact a fantasy situation.

Nevertheless, she sat down gingerly on the rug as far away from Karl as possible. He offered her the bottle of wine and she accepted it gratefully, taking a huge swig to steady her nerves. The alcohol flooded her body immediately, she had not eaten all day and instantly felt its effects. Taking another gulp she revelled in the warm glow which filled her body, making it feel much lighter and more relaxed. She lay back on the blanket soaking up the sun, unaware in her slighly tipsy state that her skirt had fallen open, revealing the tops of her thighs and most of her lace-covered mound.

Karl had noticed but still made no move towards her, taking a deep draught of wine he cut some bread and cheese, studying her as he ate.

Not a word was spoken between them. She became aware of a slight breeze caressing her exposed skin, it felt pleasant, more than pleasant in fact. Languidly she eased her body into a more comfortable position, staring at the wide expanse of blue sky and enjoying the sensation of the hot sun against her perspiring skin. She did not attempt to stop him when she felt Karl's fingers unbuttoning her blouse, parting it to reveal her smooth, brown stomach and the more lightly tanned globes of her breasts, instantly her nipples hardened and a rush of warmth engulfed her lower body. All her senses were heightened, a plane droned overhead and she heard the distant sound of sheep bleating, her nostrils quivered at the clean, soap and water smell of Karl, overlaid with the rich aroma of the earth, she could feel the ripe, juicy blades of grass between her fingers and sense his hand hovering over her. All was calm, all was still, except for the hammering of her heart as she felt Karl's gaze upon her exposed flesh and waited for his first caress.

Caught up in the exquisiteness of the moment, she didn't recognise the sound of her car on the road, or hear Dominic's footsteps on the grass. The shock of his voice piercing the blissful silence made her sit up hurriedly, automatically using one hand to shield her eyes from the sun's glare so that she could see who had interrupted them. It was too sudden a movement for someone overcome with heat and alcohol and she wobbled unsteadily before slumping backwards onto her elbows. Aghast, she stared up at Dominic's smug countenance. No longer wearing sunglasses, his hazel eyes swept over her exposed breasts and stomach, coming to rest for an indecent amount of time on her pussy. Reverting his gaze back to their shocked faces, he winked at Karl.

'While the cat's away eh, Karl my old mate,' Dominic's tone made her immediately want to strike out at him but no matter how willing her mind, her flesh was past caring.

Dominic squatted in front of her, tucking his sunglasses into his breast pocket. Once again his eyes raking over her but from much closer quarters, so close she could feel the warmth of his breath on her skin. Her vagina tingled, she hated to admit it but there was something distinctly erotic about being admired simultaneously by two men, even if one of them was the supercilious and distinctly unnerving Dominic.

Reaching for the wine bottle with a reckless, 'what the hell' feeling, she felt the first gulp of wine snake its way down to the pit of her stomach like a fiery serpent, a rush of warmth between her legs signalling the end of its journey. She eased her legs apart slightly, revelling in the attention this slight movement immediately commanded, idly she wondered if this was how strippers and exotic dancers felt, did they find it arousing to command the instant attention of their audience with a single, tiny movement? Flinging her head back, eyes closed against the sun's glare, she felt the first of the men's touches; soft fingers grazing her throat.

Not caring whose touch was upon her urgent flesh she arched her back still further, causing her breasts to break free completely from the scant covering of her unbuttoned blouse. Her nipples immediately hardened as a slight, cool breeze swept across them and she gulped hard as a pair of fingers took each one, rubbing them and squeezing them until she felt wet with desire. Was it Karl or Dominic who tormented her body in this way, would she soon learn to distinguish one man's hands from the other?

She decided she would have to look first, otherwise she would never be able to tell Karl's hands from Dominic's, or vice versa. Laying back on the blanket she opened her eyes a fraction and looked down her body. Surprisingly, Dominic was not touching her at all, merely watching as Karl trailed his fingers lazily over her stomach and breasts. In contrast with her earlier feelings, Karin found herself desperate to feel Dominic's hands on her body, accepting now that his cool demenour actually excited her more than Karl's more obvious attraction to her. Desperate for his touch, she opened her legs wider, wriggling and grinding her buttocks against the sun-baked earth. Still he confined himself to simply observing.

He must be a pervert, Karin thought to herself, a voyeur. Then a more disturbing thought struck her, perhaps he was the one who was gay!

By now Karl was sucking at her nipples, kneading her breasts in his capable hands and sending shock waves spiralling down her body. She felt her clitoris swell until it rubbed against the rough lace of her panties, urgently she willed Dominic, to touch her there. When she did eventually feel his touch upon her she was almost past caring, maddened with desire she writhed on the blanket, moaning and urging her legs further and further apart, desperate for at least one of them, either of them to slake her desire a little by fingering her pulsating flesh. Karl had steadfastly avoided feeling her below the waist and Dominic had not touched her at all. In desperation Karin had succumbed to fondling herself, stroking her own fingers between her swollen labia, desperately seeking a relief that would not come from her manipulations alone.

It was as if Karl had been merely preparing her for

Dominic, for all at once he sat back on his heels as Dominic immediately took control of her body, removing her panties with one swift movement before plunging his fingers deep inside her and bringing her to immediate orgasm. Almost screaming with ecstasy, Karin ground her hips, impaled by Dominic's fingers as he worked them deep within her, finding the magic spot behind her pubic bone that drove her to dizzy heights of pleasure. She was on fire and could not get enough, glancing down her body her swollen breasts almost obscured her vision of Dominic's blond head bent low over her pelvis, concentrating on his skilful handling of her sexual organs.

As if sensing her plight, Karl resumed sucking and stroking her nipples, his dark hair stroking her throat and chest as Dominic's caressed her thighs, it was the most unusual and exquisite sensation she had ever felt and it seemed as though it just got better and better. Not content with plunging and probing her vagina with one hand, Dominic teased her clitoris with the other, easing his fingers gently between her swollen labia and making deft, circular movements around the hub of her desire.

Wave after wave of pleasure engulfed her, tossing her into a vortex of abandonment where she quickly lost all sense of time and her surroundings, her only focus the hands and lips of the two men as they stimulated and probed every part of her feverish body. Presently, Dominic withdrew his fingers, holding them to her lips. Repelled she sat up and turned her face, feeling him paint her cheeks with her own juices. Laughing at her sudden modesty, he unzipped his jeans inviting her hands with his own to enfold his throbbing cock. She clasped it tightly, moving her curved fingers slowly and deliberately up and down its stem. Karl, meanwhile, undid the remaining buttons of her skirt and bent his head to claim new territory.

Having two men at the same time was a revelation to Karin, who had previously thought herself lucky to have one at all. Soaring to new heights as she felt Karl's tongue encircle her clitoris, she bent her head and touched her own lips against the smooth head of Dominic's penis. Allowing her tongue to drift down the full length of his shaft she found it interesting that he had been circumcised, deciding that it was extraordinarily pleasant. Dominic's fingers buried themselves in her hair, his breathing had picked up pace and, feeling encouraged, she opened her mouth wide, endeavouring to take in as much of him as possible. She had never enjoyed the rare occasions when Colin had persuaded her to fellate him, but now she revelled in it, enjoying the power that her tongue and lips wielded over this shaft of muscle.

How much more was there to enjoy between a man and a woman, she wondered? Or two men, or two women . . .? The thought had never occurred to her before but now anything seemed possible, it was as though a whole new world was opening up for her and she felt capable of experiencing everything and enjoying it to the full.

Inspired, she continued to suck hard using one hand to grip the base of his penis, whilst reaching further into his jeans to cup his balls with the other. Tentatively she stroked her middle finger along the delicate area of skin between his testicles and his anus, she remembered reading somewhere that this was a highly sensitive area. Her information was obviously correct, Dominic immediately responded, grasping her head fiercely he pulled back from her.

'I don't want to come yet,' he managed to gasp.

The sudden movement dislodged Karl's tongue, interrupting the exquisite sensations that he'd been creating within her. Disappointed, she pouted, looking from Karl to Dominic and back again. At the same time, both men glanced at the Cobra and the still deserted road, then back at each other. They seemed to have a kind of unspoken code and she wondered if they were accustomed to sharing a woman, in the same way they seemed to share a large part of their life. It was liberating to realise that she really didn't care one way or the other, she was enjoying the attentions of both, all the time feeling one man between her legs whilst the other fondled her breasts. What did it matter if this encounter was the beginning and the end of their relationship? She certainly had no desire to become involved with any man on a permanent basis.

Unexpectedly, it was Karl who took her first, with a fierceness that belied his calm, affable nature. Swiftly unzipping his jeans and sitting back on his heels, he pulled her to him, grasping her by the hips and positioning her over his erect penis. Interestedly, she glanced down at it, not having had the opportunity to view it before but Karl was obviously not interested in any further foreplay. In one deft movement he thrust himself into her and her onto him, entering her deeply before raising and lowering her body several more times. Transported instantly to cloud nine, she gripped his sides tightly with her thighs, clasping her hands around his neck and trying desperately to screw him. It was an awkward position, limiting her movement to a frustrating extent, in desperation she flung herself backwards urging him on top of her with her thighs. Miraculously, his cock remained inside her and they soon picked up a steady rhythm. Although he was clearly aroused, almost to bursting point, he continued to ride her for a long time, slamming his body against hers until she screamed out her orgasm into the stillness of the summer afternoon.

At this point Dominic, who had been stroking and teasing her breasts as he watched Karl strain within her, silenced her with a surprisingly tender kiss. It was the first time either one had kissed her on the mouth, she realised. Feeling perplexed she smiled up at Dominic, then glanced down at her body at Karl who was resting quietly between her legs. With a pang she decided she would like the opportunity to get to know them better, at the moment each man was an enigma, shy then bold, or masterful then loving. At the moment they were enacting a fantasy but what then? Who were they really?

Trying hard to push such thoughts to the back of her mind, she lay between them as they rested for a little while, sharing the rest of the wine and basking in the warmth of the sun and the afterglow of their love-making. When he returned with Karin's car Dominic had not actually mentioned whether he had succeeded in arranging for their car to be repaired but, at that moment, a car transporter appeared on the horizon. Feeling more than a little regretful, Karin moved immediately to cover herself but Dominic stopped her.

'Don't panic, believe me, no one can see you from the road. I got quite a surprise myself when I could eventually see what you and Karl were up to.'

At the mention of his name, Karl came to with a start and jumped to his feet, tucking his shirt back into the waistband of his jeans.

'I'll see to them,' he said, inclining his head towards the truck which had pulled up behind the Cobra.

Dominic nodded and as soon as he was sure that the Cobra was being safely loaded on the back of the transporter he turned his attention back to Karin.

'I suppose this is goodbye,' she tried to sound lighthearted as she began to button her blouse and skirt, groping unsuccessfully around her at the same time for her discarded panties.

Damn it where were they? In a way she felt that by allowing Karl to make love to her first she had succeeded in saving the best until last, now it looked as though she had screwed herself.

Without waiting to hear Dominic's response, she scrambled to her feet and, leaving behind the picnic things, ran across the field to the road. The last thing she wanted was to embarrass herself by allowing him to see the tears which welled up in her eyes and threatened to spill down her cheeks at any moment.

Chapter Six

By the time Dominic had gathered up the remains of their picnic and caught up with her, Karin had managed to compose herself somewhat. They joined Karl at the roadside just in time to watch the smooth curves of the Cobra stilled, silenced and strapped atop the transporter. Karin felt a brief wave of sympathy towards the car, as if it were a person.

'The garage is about ten miles away apparently. I've arranged for us to collect a hire car from there but they won't have one available until about seven o'clock.' Karl glanced at his watch, adding, 'That means we've got a couple of hours to kill yet.'

Without realising it, all three glanced behind them towards the spot they had just vacated in the field. No one could guess by looking at it now that it had recently been the scene of a small orgy. But, regretfully, they all knew it was too late to recapture that particular fantasy.

'I vote we a hitch a lift with Karin to the nearest pub,' said Dominic already striding towards her car.

Her relief was almost palpable. Far from being over, their fantasy had merely taken a new turn.

As he had drunk only a little of the wine at their picnic, Dominic offered to drive her car, while she and Karl kissed and fondled each other on the back seat like a couple of teenagers. Dominic glowered at their reflection in the mirror, Karin had somehow mislaid her panties in the field and he could clearly see the dark triangle of pubic hair through the thin material of her skirt. He glanced at the road in front of him before returning his eyes to the rear-view mirror, he felt unaccountably annoyed as he saw Karl stroke Karin's buttocks and bury his dark head in the swell of her breasts. It was not the first time he and Karl had shared a girl, but it was certainly the first time he had ever felt any jealousy.

Eventually, and with more than a little satisfaction, he espied the welcoming sight of a small country pub, unoriginally named the Queen's Head. Trooping up the crazy paved pathway, Dominic put his arm possessively around Karin's waist, if Karl thought he was going to have all the fun he could think again. But Karl merely acknowledged Dominic's gesture with a smile, holding the pub door open so that they could enter first.

Unfortunately, the doorway was much to narrow for two people to enter at the same time so Dominic was reluctantly forced to release his hold on Karin, stepping aside so that she could enter first. It was a very old pub and all three had to bend their necks to avoid hitting their heads against the low, solid oak door lintel. Inside it was traditionally welcoming, with heavy oak tables and wheelback chairs, the colour scheme predominantly red. Despite the comfortable surroundings it was far too hot to sit inside, so they carried their drinks out, through the back of the pub into the bright sunshine. They chose a table in the most secluded corner of the beer garden, both men opting to sit either side of Karin on the narrow wooden bench. Feeling very contented, she sipped slowly from a glass of iced mineral water, whilst Dominic and Karl drank non-alcoholic beers.

She felt very secure seated there between the two of them; and very happy. They alternated between making her laugh uncontrollably with rude jokes and cruelly accurate observations of the pub's other customers and subduing her with references to future plans which, obviously, did not include her. Restoring AC Cobras and making fibreglass replicas of the luxury cars was their business and they told her how they had started up their workshop several years earlier in an aeroplane hanger at a disused airfield.

'At the time we were totally skint and had to borrow from everyone we knew just to get started,' explained Dominic, adding, 'the banks wouldn't touch us with a bargepole.'

'Yeah,' shrugged Karl ruefully, 'now they won't leave us alone.'

He adopted a high pitched whine, 'Please, please, please borrow some of our money.'

Dominic laughed, 'It sounds far fetched the way Karl tells it,' he said to Karin, 'but it's not far from the truth. Now we've got full order books and customers from all corners of the globe.'

Karin was impressed, 'I've never even sat in a Cobra.'

Unintentionally she had given the men a cue to extend their relationship past the rutting in a field stage and, when she realised what she'd done, she held her breath expectantly. They didn't disappoint her.

'I've got the perfect solution,' smiled Dominic, 'what are you doing the day after tomorrow?

'Nothing I can't get out of,' she ventured cautiously. 'Why?'

Karl took over, 'I know what Dominic's getting at, we're holding a demonstration day at Silverstone, taking prospective customers around the track and letting them try out the cars for themselves.'

'It sounds great,' admitted Karin, 'but I couldn't possibly affort to buy one.'

'That's not the point,' Dominic took her hand and squeezed it affectionately, 'you'll get to drive one of our cars, eat a delicious lunch and hopefully have a thoroughly enjoyable day.'

'Well, if you're sure I won't be in the way,' she looked from one to the other as both men shook their heads emphatically. 'In that case,' she smiled happily, 'count me in.'

It was with more than a little regret that Karin dropped the two men off at the garage to collect their hire car. Much to the amusement and envy of the garage staff, both Dominic and Karl kissed her long and hard before letting her go. Then Dominic turned to Karl.

'It's no good, I can't let this lovely lady go home alone when the day is yet young, I must accompany her. You will be alone when you get home won't you?' he added, looking questioningly at her.

She nodded joyfully, enjoying the exaggerated way he spoke sometimes. Then, remembering her manners, turned to Karl, 'Would you like to come back with us for some coffee, or something . . .' Her voice trailed away, the 'or something' hanging heavily between them all.

Karl opened his mouth to answer but Dominic interrupted, 'Unfortunately my friend and partner has a prior engagement, isn't that right Karl?' His tone left no room for dispute.

'Oh yes, I'd forgotten for a moment,' he groped around for a plausible explanation but, failing to find one, simply shrugged. 'Perhaps some other time Karin.'

'Yes, perhaps,' she smiled, relieved, adding, 'I'll see you at Silverstone in two days' time anyway.'

He nodded, then took Dominic aside for a brief consultation before striding across the forecourt in the direction of their hire car, stopping half-way to turn and wave goodbye. Karin lifted her hand in response, already looking forward to seeing him again. Dominic appeared at her side.

'Ready to go?' She nodded and started to open the driver's door but he stopped her with his hand.

'Do you mind if I drive, it's just that the last time a girl drove me anywhere we ended up half-way down a ditch.'

Karin studied him carefully, he looked sincere. Tossing him the keys she made her way around the back of the car to the passenger side, just as she was about to climb in the car a thought occurred to her, 'What were you doing to make her drive into a ditch?'

'Aha,' Dominic grinned, 'you've sussed me out.'

'I'm not getting in this car until you tell me,' she countered, pretending to glare at him across the expanse of blue roof.

'Is that so? Well, in that case I'll show you what I do to women drivers.' With that he ran around the car growling, pretending to try and grab her.

Karin squealed in panic, leaping into the car and slamming the passenger door shut against invasion by his marauding hands. Unfortunately, she had forgotten the window was wide open and she found herself no match against his determination as he groped and tickled and pinched every part of her.

'Stop, please,' she lay panting in her seat, her legs falling open and her skirt pulled askew exposing the soft down of her pubic mound. Fortunately, no one else but Dominic could see her predicament.

He swallowed heavily, resisting with all his might the overwhelming temptation to touch her there, 'I think we should get you home don't you?'

Straightening herself in the seat she glanced at Dominic's profile as he drove. It seemed strange all of a sudden to be alone with him. Catching her staring at him out of the corner of his eye, he turned his head slightly and winked.

'We'll soon have you home and in bed young lady,' he joked, with mock patriarchal severity, 'but I think I may have to give you a good spanking first, you've been a very naughty girl today.'

Yes, she had, she thought to herself with glee, and the day is by no means over yet!

By the time they reached her house Karin and Dominic had both succeeded in thinking themselves into a state of extreme arousal. With no pretence at good manners, they fell upon each other as soon as the front door had closed behind them. In no time Dominic stripped off her blouse and skirt and, pushing her gently backwards so she lay against the staircase, fell hungrily onto her naked body. Like a starving man he licked and nibbled at her burning, quivering flesh, using his hands expertly to tease and torment the most sensitive parts of her body, which already throbbed frantically with unquenched lust. Kissing her deeply he stroked the hair back from her face, looking deep into her eyes.

'Not here,' he murmured in her ear, cupping her right breast in his left hand and rolling the nipple slowly between his thumb and forefinger.

Gently, she pushed him away from her and, taking him by the hand, led the way to her bedroom. Fortunately she had cleaned the whole house the day before and, although nowhere near as luxurious as Rosalinde's boudoir, her bedroom was both comfortable and welcoming, a vase of fresh flowers lightly scenting the air. Laying back against the pillows, she wallowed in the luxury of watching him undress, becoming more and more aroused as he removed each piece of clothing and, finally, his watch, placing it carefully on her dressing table. The mirror held their reflections and, for a long moment they both stared at it, taking in each other's naked body in contrast with their own. His firm, muscular, deeply tanned; hers supple, toned, the silky skin more golden in colour.

Holding his eyes to her reflection she stroked her own breasts, tentatively at first then more firmly, cupping them in both hands and snaking out her long pink tongue until she almost touched the tip against her own nipples. Disappointed, but enjoying his rapt expression as he stared at her in the mirror, she reached between her legs, carefully inserting a finger to feel the instant, insistent grip of her own vaginal muscles. This was too much for him, the time for observing was past.

With a groan of passion he fell upon her once more, this time with more finesse as he gently parted her legs further, replacing her finger with his rampant penis and urging himself deep within her. As she had expected, his love-making was exquisite, turning her insides at once to molten lava. He was at the same time tender yet forceful, guiding her purposefully to new realms of ecstasy, reaching her in places she never dreamed existed.

Clutching his taut buttocks in her hands, she thrust her hips upwards desperate to be filled totally by him and, when that still did not bring him deep enough within her for her liking, she pulled her legs back towards her chest, wrapping her ankles loosely around his neck. Instantly she became the woman in her reflection, wanton, abandoned, skilful in arousing him still further as he plundered her body. And, when she finally came with him inside her, it was wildly, without reservation, a bucking, screaming, explosion of a climax that totally eclipsed his own.

Drenched in perspiration, they lay together limply, he collapsed upon her. Like two rag dolls they lay in a heap, their breath coming in short gasps, hearts beating visibly against heaving rib cages. As her breathing regulated, she searched in her mind for something to say, whatever she thought of sounded trite and she cursed the fact that they were not more comfortable together. It only took a moment such as this to drive home the stark impersonality of a brief encounter.

Feeling a little tearful, she shifted under his weight, 'Excuse me,' she mumbled at last, when he didn't take the hint.

Still he didn't move. Now she was becoming uncomfortable, 'Excuse me,' she said again, this time a little more forcefully, pushing weakly at his left shoulder in a vain attempt to move him.

'Smmghlf,' he mumbled into her hair.

'What?' At least he was awake, thought Karin. She'd always hated the way Colin fell immediately asleep after sex.

Propping himself up on his elbows, he looked down at her, grinning, 'I said, kiss my cock and say please nicely.'

To her intense delight he stayed all night, waking her at about six in the morning to repeat his performance of the night before. She came awake slowly to the sensation of his hands caressing her back and shoulders, sliding around to the front of her body as she shifted slightly, still half asleep. Opening one eye, she glanced down to see his fingers toying with the pink buds of her nipples, her stomach contracted and she stretched, feigning sleep. His fingers worked their magic more insistently, sliding down her stomach and insinuating between her legs, rubbing gently, working their way between her labia to stroke her expectant clitoris.

Forgetting her reflection in the dressing-table mirror, she smiled and manufactured a tiny snore, believing that with her back to him he would remain convinced that she was asleep until she chose to reveal otherwise. Now both his hands were between her legs, one hand still massaging her clitoris and the other gently probing her vagina. Biting hard on her bottom lip she stifled a moan, then she felt his warm breath against her ear.

'By the way, I know you're awake.'

Her eyes flew open and, forgetting her charade she turned her head quickly to look at him, 'How?'

He silenced her with a kiss, turning her around and pulling her naked body against his. She could feel his penis, already hard, pressing against her stomach. Softly she stroked it, feeling as though it were an old friend.

'Do you have a name for it?' she asked suddenly.

He seemed surprised, 'A name for what? My cock you mean?'

She nodded, 'In a lot of the books I've read, people have had pet names for their private parts, like Mr Wobbly or something. No really, I'm serious.'

He was laughing hard now, holding his sides and pretending to be in pain, 'Mr Wobbly?' He managed to gasp, almost choking with mirth. 'I think you should start reading some serious literature young lady,' he admonished. 'There's no mention of a Mr Wobbly in *Wuthering Heights*, or *Othello* as far as I can recall.'

Now she was laughing and for the next ten minutes or so they lay on the bed, screaming with laughter as one, then the other, came up with a penis nickname for characters in great works of literature.

Laughter, she decided later as she dropped him off at

the station to catch a train home, was certainly a powerful aphrodisiac. When they finally stopped laughing they made love with a heightened passion that reflected their new found closeness. If only she and Colin had laughed a little more and rowed a little less their marriage may have stood a chance, she mused a little regretfully during the lonely drive home. Without Dominic's overwhelming presence, the car seemed very big and empty.

She hadn't told Dominic but today was her birthday. Feeling more than a little depressed, she toyed with the idea of deliberately missing her exercise session – just days before she had felt like the most desirable woman in the world, now she just felt very old and very alone. The sound of the telephone ringing greeted her as she opened the front door, sighing heavily she picked up the receiver.

'Happy birthday to you, happy birthday to you, happy birthday to the best mum in the world, hap . . .'

'Natalie!' It was a lovely surprise to hear her daughter's voice on the other end of the line, she sounded so close as though she were in the next room, not on the other side of the English Channel.

They chatted for a little while, then Colin's mother took over the phone and they had a polite but stilted conversation. This call was followed by one from her son, then another from her own mother and, finally, Rosalinde, calling to check up on her and make sure she would be going to the club.

'I'll bet you were sitting there feeling all lonely and unloved,' said Rosalinde perceptively.

'I was, as a matter of fact,' admitted Karin, 'how did you know?'

'I'm older than you remember, I've been there, felt the same way for at least the last five birthdays come to think of it.'

'Oh, great,' complained Karin, 'give me something to look forward to please. Are you telling me, in your own subtle way, that I can count on feeling like this on all my birthdays from now on?'

'Maybe,' laughed Rosalinde down the telephone, 'or perhaps by the time your next birthday rolls around you'll be living with some gorgeous man who can't get enough of you and couldn't give a damn how old you are.'

'Hmm, it's a lovely thought, although I don't know about the "living with a man" part, I rather like being my own person now, I've got used to being independent.'

Rosalinde's throaty chuckle reverberated down the phone, 'I was calling for two reasons, one to tell you that I can't make our exercise session today . . .'

'Oh, boo hoo,' Karin interrupted her, smiling, 'I expect that's really ruined your day?'

'And the other,' Rosalinde continued, ignoring her friend's sarcasm, 'is to invite you to my house for lunch today, as it's your birthday and everything,' she added.

'I'd love to Rosalinde, you are thoughtful.'

'Think nothing of it my dear, I'll start pouring the Pimms around twelve-thirty.'

Karin replaced the receiver thoughtfully, it hadn't really occurred to her before that she had changed and grown so much in such a short space of time although she didn't think it was very likely that she'd ever meet a man with whom she'd want to share her life exclusively. She smiled happily, at least the succession of phone calls and Rosalinde's invitation had lifted her spirits. Glancing at her watch she realised her exercise class was due to start in half an hour, so without further pause for contemplation she quickly showered and dressed in the new skintight leotard and leggings that were her birthday present to herself. Happiness bubbled up inside her like a glass of champagne, all of a sudden it felt good to be alive, very good in fact.

Rosalinde was waiting on the patio, glass in hand, when she arrived at the house at twelve-thirty on the dot.

'You missed a good class today,' Karin mumbled as she threw herself forward to grasp the backs of her ankles and ease the cramped muscles in the backs of her legs.

Suddenly, from behind her, she heard a babble of raised voices and turned just in time to see all the 'regulars' and staff from both her class and the salon crowding into Rosalinde's garden yelling 'Happy Birthday' at the tops of their voices. Looking around she saw she was surrounded by smiling, friendly faces – including Dominic's.

'What on earth . . . ?' Karin was totally dumfounded, they had only met the day before and it was less than three hours since she had dropped him off at the station.

Grinning broadly he stepped forward, grabbed her and flung her backwards, kissing her passionately. Arms flailing, her back almost snapping in two, she kissed him back with fervour and they were both more than a little flushed when they finally came out of their clinch and straightened up.

'Surprise!'

Rosalinde was almost jumping up and down with excitement. Grabbing Karin by the hand she dragged her into the new pool extension that she'd had built onto the house. Not sure whether to laugh or cry, Karin stared at her in amazement, set up all around the pool were tables groaning with food and drink. Brushing aside Karin's attempts to thank her, Rosalinde hissed in her ear.

'Quick, get changed and let's get the party rolling,' she urged, inclining her head toward the changing room. 'You'll find a costume in there with your name on, it's my birthday present to you.'

As she emerged from the changing room Karin couldn't help admiring Rosalinde's taste. Like all her clothes, her own choice of costume was a study in understated elegance. Simple, but beautifully cut, she wore the plain black costume as though it were a designer gown. Whereas Rosalinde looked sleek and chic, Karin appeared the complete opposite, although none the less attractive. Her appearance was bouncy and tousled, her taut curves looking as though they were striving to escape the confines of the electric blue material of her new swimsuit. It was a colour that suited her particularly well and she knew it.

One of the 'muscle men', as she and Rosalinde had dubbed the select group of *serious* exercisers from their class, had spotted her coming out of the changing room, gripped her around the waist and raised her from the ground as though she were a feather.

'You're looking good babe,' he drawled. 'How about coming back to my place for some more fun after this ends?'

Despite his extraordinarily beautiful body he really wasn't really her type, much too macho and narcissistic. She declined as pleasantly as possible, giggling and squirming in his grasp until he finally set her back on her feet.

'You an' me anytime babe, just remember that.'

Karin nodded, po-faced, forcing herself not to look at Rosalinde until she had herself under some vestige of control. When she turned around it was as she expected, Rosalinde was trying hard to smother a grin, she rolled her eyes at Karin who had to fight like crazy not to laugh aloud until he was well out of earshot.

'Anytime babe,' they mimicked and both fell about laughing.

'What's the joke?' enquired Dominic as he passed by munching from a plate of delicately cut sandwiches.

'Nothing,' responded Karin airily, shaking her head then bursting into fresh gales of laughter as she caught Rosalinde's eye and added, 'babe.'

To Dominic's confusion the two women both spluttered until, without realising what she was doing, Karin stepped backwards a little too far, straight into the warm, clear water of the newly built pool. As though it were a cue, everyone stopped what they were doing and jumped or dived into the water. It was bliss, not too cold, not too many chemicals, just perfect. Rolling over she trod water for a few seconds until she had composed herself, then crossed the pool in a lazy crawl. This was the life, friends, food, drink, sex, it was all she could ask for, although not necessarily in that order.

Almost the only person left fully dressed, Dominic called to her from the side of the pool. Karin swam over to the edge and looked up at him appealingly.

'Aren't you coming in?'

Squatting down in front of her, Dominic shook his head regretfully. 'I'm sorry Karin I can't, it's pure coincidence that I'm here at all and I really must be going.'

Karin pouted and tried to pull him into the water but Dominic was firm, although he was clearly torn between the demands of duty versus pleasure. Laughing she waved him off.

'It's okay, I don't mind, seeing you again today was a bonus. I'll still see you tomorrow though won't I?'

Dominic nodded, 'You bet, I left an official invitation and a map showing how to get to Silverstone on your dressing table.'

He blew her a kiss then turned on his heel and strode away. Karin watched his retreating figure with a mixture of wistfulness and renewed lust. Rosalinde caught her eye and winked.

'I do believe we've got some catching up to do when this lot leave,' she glanced around the packed swimming pool.

Karin grinned and nodded enthusiastically, her eyes alighting on a new object of desire. Jon had just arrived and, in one swift movement, had taken off his T-shirt and was now removing his trousers to reveal a minute pair of black swimming trunks. Diving in like a pro, he swam towards her with smooth, easy strokes, his dark, wet hair slicked back and shiny like sealskin; water droplets luminescent, like small beads of light, against the background of his bronzed skin. Under the cover of the water, he ran his hands up the outside of her thighs then slipped them under the tight elastic to clasp her buttocks. She immediately responded, groping under the water with one hand until her fingers encountered the bulge of his erect penis. There and then she fondled him, pressing her thumb against the sensitive spot below the head of his penis until he was forced to withdraw his own hands and grasp her tightly around the wrist.

'I'm about to come,' he confessed.

She was reluctant to leave the comfort of the warm water but the fact that she had aroused Jon so easily, aroused her too. Panting, she climbed the steps from the pool and, glancing around quickly to make sure no one was watching them, followed Jon as he led the way to another of Rosalinde's new home comforts, a steam room. Pausing only to lock the door behind them, he peeled Karin's dripping costume from her volatile body. It was almost unbearably hot and she could hardly see him for all the vapour. In a way it made their encounter all the more exciting, as though she were being made love to by a ghost, or the invisible man.

Soon she was seated on top of Jon, facing him and, although she couldn't see him very clearly through the fog, she could certainly feel his hard cock rubbing against her vulva. She moaned aloud, grasping his hair as he slid himself slowly up and down her crevice. Making full use of his muscular arms he grasped her hips, positioning her directly over his rampant organ, rhythmically raising and lowering her body as he thrust purposefully into her pliant flesh. From her vantage point Karin could ride him hard herself, agitatedly working her thigh and stomach muscles and gripping and releasing him with her vagina, she cried out in ecstasy as her breasts and pussy rubbed remorselessly against his unyielding, virile body. It was ravishing, sublime, the perfect start to a new year and a new chapter in her life.

A polite cough from somewhere deep in the fog, caught them both unaware. Guiltily she realised that, in their frantic state of arousal, they hadn't thought to make sure that the steam room was empty. It was obvious that their uninvited guest had deliberately waited until she and Jon had both climaxed and she didn't know whether to feel grateful or annoyed. Hurriedly, she pulled on her costume which had dried completely in the stifling heat, all she could think about was getting dressed and escaping from the room.

She felt uncomfortable about her predicament. In fact, despite her newly acquired sophistication, she was acutely embarrassed by the situation. Nevertheless, nothing could have prepared her for the shock of raising her head and coming face to face with the amused countenance of none other than the hateful Nicolai. In vain she tried to speak, groping frantically in her mind for something to say that would appear cool and casual, as though she could care less that he had witnessed her in full flow with Jon. Frustratingly, not a sound would come from her open mouth and her erstwhile lover had long since disappeared.

'The coward,' she fumed to herself, 'how dare he leave me like this?'

She was angry now and it worked, bringing words instantly to her lips, 'You could have said something,' she accused, for want of something better to say.

'What, and ruin a beautiful moment?' Nicolai responded sarcastically.

She wanted desperately to scream, or hit him, or both. But it was too late. He had already gone, leaving her alone with her embarrassment, her anger and a disquieting realisation that she wished it had been Nicolai who had taken her in the steam room.

By the time she had calmed down sufficiently to return to the party, Nicolai was fully dressed and standing next to Rosalinde talking to a couple Karin had never met before. She instinctively wondered if they were talking about her but Rosalinde gave no indication of this as she invited her to join them. Simpering like a schoolgirl, she fluttered around the other couple, introducing them as Mike and Julia, freelance beauticians who had somehow been included in the party crowd following an interview at the salon.

Although she hated to admit it to herself, it irritated the hell out of her to observe Nicolai's responses. He was obviously very taken with Julia, though for the life of her Karin couldn't understand why, the girl was far too thin, straight up and down and totally flat chested, not Nicolai's type at all she assumed. Rosalinde, in her typical blinkered fashion where her husband was concerned, didn't appear to notice his overt flirting. Although it was beginning to grate unbearably on Karin's nerves, she hardly liked to admit that she was jealous of the attention Julia was receiving from Nicolai. All of a sudden she felt claustrophobic, the only person she could usually confide in was Rosalinde but this time even that channel for release was blocked.

Feeling frustrated and upset, she wandered over to the buffet tables and picked at some food, several of the *regulars* from the salon joined her, trying to engage her in trivial chit chat. Politely, she forced herself to concentrate on their conversation but, try as she might, she found her attention wandering. Glancing across the room she saw Nicolai whispering something in Julia's ear, his hand resting lightly but possessively on her shoulder. Her stomach contracted tightly, hurriedly she put down her plate of food and gripped the edge of the table in anguish, the man was an out and out bastard, how could Rosalinde put up with him? As though he could feel her eyes upon him, Nicolai turned and smiled at her. Searching his face for the slightest trace of malice or triumph, she found none, his smile was open and friendly. Despite herself, her insides melted and she felt her cheeks glow warmly.

'God,' she thought angrily to herself, 'I must be going senile to be attracted to such a pig of a man.'

In order to lighten her mood and put some much needed space between herself and Nicolai, she wandered down to the far end of the pool where the equally new Jacuzzi was still waiting to be christened. As she lowered herself cautiously into the foam she felt the pulse of the water-jets ease her knotted muscles. Her thoughts were rolling and reeling as turbulently as the water in which she sat. Leaning back against the edge of the Jacuzzi and closing her eyes, she forced her mind to drift aimlessly, touching upon the more positive aspects of her life – she was looking forward to seeing Dominic and Karl again the following day. Her head filled with the memory of their encounter, the very thought causing her clitoris to swell and throb. It was idiotic to let herself become so wound up by one man when there were hundreds of others out there in the world who would be only to happy to pleasure her. Moving slightly she allowed the jets to pound remorselessly against her aroused flesh. To hell with Nicolai, she needed him like she needed a hole in the head. If only life were that simple.

She felt hot breath on her throat and this time, when she slowly opened her eyes, was not surprised to find herself looking directly into Nicolai's deep blue eyes.

'We thought it was time we had one of these at home,' nodding at the Jacuzzi. He reached into the water and stroked her breast, 'For something that has been designed for relaxation they can be very stimulating can they not?'

Karin jumped guiltily, why was he always catching her unawares?

'I'm a free agent, I can do what I like,' she knew she sounded petulant but it was the only response she could muster up. Shit, his manipulation of her breast was playing havoc with her train of thought.

'And you do, don't you?' he murmured, rolling her nipple between his thumb and forefinger before removing his hand and drying it on a nearby towel.

'Do what?' asked Karin, confused, hating the fact that she felt as gauche as a schoolgirl when he was around.

'You do what you like, don't you? And, you like what you do if what I've witnessed so far is anything to go by.'

'Oh, that business with Jon you mean,' she tried to dismiss the incident as inconsequential.

'Yes, there's that, of course, and then there's the other thing.'

She knew he was referring to the video tape of her previous encounter with Jon. Damn him, she had almost succeeded in forcing that to the back of her mind, confident that when the time was right she would recover it and put the whole incident behind her. But he wouldn't let her forget it.

'I must say, it makes a very enjoyable addition to an evening at home with a few business associates, several of them even asked me if I knew your telephone number. Are you interested?' He didn't wait for a reply.

Aghast, all Karin could do was stare after him, open mouthed, as he turned on his heel and sauntered casually to the far end of the room to rejoin Rosalinde, who was still deep in conversation with Mike and Julia. Making sure that Karin was watching, he pinched Julia's practically non-existent bottom causing her to squeal in delighted surprise. If Karin had not been so sickened by Nicolai's disclosure she would have been totally enraged by this action, as it was she merely sunk further into the water, willing herself with all her might not to burst into tears.

Chapter Seven

The day of her date with Dominic and Karl at Silverstone dawned bright and sunny, although it was still early the warmth in the air promised yet another gloriously hot day. Bearing this in mind, Karin opened her wardrobe and selected a strapless sundress in ice-blue cotton. As had become her custom lately, she wore no underwear other than a tiny pair of satin panties in the same ice-blue colour as her dress. As she dressed she enjoyed the way her clothing slithered sensuously over her curves, the thin material clinging to her naked breasts and hips like a sheet of transparent film and she looked forward to observing Karl and Dominic's reaction to her appearance. Although she knew its purpose was primarily business, the day held a lot of promise and she shivered in anticipation of its outcome.

With so much to look forward to she had managed to put the incident, or to be more exact, incidents, with Nicolai to the back of her mind. As far as Karin was concerned he was nothing, less than nothing in fact. It wouldn't have mattered to her if he'd watched her screwing every single man at her birthday party. In a way this was true, it didn't really bother her that she had been caught by him in *flagrante delicto* with Jon but she was concerned that he had a video tape of them, the man clearly had no morals and there was nothing to stop him using the tape time after time for his own personal gain or satisfaction. There was no way she would admit to herself that she found the idea of Nicolai sitting alone in the dark, watching Jon screw her, intensely arousing. As it was, she refused to let her mind dwell on such possibilities, she was no porn queen and if he thought she was going to let him show the tape to all and sundry he was sadly mistaken. She had already decided that the only solution was to go to the house and search for the tape herself!

She had debated whether to just come straight out with it and ask Rosalinde for the tape, taking the risk that Rosalinde knew all about Nicolai's voyeuristic activities, but something still held her back. Sometimes she baffled Karin with a code of ethics that seemed completely in contrast to her relationship with Nicolai and somehow, she felt that Rosalinde would not be too sympathetic in this case. Her responses were occasionally so unpredictable that Karin found herself wondering, at times, if Nicolai had some strange hold over his wife, like a Svengali or something. 'Never underestimate the power of the sexual weapon,' someone had once said to her, now she found herself wondering if this was at the root of Rosalinde's relationship with Nicolai. It worked both ways of course, even in the Bible women had successfully used their physical charms to enthral men.

During the drive to the race-track, she tried to work out the best way of approaching this thorny situation. It would be easy to gain entrance to the house, Rosalinde had invited her there on numerous occasions, but she had no idea how she would manage a full-scale search for the tape without arousing suspicion. There was no doubt in her mind that Nicolai would have it concealed somewhere, probably in his own bedroom, or in his study. One thing was certain, it wouldn't be lying casually on the coffee table or sitting on a shelf with Rosalinde's collection of 'Road' movies.

She was so lost in thought that she almost drove

straight past the entrance to Silverstone. Never having taken a lot of interest in motor sport, she felt quite blasé driving through the gates and following the carefully sign-posted route to the pits where the demonstrations were being managed but, as she drove over the bridge which crossed the track, she felt a small shiver of excitement, particularly as she looked down. In her mind's eye she could see the powerful cars speeding around the track beneath her and hear the roar of the crowd above the screaming engines. The imagery was so vivid that she half expected a team of mechanics to rush up to her car the moment she pulled into the pits and start to dismantle it.

It was quite an anticlimax when she found the pits almost deserted, save a few small groups of people huddled together in deep conversation. No one approached her as she slowed her car and looked around for some indication of where she should park. Eventually, as she drove around the rear of the garages, she discovered several rows of parked cars. Wondering if she'd made a big mistake in taking Dominic and Karl up on their offer, she made her way past the gleaming line of sports cars and limousines. Finally, feeling acutely embarrassed, she backed her 'old heap' into a vacant space between a Ferrari and a Lotus, without exception all the other cars looked hideously expensive. Locking her car carefully, although she doubted that anyone would want to steal it given the choice on offer, she looked around her. An arrowed route led her to a staircase which, in turn, led to the executive spectator boxes. At the first landing she paused to use the ladies lavatory and check her appearance. Admiring her reflection in the mirror she had to admit she certainly looked as though she could have arrived in a Ferrari.

At the top of the staircase the arrows led her into a vast room, on the far side of which was a wall of glass overlooking the track. Pertly pretty hospitality girls had everything under control, handing out name tags, pouring coffee from seemingly bottomless glass jugs and directing the guests to their seats at pre-arranged tables. As soon as she had presented her invitation and received her name tag Karin sauntered over to the buffet table, accepting a cup of coffee and surreptitiously grabbing a couple of biscuits. She hadn't had time to eat breakfast and so the biscuits were a welcome relief. A young man approached her and identified her as a 'group four person', indicating that she should sit at a certain table and enjoy her coffee until the briefing session began. Ignoring his directions, she walked over to the window instead, glancing down at the pits to see if she could catch sight of Dominic or Karl.

They were nowhere to be seen, so she decided to take a seat after all, feeling several pairs of eyes upon her as she crossed the room. As she sipped her coffee she glanced curiously around. So far she was the only female present, most of the guests seemed quite juvenile despite the fact that they were obviously loaded and she wondered how they could possibly manage to buy such expensive vehicles. Just lately she had been trying to work out if she could afford to buy Chris an old banger for his seventeenth birthday, now she felt guilty that she couldn't take the sting out of her split from Colin by giving him a Porsche, or something similar. Tears of self-pity sprang, unbidden, to her eyes and the sight of Dominic standing in front of her was a welcome relief.

'My God woman, what have they been doing to you,' he exclaimed, wiping away a large tear that had rolled down her cheek unchecked, 'it looks as though I got here just in time.'

Karin couldn't help laughing, 'I'm okay really, I was just thinking . . .'

'Then obviously thinking is not good for you, let's take you for a spin instead.'

Before she had time to protest, Dominic had grabbed her by the wrist, hauled her out of her seat and was dragging her towards the door. At the doorway he stopped abruptly and called across the room to one of the hospitality girls.

'Debbie, if Karl arrives before I get back please tell him to go ahead and give the first briefing, I won't be long,' he added.

The girl nodded, her lustrous red hair covering her face like a curtain. She was so pretty Karin couldn't help wondering, with a small stab of jealousy, if Dominic had had her, or was planning to.

As if he could read her mind, Dominic said, 'Debbie's a lovely girl, her boyfriend works with me and Karl, he preps the cars before they're painted.'

'Oh,' Karin tried not to look too pleased but decided she could afford to be generous, 'I think she's terribly attractive.'

'I suppose so.' To her surprise, and relief, Dominic sounded genuinely uninterested.

He led Karin through the pits until they reached an identical Cobra to the one they had been driving a couple of days before. Awed, she paused to admire its sleek lines and run her hands over the bodywork. Is this how a woman feels? she mused.

'Something like that.'

She jumped with surprise, 'I didn't realise I'd said anything aloud.'

'Perhaps I just read your mind.'

Dominic's voice was like silk, she had forgotten how seductive it was and immediately she was flooded by memories of their previous encounter. Flushed, she allowed him to tighten her safety belt, feeling the musculature of his arms graze her swollen nipples. The engine throbbed as they eased their way out of the pits then, as Dominic eased his foot down on the accelerator, they picked up speed, gliding smoothly out of the pit lane and onto the main track.

He drove fast but with the utmost care, taking the tight corners with expert precision and gunning down the straights. Her head whipped this way and that as Dominic waited until the last possible moment to fling the car into its next bend, all the time following the racing line. It was scary but thoroughly exhilarating, the wind dragging her hair into large tangles, her nails making painful indentations in the palms of her hands as she fought the urge to grip the edge of the seat. Eventually, Dominic eased his foot off the throttle and they coasted back into the pits. Karin was lost for words but Dominic was obviously expecting her to say something, his eyes were sparkling and his whole body radiated elation.

'That was . . . that was . . . amazing!'

She knew it was an inadequate use of words but she couldn't think of any other way to describe it. Nevertheless, Dominic seemed more than satisfied with her response and glowed with unrestrained pride as he led her back up the stairs to the briefing room. Karl was waiting for them impatiently, his briefing completed.

'Couldn't wait to get out on the old tarmac, eh?' He slapped Dominic playfully on the shoulder and winked at Karin, who responded with a broad grin. She dreaded to think what she must look like, as though she'd been dragged through a hedge backwards no doubt. Mind you they were used to seeing her that way. Again, she allowed her thoughts to drift back to her previous encounter with the two men, this time the memory of Karl spread-eagling her under a hedge was uppermost in her mind. Their encounter was obviously still fresh in his mind too.

'You were amazing the other day Karin, I haven't been able to stop thinking about it since.'

Karin blushed, 'How's the car, did you manage to get it fixed?'

Karl shook his head, concern momentarily creasing his brow. 'No, the problem was worse than we thought so we decided to concentrate on getting it back to the workshops where we could repair it ourselves. It'll be okay soon though,' he added, smiling at her.

At that moment they were interrupted by another of the hospitality girls, apart from her sandy blonde hair she looked, and sounded, like a clone of the pertly pretty Debbie.

'Karl, I'm sorry to interrupt you but groups four through seven are waiting to be briefed.'

Karl was suddenly businesslike again, assuring the girl that he would only be a few moments, waving a sheaf of papers at her as though to confirm the seriousness of his intentions.

'I'll make sure they've all got coffee and tell them you're on your way,' she asserted briskly, tossing her hair away from her face.

It was a mannerism which, on its own, would have exuded sensuality; combined as it was with a totally natural, genial air, it was unintentionally devastating. Even Karin was entranced. Amused, she noticed the way both Karl and Dominic watched the girl leave the room and then look at each other.

'You two are the limit,' she exploded, as soon as the girl was out of earshot, 'don't you ever think about anything else?'

'Yes,' smiled Karl, giving her an affectionate pat on the behind, 'cars.'

Pausing to pick up a clipboard from a nearby chair, he and Dominic led her into the briefing room. It was a small room, only about fourteen feet square, and all the seats were taken, apart from those directly in front of the lectern. Karl took his place at the front of the audience and motioned to Karin to be seated in one of the empty chairs in front of him. She did as she was bade, wiggling her fingers in a small wave to Dominic who moved to the back of the room.

Karl launched into his presentation immediately and Karin forced herself to concentrate as he described the hand-crafting and restoration processes that their cars underwent. By the time he got to the part where he described the layout of the track and the forthcoming demonstrations, she found her attention wandering and allowed herself a surreptitious glance at Dominic. Over her shoulder she could see him standing ramrod straight, his arms folded across his chest, wearing an extremely serious expression. She giggled to herself, he looked just like a night-club bouncer.

Although his voice didn't falter, she became uncomfortably aware of Karl's eyes boring into the back of her head. Guiltily, she turned back to face the front. As she did so, she thought she caught a glimpse of another familiar face but didn't dare to upset Karl any further by taking another look, she would just have to wait until the end of the briefing. Unfortunately Karl concluded his presentation by inviting, 'Anyone who is interested in getting out on the track behind the wheel of a four twenty-seven,' to make their way straight down to the pits. Although Karin didn't have a clue what this meant, the other guests obviously did as there was a virtual stampede to get out of the room. Dominic grinned at Karl.

'That should hook the serious ones.' He rubbed his hands together in a gesture of mock greed.

Karl nodded his agreement, adding, 'And with any luck the spread we've got lined up for lunch will weaken the others.'

The three of them trooped down the stairs to the pits which were now shimmering under an intense heat haze, it was just past midday and the sun was at its highest point. Shielding her eyes against the glare, Karin surveyed the scene. The pit area, which had been almost deserted when she'd arrived was now populated with sleek machinery and equally sleek prospective buyers. Now that the serious business was under way, the 'boy racer' element had thinned out, most of the men there now were older and obviously very well heeled. Karin was also pleased to notice a few more women had joined the throng.

Just then she spotted the man she had glimpsed in the briefing room, he was quite a long way off and standing with his back to her, yet there was something terribly familiar about him. At that moment Karl sauntered past, deep in conversaton with a much younger man who also looked familiar. Confused, she shook her head and blinked her eyes a few times, wondering if the heat was playing tricks on her. Then Karl and his companion both turned to face her, with a start she realised the young man was Jon. Rapidly her brain did a few calculations, the outcome hitting her a few seconds later like a thunderbolt, the other man, must be . . . oh, no, Nicolai!

It was the worst possible scenario as far as she was concerned and so outlandish she had to be having a nightmare, but if that were the case it was taking her a long time to wake up. There was no dignified way of looking at it, of the relatively small number of men present at the demonstration day she had had sex with three of them and another had twice caught her with her pants down, literally. Like a startled rabbit caught in the headlights of a car, she stood, paralysed in mute horror as the men bore down on her from all sides. Thankfully, it was Dominic who reached her first. Sliding his hand around her waist with reassuring familiarity he led her over to a gleaming, jet-black machine. Gratefully, she leaned her body against his, hoping in vain that the others would not catch up with them. As she sank wearily into the deep leather of the passenger seat and fastened her safety belt, she heard an all too familiar voice.

'Mind if I have a go?'

Nicolai inclined his head towards the black Cobra and looked questioningly at Dominic. In her distressed state of mind, Karin immediately thought he was making some kind of sexual proposition and motioned to Dominic to open the passenger door.

'Now just a minute,' she spluttered, wrestling with her seat-belt.

Dominic turned apologetically to Nicolai, 'I'm sorry sir I was just about to demonstrate this vehicle, however, if you wouldn't mind waiting?'

Thank God for Dominic she thought. Immediately her heart-beat began to calm down and she stopped trying to fight her way out of the car. Her relief was so great she didn't notice that Karl was whispering something to Dominic. To her horror, the next thing she knew was that Nicolai had settled himself in the driver's seat and was holding out his hand for the ignition key. As soon as she realised what was happening she started to protest but Karl hushed her.

'It's okay Karin, Mr Andreas used to race professionally at one time, he's quite a celebrity really.'

'No, he can't, I can't . . .'

She started to wrestle with her seat-belt again. Damn it, it wouldn't open. She scrabbled at the catch, breaking a fingernail in the process. It would be quite laughable really, if it wasn't so terrible, Karin thought. Poor, deluded Karl, he honestly believed she was nervous at the prospect of being driven by Nicolai because she doubted his driving ability. But thank God for that if it meant he was unaware they knew each other. She had almost succeeded in convincing herself that perhaps things weren't as black as she thought, when she caught sight of Jon leaning against the pit wall. Instantly reminded of the existence of the video tape, her heart began hammering harder than ever.

Feeling as though she were rapidly losing her self-control she stared at Nicolai, her eyes wide with panic. Calmly, he glanced down at the smooth curves of her heaving breasts, visible above the neckline of her summer dress, then back at her face, the corners of his mouth curving into a satisfied smile. The hateful swine! Suddenly feeling constricted despite her scant amount of clothing, she gasped for breath, shivering involuntarily as small rivulets of sweat snaked into her cleavage. Stroking her drenched skin with a single finger, Nicolai caught a droplet on the tip and tasted it. He looked at her for a long, long moment, saying nothing. She stared back, her skin aflame. Karl was still speaking but she couldn't hear him for the pounding in her ears. She closed her eyes in a feeble attempt to block out everything and did not open them even when she felt the car gurgle into life and throb its way out onto the tarmac. During the long, tortuous minutes as they hurtled around the twists and turns of the track she kept her eyes tightly closed, gripped the edge of the seat as though it were her last vestige of contact with sanity.

Eventually, after what seemed like an eternity, the car slowed down and glided to a halt. Trembling visibly, she looked around. Dominic and Karl were nowhere to be seen, only Jon was waiting obediently by the pit wall. His face was impassive and for a split second Karin found it hard to believe that they had both romped naked for hours. In a way she wished they hadn't, at least that way she wouldn't be forced to fret about the existence of a video tape of her exploits.

'You needn't worry, you know, your myriad secrets are safe with me.' Nicolai always sounded sincere but she couldn't trust him, although she wished with all her heart that she could.

Karin looked squarely at Nicolai, 'I don't believe you, I'm afraid.' Her voice sounded strange even to her own ears, very prim with precise, clipped tones.

'I used to have a governess who spoke like you,' murmured Nicolai, his breath hot against her ear. 'It was an incredible turn on.'

'Is there anything that doesn't turn you on?' snapped Karin sarcastically, losing her patience.

'Not unless you count beetroot and sweaty socks,' he smiled, reaching across her to open the passenger door.

'I'll be sure to wear some next time I see you,' she snarled, refusing to allow him to help her from the car.

He sat back hastily, partly to let her out of the car and partly in mock defence, 'Ouch, you're one prickly lady.'

Karin decided to ignore that remark and groped around for something to say.

'How's Rosalinde, your wife,' she added in what she hoped was a vitriolic tone.

Nicolai stopped smiling, 'She's been a bit under the weather since yesterday afternoon to tell you the truth, she'd probably appreciate a visit from you.'

Karin was immediately contrite, full of concern for her friend. After all, it wasn't her fault she had such a pig for a husband. 'Will she be at home tomorrow do you know?'

Nicolai nodded, 'I should think so, she didn't feel well enough to get out of bed this morning. I was thinking about taking her away on a short holiday, perhaps to Scotland, she loves it there,' he added.

'That's very thoughtful, Nicolai.' Karin knew she sounded patronising and felt guilty, she didn't mean to but the guy just rubbed her up the wrong way.

At that moment, Jon sauntered over, 'Everyone's going for lunch, boss.'

Nicolai glanced at his watch, 'I'm sorry Jon I don't have time, we'll have to grab a sandwich or something on the way to the airport.'

He turned to Karin, 'Please tell your friends I'll take one of these,' he smoothed his hand along the wing of the black Cobra.

Right on cue, Dominic and Karl were at her side.

'Nic . . . I . . . I mean Mr Andreas, would like one of these,' she stammered. Shit, she had almost given herself away.

Neither seemed to notice her slip of the tongue and, as they watched Nicolai striding away towards the open passenger door of a deep-blue Jaguar convertible, they winked at each other, Dominic pinching Karl on the cheek.

'Number five, number five, number five,' they sang jubilantly as soon as the Jaguar had pulled away.

She couldn't help feeling pleased for them, if anyone deserved to be successful they did. Grinning broadly like Cheshire cats, they linked arms with Karin and the three of them skipped into the building, ready to enjoy a good meal. Their blithe spirits more or less set the pattern for the rest of the day. With Nicolai off the scene, Karin was able to relax again and her afternoon at Silverstone seemed as though it would pass by more or less uneventfully. After a superb lunch, Dominic and Karl rushed off to carry out more demonstrations and take more orders, leaving Karin to wander the pits, admiring the cars for which she was developing a deep fondness and chatting to the hospitality girls.

As she sauntered around outside, soaking up the sun's rays, she found herself feeling increasingly sorry for Debbie, the red-headed girl who, so far, had been forced to spend the whole glorious day inside the building. The blonde girl had been slightly more fortunate, being able to work out in the sunshine, although she was infinitely busier than Debbie as she rushed from client, to car, to client, pausing every so often only to communicate with Debbie on a walkie-talkie.

Eventually, there was a lull, all the cars that could be driven were out on the track and the numbers were lighter by the eight people, and their drivers or wives, who like Nicolai had made a definite order. Similarly, some others had also left because they had enjoyed a free ride and free lunch but would not, or could not, place an order. Realising that she herself fell into the latter category, Karin started to feel as though she should be making tracks for home. She approached the blonde girl, whose lapel tag bore the name Natasha.

'Could you please tell me if either Dominic or Karl are around?' Karin looked about the pits as she asked, despite the fact that she was more or less certain that they were out on the track.

'Karl isn't, I saw him drive off a minute ago,' Natasha consulted a clipboard which she had carried with her all day, looking up she smiled warmly, 'According to this, right now Dominic should be showing our corporate video in the briefing room.'

Karin thanked her, deciding to pop upstairs one last time to let Dominic know that she was leaving and to thank him, one last time, for a lovely day. Once again she paused on the first landing to use the ladies lavatory and brush her hair. But this time, much to her irritation the outer door was locked from the inside, she stood outside the room waiting and, after a few moments, she thought she could hear muffled voices on the other side of the door. This was ridiculous, there was more than one cubicle inside, there was no reason why the door should be locked. She tried the handle again, just in case the door was simply jammed but it was no good, there was definitely someone inside.

Shrugging, she decided to continue upstairs but was surprised to find the briefing rooms deserted, with no sign of Dominic, a video demonstration, or even Debbie for that matter. Feeling regretful that she hadn't been able to see Dominic one last time, she started to make her way down the stairs once more, just below her to the right she could see the door to the ladies' lavatory opening. Thank goodness, now she wouldn't have to stop on the way home.

As she descended the last couple of steps she thought she could hear two voices coming through the open door. One definitely belonged to Debbie but the other was very deep, almost like a man's voice. At that moment Debbie slipped her head out of the room, surreptitiously looking around before she stepped out onto the landing, her clothes were rumpled and she had a smudge of her own bright red lipstick on her cheek. Karin smothered a grin. Well, well, well, good old Debbie, to think she'd been feeling sorry for the girl, cooped up inside on such a nice day. Debbie rushed past her up the stairs without pausing to say a word, a foot in the doorway of the cubicle indicated that her partner was about to make his getaway. There was nowhere for Karin to hide, and thus save his embarrassment, so she stood on the landing pretending to be engrossed in a lithograph of Stirling Moss, which was hanging on the wall at the side of her.

As she concentrated on the print, she sensed the man trying to sneak past her back. It was not that she had particularly sensitive sensory powers, but was more due to the fact that the landing was only about five feet square. He brushed against her, mumbling an apology. Turning slightly she recognised him immediately and whirled around.

'Dominic, how could you?'

She didn't know why she felt so angry, perhaps it was because she really liked Dominic, or maybe it was that she felt he had taken advantage of Debbie, after all he had said himself she had a regular boyfriend who worked for himself and Karl. In all probability it was a culmination of all the day's events or even, come to that, the events of the past few months. Whatever it was, she flew at him, hitting him about the chest and shoulders with all the strength she could muster.

When he got over the shock of Karin's sudden onslaught, he grabbed her by the wrists and pulled her to him, she was sobbing now, her mascara running down her cheeks in ugly black streaks.

'You bastard, how could you,' she screamed at him, dissolving into his arms.

Dominic had more understanding than she would have given any man credit for.

'Is that comment directed at me in particular, or just men in general?'

Gently, he stroked the hair back from her forehead, using his thumbs to wipe the sooty tears from under her eyes.

Realising she'd just made a complete fool of herself, Karin smiled shakily. 'I'm sorry you're right, it's not you, really.'

He didn't press her to say any more but merely nodded his understanding. Gathering her against his chest he held her tightly in his arms, rocking her gently backwards and forwards until she had calmed down completely. Karin could have stayed there for ever, it was the first time in a long time that she'd been held like that.

When she finally found her voice, she tried to explain, 'I've had to deal with a lot of stuff lately, some things I don't really understand and some I just can't handle.'

Nodding his understanding, he didn't press her to explain further. 'It's okay, it's just . . .' he looked down, releasing her slightly.

'Go on Dominic,' she prompted.

'Well, it's just, well, I like you a lot Karin but I don't want to get involved with anyone at the moment,' the words came out in a rush, tumbling over themselves.

She sensed his embarrassment, 'I do understand, I don't want a permanent involvement either,' her own realisation of the truth behind her words hit her as she spoke.

'What we had' she corrected herself, '*have* together is special and exciting and I'd like it to continue but not to the exclusion of all others, if you know what I mean?'

Dominic nodded, he looked relieved, 'You're very special Karin and I would like us to get together again very soon, if that's okay with you?'

She nodded, also smiling. Perhaps one day in the far off future she and Dominic would get it together on a permanent basis, or maybe, as was more likely, they'd enjoy great sex together and then part as friends. She was surprised to find herself thinking like that, she'd come a long way in such a short space of time she decided.

Eventually, the sound of voices drifted up the stairs, they were getting louder and more numerous, signifying that the testing part of the day had come to an end. Quickly, Dominic ushered her into the lavatory so that she could tidy herself up. When she finally emerged it was as though nothing had happened, Karl had returned and he and Dominic were both accepting deposit cheques from a pair of overweight American businessmen. Meanwhile, Debbie was rushing about, pouring coffee and handing out small corporate gifts: pens, key-rings, and the like.

Karin didn't like to interrupt Dominic or Karl, instead she forced herself to saunter casually over to Debbie and accept a free pen imprinted with their business address and telephone number. Putting it carefully in her handbag for future reference, she turned around and indiscreetly blew a kiss to the two men who responded with small, distracted waves; the Americans were obviously big spenders.

It was only when she finally arrived home, and was safely ensconced in the comforting warmth of a deep bubble-bath, that she allowed herself to reflect on the day's events. It seemed that since she'd split with Colin her life had become even more confusing and, just for a moment, she allowed herself a brief flash of doubt, perhaps she had just needed to play the field for a while, to get this unbidden, overwhelming feeling of passion out of her system. Perhaps she could learn to feel this way about her husband. Perhaps, and she hesitated to even think it, perhaps she and Colin should try again?

'NO!' she jumped up, shouting aloud.

No matter how bad things seemed at the moment, she'd had more fun, more adventure and certainly more *good* sex, in the past few weeks than she'd had with Colin during their entire marriage. For tonight she would concentrate on the enjoyable times she'd had lately and forget her problems with Nicolai and his bloody video tape. When all was said and done this was her summer of freedom, she'd earned it and she was damn well going to fly!

Chapter Eight

She awoke the next morning feeling totally refreshed. The good talking to that she had given herself the night before had done wonders for her ailing psyche. Smiling at herself in the mirror as she had showered she realised how good her body was looking now. Despite always being super critical of herself, she had to admit that, these days, she would be hard pushed to find anything major to complain about. Her figure was taut and sleek, not too rounded nor too muscular. She turned this way and that, admiring the pertness of her tight buttocks, her well-shaped legs, strong and firm, the muscles slightly more defined than elsewhere on her body.

Her breasts too were more resolute enabling her to dispense with a bra under most outfits. Rounded and pink tipped they bounced along in front of her, causing heads to turn and fingers to itch with the desire to mould themselves around each pliable, quivering mound. Totally self-absorbed, she struck various poses, emulating a centrefold – holding her hair on top of her head, pouting into the mirror, glancing demurely over one shoulder, cupping her breasts together so that her nipples jutted straight out. The only expression she couldn't quite get right was a sexy smoulder, but no doubt that would come with time.

Bringing herself back to reality she decided to give Rosalinde a call to see how she was bearing up and if she felt up to receiving a visitor. She was surprised and pleased when Rosalinde herself answered the telephone, announced she was feeling tons better and immediately invited Karin to lunch. Despite her friend's apparent recovery, Karin had a strange premonition that there was more to Rosalinde's illness than met the eye. For one thing her tone had seemed false, loaded with a sadness, which was inadequately covered with a thin veneer of enforced gaiety.

Karin sincerely hoped she had been imagining it, perhaps a vestige of her own gloomy feelings from the day before had lingered on and intruded into their conversation. Maybe it was herself who was the one trying hard to appear happy. Her thoughts immediately returned to the problem of the video tape, it really was blighting her life at the moment but, with a bit of luck, perhaps at some point today she'd be able to sneak into Nicolai's room and retrieve it. She hoped that would then be an end to it.

Any doubts she had had about Rosalinde's recovery were dispelled as soon as she arrived. Far from looking as though she were just recovering from an illness, Rosalinde looked positively glowing with health as she flung open the front door.

'Hi Karin, you look gorgeous.'

Karin was wearing the same all-white outfit that she'd worn on the day she met Dominic and Karl for the first time. Automatically, she ran her eyes approvingly over the tobacco and black patterned sarong and matching bandeau top that graced Rosalinde's lithe, mahogany body.

'So do you,' she responded, feeling relieved that her friend was looking so well. 'I feel as though you've got me here under false pretenses.'

'I have been less than honest,' admitted Rosalinde, leading the way through the house and out onto the patio. 'Not so much with you, but certainly with Nicolai.'

She stopped speaking abruptly as Jon strutted past them, unreservedly oozing virility, his well-conditioned body stripped to the waist and his mane of hair tied back in a pony-tail. Both women automatically followed his movements with their eyes, Karin unable to conceal a small gasp as the muscles on his back and shoulders rippled enticingly under a thin sheen of sweat.

'Fancy a replay, eh?' Rosalinde smirked.

Karin whirled round to face her, aghast, 'Wha . . . what do you mean?' All she could think about was the bloody video tape. There was no way she could accept finding out now that Rosalinde had known about it all along. But her expression was open and innocent.

'You know,' she smiled and then, as though she realised that she'd made a *faux pas*, 'oh, I'm sorry Karin, you feel embarrassed that you told me, perhaps you'd rather I forgot it?'

Relief flooded her, Rosalinde obviously didn't know anything about the tape after all. Misunderstanding the panic-stricken look on Karin's face, Rosalinde leaned across the table and patted her arm.

'It's OK, I won't ever mention it again.'

Nodding weakly, Karin accepted Rosalinde's offer of an aperitif, breathing a huge sigh of relief as she went inside the house to fix their drinks. By the time Rosalinde returned, bearing two huge glasses of Pimms, Karin was totally composed.

'Goodness, what a lot of fruit, I shan't be able to manage lunch,' she sipped her drink gratefully, it was turning out to be another stiflingly hot day.

Karin regaled her friend with the story of her meeting with Dominic and Karl, omitting nothing and then the details of her day at Silverstone, although this time she left out the part about her encounter with Nicolai. When they had exhausted the latest developments in Karin's sex-life they chatted for a while about inconsequential things, mutual acquaintances from the health club, diets, clothes and so forth. Eventually, they fell silent, wilting more than a little under the intense heat of the noonday sun.

'We can go for a swim before lunch if you wish,' Rosalinde stood up, casually removing her sarong. Underneath she wore an identical pair of bikini bottoms.

Karin smiled approvingly at her, she really was a beautiful woman. Rosalinde was now leading the way across the lawn to the pool extension. Through the open glass doors Karin could see cool, blue water lapping invitingly against the mosaic surround. Rosalinde pointed an elegant, perfectly manicured finger towards the changing room.

'You'll find a selection of swimsuits in there, or you can skinny dip if you'd prefer.'

Karin decided her safest option would be a swimsuit, she didn't want to run the risk of bumping into Nicolai again unless she was at least wearing something. All the swimsuits hanging in the changing room were gorgeous, making it difficult for her to choose one, eventually though she settled on a minuscule, white G-string bikini. Feeling Jon's eyes upon her as she stepped out of the changing room she ran quickly to the pool and dived straight in. The shock of the surprisingly cool water against her burning flesh made her gasp and she almost went under.

Rosalinde swam over to her, with long easy strokes, 'Are you okay?'

Karin nodded, 'Yes, really, I'm fine, the water feels a little cold that's all.'

To prove to her friend that there really was nothing wrong with her, Karin struck out boldly for the far end of the pool. For several lengths she and Rosalinde swam side by side, neither of them saying a word. Presently, Karin sensed that Rosalinde was trying to build up the courage to tell her something monumental. She wasn't wrong.

'By the way, I'm divorcing Nicolai.' Rosalinde trod water, smoothing her hair back from her forehead, affecting such an air of innocent calm that Karin thought she must have misheard. Perhaps she had water in her inner ear, obscuring her hearing, she shook her head hard in an effort to dislodge it.

'What did you say?' Karin immediately stopped paddling, almost going under in the process. Noticing her friend's discomfort, Rosalinde motioned to her to swim over to the side of the pool, once there they heaved themselves out of the water and sat on the side, idly paddling their feet.

Eventually Karin found her voice again, 'I'm sorry Rosalinde, it's just that I thought for one crazy moment you said you were planning to divorce Nicolai.'

'I did,' Rosalinde looked at Karin, her face was intensely serious. 'You don't have to act surprised Karin, I know what sort of a man he is and I know how you must despise me for putting up with his behaviour.'

Karin desperately wished she could deny Rosalinde's accusation but it was almost true, 'I could never despise you Rosalinde, you're too good for that.' And definitely too good for him, she wanted to add.

'I don't blame you for feeling the way you do, or for hating him, he is a complete and utter pig who cares about no one but himself,' Rosalinde was matter of fact.

Karin wondered if this would be a good time to mention the tape, but now Rosalinde had opened the floodgates she was in full flow. All through lunch she poured out such a litany of Nicolai's bad deeds that Karin's temples began to throb. Most of it was the usual unfaithful husband stuff, the lies, the excuses, telephone calls last thing at night to say he would be working late, mysterious callers who hung up when Rosalinde answered, unexplained 'gifts to himself' – a new tie, or underwear, some of them in such appalling bad taste that she knew beyond a shadow of a doubt that Nicolai would never have chosen them.

She was more intrigued, however, when her friend touched upon more interesting transgressions, particularly those involving their own sex-life which, apparently, had not diminished one iota during the times that Rosalinde was certain he was seeing someone else. Try as she might, Karin could not quell the thrills of vicarious excitement that flared within her as Rosalinde described the times he had tied her to the bed and lightly whipped her, or the many occasions he had asked her to accompany him to a sex-show or strip joint then enact what they had seen afterwards, in the privacy of their own home. Karin felt her mouth becoming dry as she listened to her friend's frank outpourings, it seemed as though Nicolai enjoyed an extensive repertoire of mildly deviant sex games. At each disclosure she did her best to sympathise with Rosalinde but in reality found herself becoming more and more aroused, perhaps it was this *dangerous* side of Nicolai that really attracted her to him despite her better judgement. Eventually, there was a lull and Karin, finding her voice, ventured to speak.

'How did he take the news, Nicolai I mean?' Although she didn't like to believe he was capable of such behaviour, she half expected Rosalinde to say that he'd gone berserk and hit her.

'That's just it,' Rosalinde murmured, toying with her straw, 'he doesn't know yet.'

Karin let out a low whistle, 'My God Rosalinde, when were you planning to tell him exactly, or did you think you could just leave him a note?'

Rosalinde was affronted, 'I'm no coward, Karin.' She stood up and began pacing up and down the patio, pausing every so often to check that Jon was not in earshot.

'I admit that during the past few days I haven't been ill as such,' she stopped and looked out over the gardens, her expression strained, she seemed to be struggling to find the right words. 'But I had to take some time out to think things through and, wouldn't you know it, Nicolai has actually been at home a lot during the past couple of weeks; it was the only way I could give myself some space.'

She looked down at her hands and then back across the gardens, tears forming just behind her lashes, 'It's ironic really but Nicolai seemed really concerned about me.'

Karin got up and walked over to her friend, placing

her hand gently on her shoulder. 'Are you absolutely sure about this Rosalinde, is it really too late for a reconciliation?'

Rosalinde sniffed and laughed ruefully, 'Believe me Karin despite what I've just told you, you still don't know the half of it. Nicolai is not a normal man.'

Feeling even more intrigued by this remark, Karin was, nevertheless, far too concerned about Rosalinde's feelings to press her any further.

'Besides,' Rosalinde was smiling now, all traces of tears gone from her eyes, 'I've found someone else.'

If Rosalinde had said she was planning to spend the rest of her life living on Mars Karin couldn't have been more surprised.

'Rosalinde . . .?' It was the best she could manage at short notice.

Karen would never have thought this cool, elegant woman could be capable of smirking, but she was. Not only that, but she was practically jumping up and down with excitement like a young child on Christmas morning.

'It's no good, I have to tell someone,' she looked as though she was about to burst.

'Well, go on then,' Karin urged in mock resignation.

Rosalinde quickly scanned the gardens to make sure no one else could hear what she was about to say, putting her mouth close to Karin's ear she whispered, 'It's Mike.'

Karin looked blankly at her, then realisation dawned, 'Not . . . from the party?'

Rosalinde nodded, her cheeks glowing bright pink even through her tan. 'The same and, ooh . . . Karin, he's got a lovely body.'

The plot was thickening beyond the limits of her comprehension, 'But I thought he was with that other woman, you know the skinny one, really flat chested, oh what was her name?' Karin groped around in her mind in an abortive attempt to recall the name of Mike's companion, at the same time trying, equally unsuccessfully, to obliterate the memory of Nicolai's obvious attraction for the young woman and how it had made her feel at the time.

'Do you mean Julia?' Rosalinde was totally calm now and had reverted to her quiet, controlled voice once more.

Karin nodded in answer, then nodded again as Rosalinde picked up the pitcher of Pimms and looked at her curiously.

Totally in control of herself once again, Rosalinde poured them both another glassful. 'She's not interested in Mike in that way, she's gay.'

'What . . . completely, with other women you mean?'

'Is there another way to be a lesbian?' Rosalinde's dry humour had returned with a vengeance. 'Mike and she are, literally, just good friends. Nicolai invited them both out to dinner with us that same evening, after the party, and Mike and I just sort of hit it off.' She looked thoughtful, remembering all the details, a small smile playing around the corners of her mouth. 'Nicolai didn't suspect a thing, he was far too preoccupied trying to woo the lovely Julia. Poor bastard, I almost felt sorry for him, he nearly turned himself inside out trying to attract her and all the time she was making furious eye contact with one of the waitresses at the restaurant.'

'Talk about perfect justice,' Karin couldn't help gloating, it was about time Nicolai got his.

'Yes, well,' Rosalinde looked subdued again, 'I've still got to break the news to Nicolai that I'm leaving him.'

'When are you planning to do it Rosalinde? I know from my own experience that there's never a right time for something like that.' Karin sipped her drink thoughtfully, remembering briefly how traumatic it had been when she and Colin had finally made the break, even though by that time they both knew their marriage was well past the point of no return.

'He's taking me to Scotland tomororw, I'll wait until we get there and get settled in and then I'll tell him. Mike knows all about the trip and what I'm planning to do there, if there's any problem he'll be there on the next flight.'

It seemed as though Rosalinde had her life under control but Karin couldn't help feeling a small shiver of apprehension, something about this situation just didn't seem right but, try as she might, she couldn't put her finger on it. At that point Madge arrived to announce that lunch was served on the patio. Karin swallowed hard, the last thing she felt like was food. Rosalinde's news had really shaken her and not just for the noblest of reasons.

She felt an enormous amount of empathy for her friend, of course, but she also had her own concerns. If Rosalinde left the house, or Nicolai for that matter, there was no way she'd ever be able to recover the video tape. If she was going to act it would have to be sooner rather than later. For the next hour or so, Rosalinde chattered on incessantly about Mike. She was so wrapped up in her own plans and dreams she didn't notice that Karin was hardly listening to a word she said. In the meantime Karin had been thinking hard and fast, finally she was satisfied that she had come up with a viable solution to her problem. With Rosalinde and Nicolai away in Scotland it would be the perfect, and possibly only, opportunity for her to recover the video tape.

Karin realised that she would have to plan her visit to the house very carefully, she couldn't afford to run the risk of anything going wrong. Rosalinde would be leaving for Scotland the following day and, according to her friend, her husband was definitely planning to travel with her. The only real drawback was that they had decided to go by train so Jon would not be driving them up, although she quickly realised that this particular *problem* could actually turn out to be a blessing in disguise.

She had forced herself to resist the temptation to ask Rosalinde any leading questions which may have aroused her suspicions and eventually settled on the simplest of plans so that there would be less risk of anything going wrong. The first step, persuading Jon to invite her to the house, was so easy she almost cried with relief. She trusted that his ego was so immense he would be only too willing to believe that Karin couldn't stop thinking about him and had to have him again. It was a foregone conclusion. Boldly, she invited herself to the house for seven-thirty the following evening.

The second major hurdle was Madge the housekeeper. Although she and Rosalinde had become very friendly of late, she was still a virtual stranger as far as Madge was concerned. Remembering Rosalinde's reference to Madge's love of soap operas, Karin had scanned the television pages with interest. That particular evening's programming schedules were crammed with them and, if Madge was as fanatical about soap operas as Rosalinde had led her to believe, there was no way she would forego any of them to keep an eye on her and Jon. The only thing she hadn't succeeded in working out in advance was how she would distract Jon so that she could search for the tape, deciding it would be easier to play that part by ear. If the worst came to the worst, she would tell Jon about the tape and bribe him, if necessary, to help her retrieve it.

By the time the following evening rolled around, Karin was a complete nervous wreck. She'd dressed with care, bearing in mind that she was supposed to be seducing a much younger man, and was more than pleased with the result. She'd come across the black suede mini-skirt months before in a boutique in town but had never had the courage to wear it. Now that her figure was trimmer and tighter she dared to try it on, matching it with a tightly laced corset in black leather. Black silk G-string panties, hold-up stockings and high heels completed the outfit. A last look at her full-length reflection confirmed her aspiratons, the whole ensemble was outrageously whore-like, precisely the stuff a young man's wet dreams are made of.

'Pity I don't have a whip,' she giggled to herself as she pouted in the mirror, applying yet another coat of blood-red lipstick. Her eyes were carefully shaded and outlined, the lashes heavily mascara'd into spikes. She teased and back-combed her hair into a cloud of wild blonde curls, turning her head this way and that to admire her handiwork. Deciding that she looked like a modern-day version of Barbarella, she covered her creaking outfit with a long raincoat, she didn't want to risk upsetting Madge as soon as she arrived.

Glancing down at the picnic basket on the passenger seat beside her and the cool-bag containing several bottles of wine on the floor, she mentally went over her plan, such as it was. She'd told Jon not to worry about food, adding, lasciviously, that he should concentrate on building up his strength.

Rosalinde and Nicolai were definitely in Scotland; she'd telephoned Rosalinde early that morning before they left just to confirm that the trip was still going ahead as planned, and had repeatedly tried ringing the house throughout the afternoon. Using a variety of disguised voices she'd asked for Mr or Mrs Andreas only to be told on each occasion, by an increasingly irritated Madge, that 'the Master and Mistress are away in Scotland.'

A few miles from Rosalinde's house, she started to feel jittery. Everything had gone so smoothly up until now, she didn't know how she would handle it if something went wrong. She was surprised to find that, despite the real reason behind her visit, she was actually looking forward to seeing Jon again and was particularly interested to see how he would react to her outfit. Although it had only been a couple of days since her last sexual encounter the frustration was definitely beginning to have an effect on her; to her own amazement she'd found herself eyeing almost every man she came into contact with, from the young window cleaner to old Mr Fergus at the Post Office.

At last she was turning into the driveway, she gulped hard, in a few minutes there would be no turning back. Resolutely, she picked up the wine and picnic basket, locked the car and marched up to the front door. She was just about to press the doorbell when she saw Jon standing at the side gate beckoning to her.

'It's OK, you don't have to look so worried, Madge and Bill aren't here. Mr and Mrs Andreas said they could spend a few days on the Isle of Wight with their daughter, you probably passed their car in the lane.'

Karin could not believe her luck and let out an audible sigh of relief. Jon, however, didn't appear to notice, he was too intent on eyeing Karin's outfit as she shrugged off the raincoat.

'Wow, you look hot,' he stepped forward and ran his hands down her leather-clad sides and over her hips, clasping her buttocks in both hands. Almost losing her balance, Karin melted into him and they kissed long and hard. Finally she broke away, a swift glance around her revealed that the table on the patio had been set with plates, glasses and cutlery. She handed Jon the cool bag which she was still holding in her left hand whilst, with her right hand, she stroked his long, tawny hair, lifting it and feeling the weight of it entwined between her fingers.

'I've just washed it and now I can't do a thing with it,' he laughed at the old cliché, moving over to the table to uncork the wine.

Karin eyed him approvingly as he poured their drinks. He was quite casually dressed, in light blue Levis and a white, heavy linen shirt, but he looked superb. His skin was tanned much darker than she remembered and she could see his back and shoulder muscles rippling under his shirt, despite the thickness of the material. Karin decided that she could allow herself to relax a little, make the most of her evening with Jon. After all, with everyone else away, she'd have plenty of time to look for the tape.

For a little while they sat next to each other without touching, sipping their wine and enjoying the stillness of the warm summer's evening. Karin was entranced as a pair of squirrels skipped across the lawn barely two feet in front of her as, from a long way off, a church bell tolled. The whole scene was absolutely idyllic and it was with more than a little regret that Karin realised she probably wouldn't be visiting that house again. She doubted that Nicolai would let Rosalinde keep it as part of her divorce settlement, he was much too malicious for that.

Lazily, Jon ran his fingers of one hand up and down her right leg. Karin glanced at him from under her lashes, he was leaning back in his chair surveying the scene in front of him as Karin had, his flowing mane of hair suiting his temporary position as king of all he surveyed.

'It must be very hard work keeping these gardens up to scratch,' Karin murmured.

His hand stopped moving abruptly. Thinking that she must have upset him in some way, possibly by reminding him that he was only the hired help, she turned to him, struggling to find the right words to appease him. To her intense relief he did not seem unduly perturbed, although he was looking at her strangely. As she turned her head back he surprised her by grabbing her bodily, lifting her out of her chair in one swift movement and gathering her up in his arms. She could feel his heart pounding with desire through his shirt and her own bodice. Feeling her breath quicken in response, she leaned her head weakly against his shoulder.

Carrying her only a few paces he set her down on the lush grass, his hands pushing her skirt higher up her thighs. She felt his fingers close around the elastic on her panties, yanking them free, allowing the warm evening air to bath her naked skin. The scent of rose petals mingled with the musky aroma of his excitement and she slipped one hand down between their bodies to feel the cool, smooth, hardness of his cock. Salaciously she rubbed it back and forth along her stockinged thigh, waiting until her thumb caught the first tell-tale drop of his juices before bending her knees as much as possible to allow him easy entry.

Without any preamble he followed her cue, thrusting

deeply inside her in one, long, smooth movement, filling her pelvis with an incandescent glow. Running her hands greedily up under his shirt, she allowed them to travel over the hills and valleys of his muscles, pinching and rubbing the sinews and pulling him closer to her with every thrust. Lifting her hips to meet his she felt his lips upon her shoulders and throat, teasing her with little nips and kisses. She felt her nipples swell beneath the constricting leather, the intensity of their arousal disturbing the rhythmic movements of her lower body. Now all her senses were focused on her breasts. Releasing her grip she felt the springy turf beneath her buttocks, the longer blades of grass probing and tickling her most sensitive parts.

Sensing that her attention had wandered slightly, he suddenly rolled over onto his back, taking her with him. Sitting astride his powerful body, her knees gripping his sides, she looked as wild as a Valkyrie as she rode him mercilessly, her hair flying in all directions. She could feel he was almost ready to come but she wasn't. Slowing down, she leaned over him, inching her body forward until the tip of his penis was all that remained inside her. Grinding her hips slowly she teased him, reaching behind her to cup his balls in her hands. He began to moan and reached up to rub her breasts through the cold but malleable leather of her corset. She wished she were not wearing any clothes, so desperate was she to feel his hands on her bare flesh. Her nipples chafed against the rough reverse-side of the leather and she cursed the fact that she had chosen a garment which was so complicated to undo.

Tiring of feeling her through her clothing, Jon reached behind her, rhythmically squeezing her buttocks as she ground against him, every now and then allowing a finger to slide between them and stimulate her anus. It surprised her to learn how pleasurable this could be, having always discouraged Colin from going anywhere near that part of her body. All too soon, she found the last vestiges of her self-control dissolving under his expert caress, now she too was ready. Bracing her hands against Jon's chest she raised her hips several inches from his body and, without releasing him fully, began to move quickly up and down. The heat was gathering within her rapidly, losing all pretence at finesse she sank down hard on him, provoking a lusty groan of pleasure. She felt him climax inside her and gripped his sides, marking him deeply with her fingernails as she rode out the waves of her own orgasm.

It had been stupendous and all either of them could do for a long while was to lay on the grass, spent but happy. Eventually, Jon got up and padded over to the table, returning with full glasses of wine for both of them. Karin accepted her glass from him and rolled over on her stomach, still waiting for her laboured breathing to subside. Stroking back a tendril of hair from her cheek, Jon stared deep into her eyes, for a moment looking so serious that Karin wondered what on earth he could be about to say. She didn't have to wait long.

'Now that was okay for a starter darlin' but when do we get to the main course?'

For a moment she wasn't sure if he was serious but one look at his grinning face told her otherwise. Forcing herself not to laugh, or even smile in response, she tried her best to appear prim and proper as she sat up and straightened her clothing, covering herself as best she could with the short length of suede she laughingly called a skirt. It wasn't an act she could keep up for long. Giggling, she groped around for her panties, leaning over to kiss Jon on the arm. Tantalisingly she allowed her tongue to snake a trail up and down the deep bronze skin, savouring the flavour of sweat, seasoned with fresh grass.

'I need to use the bathroom before I do anything else, otherwise . . .'

'Yeah, sure, you may as well use Rosalinde's, I . . . I mean, Mrs Andreas' bathroom,' he looked down guiltily, reminding her of the time Rosalinde had described Jon as being rude.

'Still waters run deep,' Karin murmured to herself as she climbed the staircase, ostensibly to use the bathroom.

She'd decided that Jon was far too fatigued to come chasing after her for a while. Despite his crack about starters and main courses he'd been almost dozing when she left him on the lawn, giving her a perfect opportunity to look for the tape. Nevertheless, she prayed there were no closed-circuit TV cameras in the garden, otherwise she might find herself having to come back yet again to look for *Karin and Jon Part Two*.

Cautiously, she pushed open the door to Nicolai's bedroom and glanced around. As far as she could tell, there was nothing out of place and no sign of any video tapes. Closing the door carefully behind her, she walked tentatively across the room to the wardrobes, confident that the tape would soon be in her possession. Unfortunately, it seemed they held nothing but clothes. Feeling disappointed and more than a little desperate, she moved to a large chest of drawers, rifling purposefully through each drawer in turn, she came up empty handed. Equally, there was nothing untoward in his bedside cupboards, nor in his bathroom cabinet. She even checked his weight racks just to make sure there was nothing concealed behind the precisely graduated stacks of dumb-bells. Wherever the tape was, it wasn't in Nicolai's bedroom, she thought grimly, crawling backwards out of the bedroom on her hands and knees to obliterate the obvious marks her feet had made in the deep pile of the carpet.

Almost in tears she inched her way out of the room. In her wildest expectations she'd imagined she would find a concealed TV and video unit, the player complete with the offending tape. As it was, she would have to search his study as well, which was a prospect that she was even less keen about. Although being on the ground floor the room would be much more accessible to her, it would also put Jon within earshot of her activities. Deciding that she would have to simply rely on an opportunity presenting itself later in the evening she made her way to Rosalinde's room. A quick glance at the clock told her she'd been gone a long time, if Jon wasn't already wondering where she was he soon would be. Quickly she cleaned herself between her legs and pulled on her crumpled panties, carefully shaking the blades of grass into the toilet bowl and flushing it.

It was just as she was leaving Rosalinde's bathroom that she heard the voices. Several different tones drifted up the stairs, assaulting her ears, she couldn't make out all of them but she knew for certain none of them belonged to Jon. She was equally certain that one was Nicolai's and she could also hear at least one woman speaking, although it didn't sound like Rosalinde.

Oh my God she wanted to scream.

Once again Nicolai had caught her doing something she shouldn't, only this time it was much worse. She wasn't merely *in flagrante* with his gardener, this time it was serious, she'd been about to steal from him. She knew without doubt that she was trapped, there was no way she could escape over the balcony and if she used the stairs Nicolai would be bound to catch her. There was only one thing for it, it looked as though she would have to brazen it out. Tossing back her hair and looking directly ahead she marched boldly down the stairs, straight into Nicolai's arms.

Chapter Nine

If Nicolai was surprised to see her there he certainly made a good job of concealing it, although he didn't pass up the opportunity to run his eyes up and down her body, taking in every detail of her slightly outlandish appearance.

'My dear Karin, what a pleasant surprise,' he stepped backwards, allowing her to descend the last couple of stairs on shaky legs.

Gripping the banister firmly for support, Karin tried hard to quell her rising panic by steadfastly maintaining eye contact with Nicolai for several moments until, inevitably, she finally conceded. Allowing her gaze to falter slightly, she took in the interested stare of his female companion, whom Karin had never met before. Standing next to Nicolai, and almost a head taller than him, was a statuesque blonde. Karin noticed how, with her stunning appearance, this amazing creature almost overpowered him, her closely cropped hair serving only to accentuate the most perfect bone structure she had ever seen. Noticing Karin's curiosity Nicolai introduced the girl to her simply as Rakel, adding that she was from Sweden. Karin was not surprised at the girl's Scandinavian origins, large breasted but with a narrow waist and hips she was a sensational combination of the very best her heritage had to offer. Timidly, Karin extended her hand but Rakel merely inclined her head, saying nothing.

Just then the sight of Jon hovering in the background caught Karin's eye, wide awake now he looked extremely nervous. Not for the first time she suspected that, as employers go, Nicolai was a hard taskmaster. She was sure Jon wished he could escape this tricky situation as much as she did, perhaps they could both make a run for it, she thought idly, but it was already too late. Without turning around Nicolai commanded Jon to step forward, his tone icy as he flicked his gaze impassively between the trembling figures of Karin and his deviant employee.

'I hardly need to ask what has been going on here.'

He glared hard at Jon for a few seconds and then, to everyone's overwhelming surprise and relief, threw his head back and laughed loudly, clapping Jon on the back and winking at Karin and Rakel. Rakel remained expressionless, it was difficult to discern whether her apparent disinterest was because she hadn't understood the finer points of what had just taken place, or were merely humourless. Despite her trepidation, Karin managed a small, shaky smile. She was dying to ask Nicolai about Rosalinde but didn't dare to, it was obvious that, for one reason or another, she and Nicolai had parted company fairly near the start of their trip to Scotland.

'I . . . I should be going,' murmured Karin, looking wistfully in the direction of the front door, it seemed a terribly long way off and Nicolai was blocking her path.

'Nonsense,' Nicolai turned and took Rakel's arm, 'the night is yet young, let us all have a drink and get to know one another a little better.'

Although all her instincts urged her to refuse, something more powerful compelled her to follow Nicolai and Rakel into the large, elegant sitting room, Jon followed hot on her heels. Despite her nervousness, Karin took a few moments to survey her surroundings, appreciating what she saw. Spacious yet congenial, the room was extremely well appointed, with an abundance of overstuffed leather sofas and chairs, thick antique rugs and valuable artefacts. She couldn't help wondering, of Rosalinde and Nicolai, whose sense of taste and style was ultimately responsible for achieving such an effect.

With apparent indifference to the gentility of her surroundings, Rakel flopped into a deep leather chair next to the fireplace, carelessly splaying her long legs so that it was immediately apparent to everyone she was wearing no panties. Feeling slightly annoyed, Karin observed Jon's licentious expression and the way he deliberately chose the seat directly opposite Rakel. As an act of defiance, Karin emulated Rakel's audacity, sprawling voluptuously on the sofa, a good expanse of tanned thigh visible above the black lacy tops of her stockings. As acts go it was a command performance, and one which didn't go unnoticed by either Jon or Nicolai, she noticed with smug satisfaction.

Her elation was short lived. In no time she realised she was starting to feel a little woozy, she hadn't eaten all day and the wine she'd shared with Jon earlier had gone straight to her head. Desperately wanting to refuse when Nicolai crossed the room and handed her a glass, she nevertheless accepted it meekly, staring bleakly into the clear depths of the gin and tonic contained within. Without asking Rakel what she would prefer to drink, Nicolai also poured her a glass of gin and tonic, then prepared a measure of Scotch and soda each for himself and Jon.

'Cheers,' he smiled, raising his glass to his lips and taking a large gulp of the amber liquid.

Everyone nodded in reply and likewise raised their glasses. Karin sipped her drink slowly thinking that, under different circumstances, the evening would have had the potential of being very enjoyable. No one spoke, although Rakel's body-language was deafening, she was making an open play for Jon and he was falling for it hook, line and sinker. Karin knew she didn't have any claims to him but felt affronted just the same. Covertly, she eyed Nicolai, wondering how he would react to this little display. Typically for him, if he was at all disturbed by it he was doing an excellent job at covering it up.

Deciding she must still be very naîve, believing that couples should at least remain faithful for the duration of the evening, Karin decided to relax and treat the experience as just that, an experience. She would have a few drinks, enjoy the floor-show for a little while and then go home. It was a shame she would be going home without the video tape as a souvenir but, *c'est la vie* . . .

At that moment she was startled by the unexpected sound of someone ringing the front door bell. Nicolai glanced at Jon, slightly raising one eyebrow by way of a command, Jon immediately jumped to attention, exiting the room in a few strides. Once again muffled voices filled the hallway, whoever it was Nicolai was obviously expecting them. Nodding almost imperceptibly to himself, he put down his glass and walked across the room to the sitting room door, opening it wide to welcome his guests. Intrigued, Karin craned her neck to catch her first glimpse of the new arrivals, a man and a woman.

Although equally stunning the woman was, in terms of appearance at any rate, the complete opposite of Rakel. Very small boned and dark, she looked almost but not quite oriental. At first glance she appeared to have originated from the Philippines, her exquisitely fragile, elfin face was framed by a sleek chin-length bob and dominated by large, almond shaped eyes. Although fascinated by her whole appearance, Karin found herself especially drawn to this woman's eyes, noticing eventually that what made them particularly unusual was that they were slightly slanted but also, like Western eyes, deep-set and fringed with thick, dark lashes.

Despite the overwhelming visual evidence that she possessed genes which originated in the Pacific region, this misconception was quickly dispelled when she spoke, for her tones were unmistakably pure Texan drawl. In no time at all Karin came to realise that, not only was she visually quirky, her personality was also in complete opposition to her appearance. Outspoken and a natural leader she was someone who, despite her diminutive stature, seemed to fill the room with her natural effervescence. All in all, it was a stunning combination.

Almost paling into insignificance beside her was her male companion who, as soon as he spoke also gave himself away as an American, although his accent was plainly not from the same state as the woman's. Taller than either Nicolai, or even Rakel, he towered over all of them at well over six feet. Karin thought he looked typically American, like so many Hollywood stars she had seen in films, or up and coming young senators. Perfectly even, white teeth forming a winning smile within the setting of a strong, boyishly handsome visage, which was crowned by thick, collar-length, mid-brown hair, slightly waved and slicked back from his temples. On his lean, well proportioned body he wore a smart business suit, unconventional in cut and colour – a deep turquoise – he wore it with casual aplomb, perfectly complementing his easy going, relaxed demeanour.

Although he was not automatically *her type*, Karin decided on the spot that she liked this man and found his congenial nature disconcertingly attractive. Nicolai cleared his throat, preparing to make the necessary introductions but the other man beat him to it.

'Hi, I'm Kurt,' he stretched out his hand towards Karin and nodded towards his companion who was already helping herself to a drink, 'and that's Gloria.'

Karin took his hand, noting how strong and capable it felt, 'I'm Karin, hi yourself,' she murmured in what she hoped was a seductive tone. The atmosphere in the room had changed considerably with the arrival of Gloria and Kurt. Instantly Karin started to feel relaxed and was gratfied when Kurt automatically sat next to her on the sofa, casually laying his arm along the back of the seat. Gloria smiled in her direction and raised her drink, nodding pleasantly in reply, Karin did the same with her own.

'Bottoms up,' said Rakel, smirking.

Her voice gained the instant attention of the whole room, it was the first time she had spoken all evening and Karin was surprised to hear how good her English accent was. Jon had resumed his seat opposite her but Rakel was now sitting with her legs crossed demurely, no doubt to his immense disappointment Karin thought smugly. Turning her attention back to her own immediate vicinity, she was uncomfortably aware of the heat emanating from Kurt's body. With a shiver of uncontrolled desire she remembered feeling exactly the same way a few weeks earlier when she'd been seated next to Nicolai.

There was no doubt about it, the three men present were extremely attractive by anyone's standards. Nicolai, with his overtly Mediterranean swarthiness and deep blue, *bedroom* eyes, Jon with his youthful, self-assured, leonine masculinity and Kurt, with his undeniably mischievous charm. Definitely 'cute' as the Americans themselves would put it, thought Karin as she surreptitiously moved a little closer to him.

For a while everyone sat in silence, sipping their drinks from time to time and exchanging eye contact with one another, or furtively watching the others to see who was eyeing who. Karin noticed that Gloria was already pouring herself a second drink. Picking up the gin and Scotch bottles in each hand, she waved them around.

'Anybody?'

The honeyed tones of her accent sliced smoothly through the oppressive silence like a knife through butter. Karin, Jon and Kurt shook their heads but Nicolai sauntered over to her, taking possession of the bottle of Scotch.

'I'll have another.'

He added several ice-cubes to his glass and filled it to the brim, looking meaningfully into Gloria's eyes as he did so. Karin felt her stomach muscles contract and she blushed involuntarily as she felt the now familiar tingle between her legs. Her flushed cheeks didn't go unnoticed.

'I think some of us are feeling a little uptight this evening.' Nicolai looked straight at her, his words hardly more than a murmur, yet to her they felt as intimate as a caress.

Although Nicolai made no move towards her, Kurt took his cue. Leaning back slightly from Karin, he began to massage her shoulders with firm but gentle strokes. She wanted to protest, aware that she had become the centre of attention and feeling thoroughly foolish because of it, but gradually the pressure of Kurt's fingers began to work their magic, her limbs turned to water and her stomach to jelly. If he had wanted her right there and then he could have had her.

Disappointingly, in Karin's view, Kurt's fingers did not stray from her shoulders to any other part of her body but maintained the same, hypnotic rhythm. Nevertheless, she noticed there was a subtle change in the atmosphere, it had moved out of the polite stranger zone and into the much more interesting, possibly dangerous, territory of erotic expectation. Nicolai was standing very close to Gloria, almost touching but not quite, their bodies slightly inclined towards each other, as though drawn inevitably together by magnetic attraction. Her almond eyes glinted in an otherwise impassive face as she glanced slyly sideways at Nicolai, acknowledging his presence, the only indication that she was at all stirred by his closeness was the hardening of her nipples, clearly defined through the gossamer thin silk of her camisole top.

Rakel had resumed her provocative position, her tight, white mini-skirt hiked well up her legs, revealing the full length of her lean, brown thighs and providing the whole room with a clear view of her pale blonde pussy. Karin swallowed hard, for some reason she could not tear her eyes away from Rakel, or rather, from her exposed flesh, she had never seen that part of another woman, except in magazines, and Rakel's bush was so fair that she almost looked as though she had no pubic hair at all. She felt the heat beginning to gather deep within her, her clitoris pulsating in time with Kurt's manipulations.

The sexual dynamics were clearly getting to all the women. Rakel took a long draught of her drink, draining her glass which she then set down carefully on a side table. Gloria firstly licked her lips, the pink tip lingering at the corners as though her mouth had suddenly gone dry, then ran her hands down her body, smoothing imaginary wrinkles from the short, red velvet skirt she wore, running her hands slowly and provocatively over the slight curve of her hips and buttocks.

Jon was the first to break the tension, with one easy movement he crossed the room and sat at Rakel's feet. Staring at Karin's rapt expression, he slowly ran his fingers up and down Rakel's legs, from ankle to thigh and back to ankle, first the left, then the right, not taking his eyes once from Karin's face. She felt the tell-tale flush creeping up her neck, once again suffusing her cheeks, but could not tear her eyes away from Jon's fingers. Shifting in her seat, she held her breath as his fingertips crept up the length of tanned flesh, easing themselves over her kneecaps and stopping just short of the blond 'vee' where the inside of Rakel's thighs almost met.

With an enormous effort she forced herself to avert her gaze, alighting her eyes instead on Nicolai. Straight away she wished she hadn't. With an intense pang of jealousy, she noticed that Nicolai was now standing behind Gloria, his hands resting lightly on her shoulders as he towered over her. When he caught Karin's eye he smiled disdainfully, patently enjoying her look of yearning as he eased down one of the straps on Gloria's camisole in order to stroke his finger the length of her collar bone. Bending his head to kiss her shoulder, he slid his powerful hands further down her body encompassing her diminutive breasts in a single fluid motion. Shocked to the core by such an overt display, and wishing desperately that she could take Gloria's place, Karin gave a small gasp.

All of them laughed, Gloria tossing her head back and gurgling deeply, Rakel giving a short, sharp, 'ha!' and Kurt, Jon and Nicolai making deep, throaty sounds of varying pitch. Nicolai caught Kurt's eye and nodded at Karin.

'Don't let this young lady fool you, she's not quite as easily shocked as she would have you believe.'

Karin held her breath, even in her, albeit limited, experience of this man she knew he never said anything simply for the sake of it, Nicolai was leading up to something and she dreaded to think what it might be. She glanced at Jon, wondering if he knew about the video tape and, if he did, if he was nervous of the possibility that Nicolai may choose to show it that evening. But the thought had obviously not even entered his head. Having quickly tired of playing games, he now had his hand between Rakel's legs, parting them as much as the chair would allow. In horrified fascination Karin watched as her lover of barely an hour earlier plunged his fingers deep into the other girl, inducing a low moan of pleasure. In her profoundly confused state, Karin wasn't entirely sure if the sound came from Rakel's throat, or her own. Involuntarily, she felt her own legs part, deep within her was a smouldering passion that was in danger of being unleashed indiscriminately.

Although slight, this movement did not go unnoticed. Nicolai in particular stopped fondling Gloria and stared at Karin with a new expression which she hoped was lust. It went against all her finer instincts but she felt extraordinarily pleased at such a positive reaction from him. Without wanting to admit it to herself, she had developed a deep yearning to be desired by the nefarious Nicolai; to be able to exercise her physical power over him. Without taking her eyes from his face, she executed a sinuous wriggle which almost dislodged her breasts from their black leather corset.

In the hope of further inflaming him, she crossed her legs, slowly and deliberately, enjoying the sensation of friction between her stocking-clad legs. She was so intent on Nicolai's reactions that she had temporarily forgotten about Kurt, who had stopped massaging her. Turning her head to look at his face, she saw that he was watching Gloria as she swayed gently from side to side, rubbing her buttocks against Nicolai's thighs. Nonplussed, Karin took several sips of her gin and tonic. It seemed as though each person in the room had deliberately set out to attract one of the others in some way, with the intention of provoking yet another person into a sexual or jealous reaction. One thing was certain, there was a lot going on under the surface that she didn't know about and all her instincts screamed at her to leave, to get out now while things were still on a relatively polite, sociable footing.

It was already too late. Announcing that dinner was served, Nicolai led the way into a much larger room, again furnished with huge leather sofas but with the addition of a long mahogany table laden with tasty titbits. It all looked very inviting, although Karin couldn't help wondering when he had arranged all this, and who had prepared it. As if he could read her mind, Nicolai moved to her side and murmured in her ear.

'There's an excellent little catering company just around the corner from my office, I can always rely on them to come up trumps at short notice.'

He held out a stuffed date to her, touching it gently against her lips, feeling slightly foolish she took it between her teeth, it was delicious. Smiling, Nicolai put his arm around her waist, his thumb slightly brushing the side of her breast. Inexplicably, she felt relieved that her reaction had obviously pleased him. Although she still felt nervous when he was around, she had finally confessed to herself her desire for him, it was as though Rosalinde's announcement that she was leaving Nicolai had liberated Karin's true feelings. As there was no possibility of her leaving the party, she decided she might as well try to relax and enjoy the evening. When all was said and done, they were simply ordinary people and Nicolai, although slightly disconcerting at times, was no Marquis de Sade.

The food was absolutely delicious and for some time everyone hovered around the table, picking at tasty morsels and making smalltalk. Karin tried not to feel repulsed that Jon had not washed his hands first as she watched him scoop up some anchovy relish with his forefinger and lick it off, all the time staring at Rakel. Glancing across the table she noticed Kurt watching Jon as he did this and a shiver coursed down her spine, surely such a gorgeous man couldn't be gay. In Karin's sheltered world people were either heterosexual or homosexual, there were no grey areas, no overlapping tendencies. It was an illusion which would soon be shattered.

The banquet was washed down with copious amounts of wine, after her third glass Karin stopped being discriminating and happily sloshed a measure of whatever came to hand into her glass. She was really starting to enjoy herself and found Gloria particularly entertaining. She was full of wisecracks and quick rejoinders and had a varied repertoire of jokes which veered from the slightly risqué to downright crude.

One by one they drifted away from the table, making themselves comfortable once more on the leather sofas which seemed to be a hallmark of the house. When everyone was seated, Gloria walked across the room to the open liquor cabinet. Helping herself to a bottle of coffee liqueur she asked Nicolai if he had any whipped cream. Jon immediately piped up that he knew where Madge kept some and offered to go and fetch it. While he was gone Gloria rummaged around in her copious handbag, with a smile of triumph she produced three identical drinking glasses.

Karin studied them as she set them out on a table, half filling each one with the liqueur. They were more like test tubes, about an inch and a half in diameter and six inches tall. They were all intrigued, wondering what Gloria was about to do. The sound of the door opening and closing signalled Jon's return, he was carrying a large aerosol can of whipping cream.

He handed it to Gloria, 'Will that do?'

Gloria nodded, 'It's perfect, Jon, thank you.' As a reward she reached around the table and squeezed his balls, 'Mmm, nice,' she murmured, almost to herself.

Jon had the grace to blush but no one except Karin noticed, they were all too busy watching Gloria, wondering what she was about to do next. She looked at all their faces, then smiled at Karin and Rakel.

'Haven't either of you ever played *Blow Job* before?'

They both shook their heads. Gloria motioned to them to come forward to the table. Walking down to the other end of the room she picked up a dining chair.

'It's more comfortable if you're sitting down,' she explained, positioning the chair in front of one of the glasses.

Karin and Rakel followed suit, now the three of them were seated around the table, one of the glasses of coffee liqueur in front of each of them. Swiftly, Gloria shook the can of cream and swirled it around the top of the glasses, making sure that it peaked above the tops as high as possible. With one hand she gathered her hair into a pony-tail at the nape of her neck, holding it away from her face as she bent her head over the glass in front of her.

'Now watch and take note, girls,' she commanded.

Karin and Rakel fixed their eyes on Gloria with rapt attention, Jon remained hovering by the table, Nicolai and Kurt were the only ones not watching her. Their heads close together they were deep in whispered discussion. Suddenly the pink tip of her tongue appeared between Gloria's slightly parted lips, delicately it touched the cream, lingering tantalisingly on the very peak before swirling gracefully around the outer edge. Momentarily it disappeared back inside her mouth as she tasted the cream, then it snaked out once again encircling the point where the cream had already started to wilt over the edge of the glass. Methodically, starting at the bottom of the glass and working her way upwards, she caught each milky trail. Gradually the cream began to sink into the dark liqueur in biscuit coloured strands. She looked up.

'I guess you've probably got the idea by now,' she downed her drink, nodding to Karin and Rakel to do the same.

'Now I'll get us all a refill and we can have a contest, get the guys to award marks out of ten or something for licking and sucking.'

At the mention of the words 'licking' and 'sucking' Kurt and Nicolai looked up expectantly.

'Did we miss something?' Kurt craned his neck to see what the girls were up to.

Gloria was just putting the finishing touches to the last glass.

'You will if you and Nicolai don't get your butts over here. Like now,' she commanded.

Obediently Kurt, Nicolai and Jon fetched chairs for themselves and soon all six people were seated around the table, boy then girl fashion. Gloria glanced around the table.

Looking at Karin and Rakel she said, 'Now you can only use one hand, and that's just to steady the glass, no wanking please.'

Karin giggled but Rakel looked confused, Nicolai leaned across the table and whispered something to her.

'Ha!' Rakel's strange laugh suddenly exploded from deep within her, almost toppling the glasses.

Gloria gave her a mock glare, 'Careful please, this is a serious business.'

She turned to look at Kurt, Jon and Nicolai in turn.

'Now guys we're depending on you to judge this thing fairly, that means no favouritism just to win brownie points with the lust of your life.'

She looked meaningfully at Jon and then across to Rakel. Gathering up her hair once again, she smiled at Karin who followed suit with her own blonde curls.

'Okay, ready, set, go!'

Immediately all three bent their heads, tongues licking and caressing the cream laden glasses. Rakel went straight for the kill. Forming a perfect 'O' with her lips she lowered her mouth over the glass, taking in the full length and moving her head rhythmically. Each of the men sucked in their breath sharply, she certainly knew what she was doing. Karin, less skilled in that area, decided to opt for the sensitive approach, delicately lapping at the top and edges of the cream with deft strokes of her tongue. Soon all the women were totally intent on their task, licking and sucking as though the glasses genuinely were the real thing. Karin, naturally, imagined her glass belonged to Nicolai, she wondered if, later on in the evening, she would look back on this and realise that she had been practising for what was to come. With a thrill of excitement at the thought, she allowed herself to look up and immediately found her eyes locked with those of Nicolai, the very object of her desire. With renewed lust she attacked her glass and was pleased when the men voted her 'most seductive cock sucker'.

The game had succeeded in setting the tone for the rest of the evening, there was no going back Karin realised and she hoped, if they ended up pairing off, she would find Nicolai as her partner. It certainly seemed as though Jon and Rakel were destined to have one another before the night was out, one glance at their body-language was enough to confirm that, but she wasn't sure if Kurt and Gloria were romantically involved, or merely friends. She sensed a camaraderie between them but otherwise they had shown no sign of mutual attraction.

The combination of good food and plenty of alcohol had resulted in everyone feeling much looser and more relaxed with each other. Karin no longer found it disturbing that Rakel chose to display the most intimate part of her body to the rest of the room, nor was she shocked by Gloria's earthy demeanour and crude expressions. In contrast to her previous attitude, Karin now felt a grudging respect for the two women and their almost primitive inclinations. Certainly Nicolai did not seem to be put off by Gloria's vulgarity, which was the complete opposite of his wife's refined demeanour. Or perhaps that's why he likes Gloria, Karin thought to herself in a flash of inspiration.

While she was thinking, the others were drinking, and laughing, and talking, and she suddenly realised that she had missed something interesting.

'What was that?' She shook herself out of her reverie, addressing no one in particular.

'Nicolai was just telling us that he has amassed quite a collection of erotic movies.'

Gloria leaned comfortably against the back of the sofa, stretching her slim legs out in front of her. Karin paled, just when she was starting to enjoy herself she was suddenly brought back to reality with a jolt. Nicolai stood up, stretching slowly like a cat, his arrogant smile taking in Karin's shocked countenance. He walked across the room to a tall mahogany cupboard, flinging open the doors he revealed row upon row of video tapes. Tapping his forefinger against his lips he pretended to consider all of them, although Karin knew that he knew full well which one he intended to choose. Pretending to have come to a difficult decision he reached to the top shelf, selecting the only video in a red case. With annoying slowness he removed the tape, taking care to brush imaginary dust from it before inserting it into a player which was also concealed within the cupboard.

Her mouth had gone completely dry and she was having difficulty breathing steadily. Taking a large sip of her drink she watched him carefully, like a small animal wary that it is being stalked by a predator. There was no sign of a TV in the cupboard. She looked around the room at the others, no one else appeared to be interested in Nicolai's movements. Kurt and Gloria were whispering intently to each other, whilst Jon and Rakel kissed and fondled, seemingly oblivious to the rest of the party. Nicolai clapped his hands together twice.

'Ladies and gentlemen,' he began, assuming the role of ringmaster, or master of ceremonies. 'For your delight and delectation I present a home-grown number, Karin and Jon!'

With that he removed a large painting which hung over the fireplace, revealing an expanse of television screen and pressed a button the remote controlled handset which he held in his left hand. Automatically the lights dimmed and the screen flickered into life.

Chapter Ten

It was a relief that the lights were so low, Karin thought, at least no one could see how red her face was becoming as the first scene unfolded before them. It opened, of course, with Karin entering the bedroom and looking around. Nicolai had obviously edited the film because this part was extremely short and there was no shot of her going out onto the balcony, or speaking to Rosalinde on the telephone. Instead, the Karin on the film, walked over to the bed, stripped off her outer clothes and lay down, falling immediately into a deep sleep. Cut to Jon entering the room and finding Karin's sleeping figure, watching her for a few minutes as she writhed against the coverlet.

Trying hard to view the tape dispassionately, Karin was intrigued to see how seductive *the girl*, as she considered herself, looked in her peach, cotton underwear. The thin material moulding itself to her damp, perspiration soaked body. Looking at herself through Jon's eyes, she realised how little effort she really needed to make in order to attract a man. Feeling calmer now and more self-assured, she turned her head to see what effect, if any, the film was having on the others.

At the mention of his name, Jon had stopped kissing Rakel, automatically raising his tousled head to look at the screen. From the expression on his face, it was obvious to Karin that he hadn't known about the tape after all, although he didn't seem at all perturbed that the whole room was about to watch him in action. On the film he was now stroking *the girl*'s body, although she was still asleep at this point. Rakel was looking more than a little interested in the film's content. Glancing sideways at Jon, then across to Karin, she grinned broadly and winked.

Feeling quite pleased with this reaction, Karin turned her attention back to the screen, *the girl* was now awake and obviously enjoying her encounter with Jon, arching her back so that her breasts nudged his face, spreading her legs wide to encourage his exploring fingers. The action was becoming a little more intense now, renewing Karin's embarrassment. Cautiously she glanced at Kurt and Gloria, who were both sitting side by side, staring at the screen with similar expressions of rapt attention.

For some unknown reason she had deliberately avoided looking at Nicolai. After all, the video could hardly be considered as a new item of interest as far as he was concerned. Glancing back at the screen she saw Jon and *the girl*, well and truly absorbed in the first, frenzied bout of intercourse. She was thankful for the limitations of the closed-circuit camera, unlike a typical blue movie this film featured no embarrassing close-ups, awkward angles, or over exaggerated soundtrack. The camera was obviously positioned discretely in a corner above the bed, as the film was taken from a slightly angled, overhead perspective. The only sounds were the faint moans and gasps which they emitted from time to time, and the gentle 'slap, slap, slap' of Jon's thrusting pelvis against Karin's pliant flesh, although Karin remembered that her moans had turned to screams of ecstasy as their love-making continued unabated.

She sensed Nicolai moving to sit beside her, keeping her eyes firmly fixed on the screen she tried to ignore the heat of his thigh against hers. Her heart pounding against her ribs under the restrictive leather corset, she felt her breasts swell and her nipples harden. Taking a deep breath, she turned her head to look at him. His eyes too were intent on the film, small beads of sweat were forming on his brow and, she noticed with satisfaction, something in his trousers was beginning to stir.

'The natives seem restless,' she murmured to herself, surreptitiously inching even closer to his, firm, unyielding body.

She was rewarded by the touch of his hand upon her leg. Gently kneading the flesh just above her knee, gradually it moved higher and higher until it came to rest on her inner thigh, his fingertips gently insinuating themselves just inside the top of her stocking. Her leg burned where he touched her, as though small drops of acid spilled from his fingertips. Gently, she flexed her right hip, allowing the leg to part company with her left thigh and revealing a small triangle of black silk. Seemingly without taking his eyes from the screen, Nicolai stroked her inner thighs, first one leg then the other, pausing a fraction before they touched the hub of her desire then stroked downwards once again. It was maddeningly erotic and she felt her stomach grip tightly and her breathing stop each time he approached her crotch.

She longed to hurl herself into his arms, rip off her clothes and rub herself against his face and body, plunge her hands deep into his trousers and torment him until he begged to be allowed to take her. Then the telephone rang and he was gone, yet again the moment, *their* moment had been cut short.

Almost pushed to tears by the force of her disappointment, she drained the last of her drink. She glanced around her, everyone else had dispensed with formality long ago, helpong themselves to drinks as and when they wanted them. On screen Jon and *the girl* had just emerged from the shower, she damp but radiant, he strong and overtly masculine, still pulsating with unleashed virility. If she remembered rightly they were minutes away from screw number three, or was it four, she couldn't quite remember? For some reason this reminded her that there was still plenty of time for her and Nicolai to get their act together.

Filled with renewed expectation, she sauntered over to the drinks cabinet to fix herself another gin and tonic. Rakel had obviously had the same idea as they brushed against each other whilst reaching for the bottle of tonic.

'Soo sorry.'

Rakel's accent was more pronounced now that her tongue had been loosened by alcohol. Karin decided she preferred hearing her speak with a Swedish accent, it had a pleasant sing-song quality that she found endearing and she couldn't help thinking that, if she were a man, she would be very attracted to this extraordinary woman. Groping around for something to say, Karin reached up and touched Rakel's hair.

'I do like your haircut, it's so daring.' She grabbed a handful of her own tousled curls, 'I often wish I had the courage to have it all cut off.'

Rakel smiled, taking a tendril of Karin's hair and rolling it between her thumb and forefinger.

'It would not suit you I think, to be having the shorter hair, you are more beautiful like this.' She looked thoughtful for a moment, appraising Karin, 'Yes, rather lovely. I like.' She looked towards the door as Nicolai entered the room.

'Nicolai, I like.'

Nicolai looked at them, nodded in Rakel's direction and smiled at Karin.

'She likes,' he said simply.

Karin didn't now how to respond. 'Um, er, thank you, Rakel, I like you too.'

This seemed to please her enormously and she clasped Karin to her in an overtly friendly gesture.

'I think we are having the nice time together, you, me and Gloria, no?'

'No, I mean, what?'

Karin was confused now, she looked around, Gloria wasn't even in the room although she hadn't noticed her leave.

Noting her confusion, Kurt was by her side like a shot.

'Another drink Karin?'

She accepted gratefully, taking a large swig before handing her glass to Kurt for a refill. Nicolai glanced at them, nodding approvingly at Kurt, again it was an action that didn't go unnoticed by Karin but she didn't understand the significance of what was going on.

Nicolai's probably just pleased that I'm getting on well with his friends, she thought to herself.

Although not entirely convinced, she couldn't think of any other explanation for their disconcerting behaviour. Kurt handed her the drink and after a few more sips she felt herself relaxing again. Rakel whispered in her ear.

'Shall we look for Gloria?'

Unable to think of any reason why she shouldn't, Karin agreed, following behind Rakel as she undulated across the room to the doorway. Just as they were about to leave the room, Rakel stopped and turned.

'Bye, bye, boys.'

Each of the men held up a hand in a silent wave, looking from one to another with a collective expression that Karin couldn't fathom. Rakel led the way to an adjoining room, holding the door open so Karin could enter.

'Gloria is in here, I think.'

The room was dimly lit but, when Karin's eyes finally adjusted to the gloom, she wasn't prepared for the sight that greeted her. Almost two-thirds of the sparsely furnished room was taken up by a huge double bed, covered only with a black satin sheet upon which Gloria lay, naked, pleasuring herself with a vibrator. If she heard the other two women enter the room, she gave no indication of it, intent as she was on her own enjoyment.

Rakel immediately crossed the room, stripped off her skirt and T-shirt in a single, decisive movement and sat down beside her on the bed. Gloria moaned as Rakel began to stroke her breasts, gently at first and then with more passion, teasing the nipples between her fingers and thumbs. Karin watched in appalled fascination, her eyes fixed on Rakel's large, pale, fine-boned hands as they fondled Gloria's pert brown breasts. Despite her initial revulsion she could feel herself becoming aroused, an intense heat growing and spreading throughout her whole body. Luckily, she was still holding her glass. Downing the entire contents in a single gulp she put out her hand to steady herself. There was nothing to hold on to. Unsteadily she sat down on the foot of the bed, taking care not to sit too close to Gloria and Rakel. Gloria was now in the throes of a gigantic climax, rocking and moaning as she slid the vibrator deeper and deeper into her own body.

Rakel's hands moved slowly down Gloria's delicate frame, expertly kneading and stroking the pliant flesh until they came to rest on her upper thighs. Trying to avert her eyes, Karin found herself staring instead at all three of them reflected in every detail in a large, ornate mirror which covered one whole wall. Gloria was so petite she was hardly visible, overshadowed as she was by Rakel's voluptuous form. For a second, Karin allowed herself to admire Rakel, envious of her full, firm breasts, narrow waist and hips and endless legs. Then she turned her attention to the third figure in the mirror. She didn't recognise herself as herself, or even as *the girl* in the video, this woman who stared boldly back at her could not claim to be innocent in the ways of the flesh, or ill-equipped to deal with her predicament. This woman, this particular woman clad in black animal skins was wild, wanton and ready to run with the pack.

Turning away from the mirror, she looked across the bed at the writhing figure of Gloria. Despite her knowing ways she was so petite, so delicate, that she almost looked like a young girl embarking on her first sexual experience. Rakel, on the other hand, looked magnificently bold and in control. She had now taken command of the vibrator, moving it tantalisingly up and down between Gloria's legs, teasing her vulva with the shuddering tip, encircling her clitoris and the outer edges of her vagina. Kicking off her shoes, Karin climbed right onto the bed, moving closer to the other two women in fascination, leaning forward to watch Rakel's hands as they parted Gloria's labia, the pink fleshy folds opening out like a flower to reveal the hot, swollen bud that lay within. Gloria was too far gone to notice Karin's interest, tossing and turning under her partner's expert manipulations. But Rakel looked up, her hands still moving, stimulating the woman beneath them, as her eyes locked with Karin's.

As she continued to massage Gloria with the vibrator, Rakel reached out her other hand towards Karin. Deftly insinuating her fingers beneath the tight leather corset, she cupped one of her breasts. The nipple immediately hardened on contact with Rakel's fingers and Karin swallowed hard. She didn't know what she was supposed to do now, should she let this continue, or jump up from the bed and make a dash for the door? No one was holding her against her will, it was her own curiosity and lust that compelled her to stay. Reaching behind her back, Karin slowly unhooked the corset, allowing it to drop onto the bed. Continuing to stimulate the same breast, Rakel allowed her eyes to wander over Karin's body. She smiled and nodded approvingly.

'It eez all right to do this Karin, I won't hurt you.'

Feeling extremely warm under her penetrating gaze Karin detached herself from the other woman's touch. Swallowing hard, she came to a decision. Now Gloria was watching her too, the vibrator, temporarily forgotten, buzzing uselessly against the black satin like a bee that's used its sting. Resolutely Karin stood up, stretched slowly and, with slightly trembling fingers, unzipped her skirt, allowing the black suede to slither down her stocking-clad legs to the floor. She stepped daintily out of it, leaving it where it fell. Wearing only her stockings and brief panties she stood nervously before Rakel and Gloria, conscious of the fact that women were naturally more critical of other women. A man would probably have looked past her underwear but they were sizing her up.

She felt as though she had gone crazy, worrying that the two women may not find her attractive. The words of the song by Madonna drifted into her head, 'Like a virgin, touched for the very first time.' It was funny, she thought, that's exactly how I feel now. Gloria stretched out her hand to her, Rakel smiled. It was okay, they wanted her after all. Tentatively she climbed back onto the bed. As though there had been no interruption, Rakel resumed her massage of Karin's breast, with long easy strokes she covered every inch of the quivering flesh, teasing the nipple with her thumb until Karin felt it would burst with the craving for more direct stimulation. Gloria licked her lips thoughtfully, like a glutton for forbidden fruit. Slowly, deliberately she also put out a hand to touch Karin and was immediately rewarded by making contact with her other breast.

Each of them had a very different, very distinctive touch and, for a brief moment, Karin was reminded of her encounter with Karl and Dominic, how strange that had felt to have two different men touching her. Now it was two women. She gave herself up willingly to the new sensations that coursed through her body as each woman kneaded and fondled her aching breasts. Eventually Rakel bent her head. Taking a nipple between her lips she sucked hard, the already swollen teat feeling as though it would burst into flames. It was exquisite torment and Karin's keen appetite for satisfaction soon had her craving for extra stimulation. Arching her back, she urged the women to fondle more than her breasts. Moaning and grasping at the sheet as wave after wave of desire coursed through her, she parted her legs, immediately feeling the softest of caresses between them.

Closing her eyes dreamily, she felt herself drowning deeper and deeper in a sea of pleasure. Tossing and turning on the crest of each wave, she floundered at first, unwilling to let herself go completely. It could never be like this with a man, she thought as she sensed, rather than felt, Rakel's sweet breath on her stomach. Everything about this experience, every feather-light touch, every perfumed kiss, every perfectly choreographed movement was sheer poetry. No matter how thoughtful, or how loving a man might be, the women's touches were a mere nuance compared with the hard insistence of a masculine caress. Looking down her body, through half-closed lashes she watched, spellbound, as Gloria removed her panties, sliding them gracefully downward, her hands following them over the curves of Karin's body.

Karin felt her eyes drawn to the mirror, watching as though she were a third party as Gloria gently parted her legs still further. Working in wordless unison, Rakel supported the top half of Karin's body, fondling her breasts with one hand as she slid the other down the length of Karin's torso until her fingertips made contact with a few stray curls of pubic hair. Gloria lay full-length on the bed, her head between Karin's legs, not touching, just looking. Glancing down at herself once more, seeing Gloria's dark, silken head between her thighs, Karin could feel the wetness surge from her, drying on contact with the warm air.

'You are surely beautiful, especially here and here . . .' Gloria brought her hands up and, resting her arms on Karin's thighs, delicately eased apart her labia and stroked her throbbing clitoris. Karin jumped.

'Now, now, no need for that, missy, we're all goin' to have a real good time.'

Gloria's Texan drawl was as soothing and hypnotic as her touch. Using both her thumbs she massaged around the swollen flesh, pausing every now and then to kiss it lightly, almost imperceptibly moistening the pink, wrinkled skin of Karin's labia with a brush of her lips. Gracefully, Rakel manoeuvred herself from under Karin, instead laying full length alongside her so that her pubic hair tickled Karin's shoulder. From the moment Rakel's fingers entered her, Karin felt the last bastions of her reserve crumble. Moaning and writhing against the manipulations of the two women she allowed herself to come in a shuddering climax that peaked, then peaked again, seemingly without end.

As the waves of her orgasm gently subsided neither Rakel nor Gloria stopped what they were doing to her, the eroticism of the moment was divine and she felt she wanted to pleasure them as they were pleasuring her. Cautiously, she moved her arm until her fingers were grazing Rakel's vulva. She expected it to feel strange and she was not disappointed, nor was she repulsed, it certainly wasn't the same as stroking a man's scrotum, this was much more interesting. Cautiously, she explored with her fingers, encountering an abundance of warm crevices and deep, moist places. Gradually she became more daring.

Of course, she had felt herself extensively but it was not the same as this, not at all. With a thrill of excitement, she sensed Rakel responding to her touch, felt her labia swelling and opening out, her vaginal entrance enlarging, inviting her fingers to enter that secret, perfumed, mysterious place. Gloria was quick to take in what was happening and was eager for some action of her own, raising herself to her knees she boldly took Karin's other hand, placing it between her legs, clamping it firmly in place and grinding her hips. Rakel moved slightly. Without disturbing Karin's probing fingers she propped herself on one elbow and reached out to rub Gloria's breasts. For what seemed like hours, the three women probed and rubbed and caressed each other into a series of climaxes, some earth-shattering and some no more than a surge of warmth and calm.

Although she was happy to explore Rakel and Gloria with her fingers, Karin didn't feel comfortable about using her tongue to investigate and stimulate. But this didn't seem to bother either of them, though they had no qualms about licking each other, or Karin for that matter, into a frenzy of uncontrolled excitement. The heat of these especially fervent orgasms spread through their bodies like wildfire, each one more intense than the last. Eventually, however, they lay replete, a tangle of arms and legs, their bodies soaked in a film of musky perspiration. Gloria was the first to break the silence.

'I bet the guys sure got their kicks from that one.'

Rakel nodded, 'I think, yes.' She smiled at Karin, stroking a tendril of hair away from her eyes. 'How do you feel about it, I think you were not so experienced with women?'

Karin wasn't sure how to respond, if there were words that could adequately describe the way she was feeling they weren't part of her vocabulary.

'It was different,' she ventured carefully, 'but very nice,' she added quickly, not wishing to offend either of them. She hoped her expression came across as more enthusiastic than her words.

'Let us see if the boys think it was nice,' said Rakel, moving to the edge of the bed and stretching.

Horrified, Karin saw her wink at the mirror. Comprehension hit her straight between the eyes like a thunderbolt. Surely they couldn't . . .? They wouldn't . . .?

Leaping up, aghast, Karin started to pull on her clothes. This corset top is a damn nuisance, she thought angrily, her fingers trembling so much that she couldn't do up the hooks and eyes. Gloria crawled leisurely across the bed, still naked, and began to assist her.

'Don't tell me you didn't realise they were watching?'

She glanced over at the mirror, as though she could see the men on the other side, watching and shrugging. Karin exploded.

'No, I did not. I'm not used to this kind of thing.' Jamming her feet angrily into her shoes she strode towards the door. 'And now I'm going home.'

'I think not.' Nicolai was standing in the hallway as she strode out of the door straight into his waiting arms.

'Yet again,' she fumed to herself.

She was definitely beginning to detest him anew, angered by the way he always turned up when she least wanted him to. Grasping her firmly by the elbow, he escorted her back into the other room. Kurt eyed her with interest and Jon with grudging admiration as she sat down petulantly on the only vacant sofa. She forced herself not to look towards the two-way mirror which had now been revealed, having previously been screened by a pair of heavy velvet drapes. Nicolai walked over to her, handing her a fresh drink.

'There is no need for you to act so modestly, you have a good body, why not flaunt it a little?'

'That's not the point and you know it,' Karin hissed back at him through clenched teeth.

My God, the cheek of the man, she thought angrily, who the hell does he think he is? But Nicolai had not finished with her.

'You must also remember, I have already encountered your, ehm, activities, on a couple of occasions and Jon has carnal knowledge of you also.'

Karin couldn't help noticing that his voice tended to slip into a slight accent when he was agitated, which made her wonder if he was not feeling quite as calm as he tried to make out.

'The police might be interested to know what you get up to,' she gambled, hoping this would prove to be his Achilles' heel.

'I think the police know you better than they know me,' he was smirking now, one eyebrow raised in a supercilious fashion. 'One Inspector Maddison may even believe that you are the corrupt one.'

If he had physically hit her she could not have been more shocked. How on earth could he possibly know about her and the inspector? Try as she might, she could not come up with a reasonable explanation for his knowledge and her confusion silenced her temporarily. Now she wasn't sure what to think any more, or which way to turn. She waited for Nicolai to say something else, to either justify his wild accusation or twist the knife still further with another incisive remark. But his attention had shifted to Gloria and Rakel as they returned to the room. He clapped slowly and they both turned, smiling. Rakel bowed and blew kisses and Gloria executed as perfect a curtsy as her tight skirt would allow.

Try as she might to understand, Karin found their

viewpoint difficult to fathom. She wasn't a prude by any stretch of the imagination but their *laissez-faire* attitude to sex disorientated her, she couldn't see where they put their boundaries. Perhaps there weren't any, she decided, maybe people like them just see something they want and go for it, regardless of the possible consequences. In a way she admired them but felt, that for her at any rate, it was necessary to follow some moral guidelines however slight. Wistfully, she cast her mind back to the days when she had just one lover. Could she ever go back to that way of life, she wondered?

Gloria sashayed over to Nicolai and asked him to fix her another drink, whilst Rakel targeted herself at becoming reacquainted with Jon. Feeling very alone, Karin sank deeper into the sofa, wishing that she could bury herself completely. Noticing her distress, Kurt approached her. Sitting down beside her he covered her hands with one of his own.

'Don't worry Karin, Nicolai just gets a bit carried away sometimes.'

'But you don't understand . . .' She felt herself becoming perturbed again but Kurt silenced her.

'It's you who doesn't understand, that's why you're afraid right now.' Gently he stroked her hair, calming her down as if she were a frightened animal.

His tone was soothing, 'Relax Karin, trust me and let it go.'

Despite her agitation, she felt the tension being released under the soporific effect of Kurt's touch. Feeling her body turn to water, she allowed herself to slump against him, letting the warmth from his body revive her as though she were somehow absorbing his life force. Nicolai walked over to them, Kurt immediately started to leave.

'Don't go,' Karin looked at him imploringly, she didn't want to be left alone with Nicolai again.

He sat down again. Nicolai seated himself next to Karin at the other end of the sofa. When Nicolai spoke his tone was surprisingly gentle.

'I apologise Karin, I should not have spoken in that way to you.' He glanced down at his hands. 'There are things that you don't understand. I shall tell you, eventually, but for now you will have to endure our secrecy.'

He glanced at Gloria, who nodded her head in agreement. Whatever it was, Karin thought, Gloria, Kurt and Nicolai were in on it but she didn't understand where Rakel fitted into things. One thing she did understand was that both she and Jon had stumbled into the middle of whatever the situation was by accident and were being taken along for the ride. She didn't know what prompted her but she suddenly had an overwhelming desire to satisfy her curiosity about one thing. She turned to face Kurt.

'Are you gay?'

She hadn't meant to blurt it out in quite such a blunt fashion. Far from being insulted, Kurt threw back his head and roared with laughter.

'Hell no, what on earth gave you that idea?'

Embarrassed at her *faux pas*, Karin blushed bright red and wrung her hands. Thinking he deserved some sort of explanation Karin answered in a voice so small it was barely a whisper. 'I . . . don't really know. It's just . . . it's just—' She gave up, intelligent speech was simply beyond her capabilities at the present time.

Kurt nodded his understanding, 'It's just that I haven't made a pass at you, or the luscious Rakel, or Gloria for that matter.'

Karin blushed harder, he was more sensitive than she would have given him credit for. 'Yes, I suppose it is,' she managed to squeak.

What Kurt did next took her completely by surprise. Reaching over her he slid his hand under her buttocks and lifted her onto his lap. Before she had time to say, or do, anything he kissed her, hard, his tongue exploring her mouth and his hands roaming over her body as he did so. 'Would you like me to take you back in the other room and fuck you now?' He murmured into her ear. 'I could you know, I'm quite ready to show you that I'm all man.'

With that he grabbed her by the wrist and thrust her hand down between their bodies forcing her fingers around the bulge in his trousers. Shocked, she pulled her hand away instantly, then, deciding to call his bluff, at least in part, she put her hand back there, feeling the length of his firm penis with her fingers. She was amazed, not only was he rock hard but his cock just seemed to go on and on. It was very tempting to take him up on his offer, the thrill which had run through her just as he said the words had almost made her come, but her sensible self felt that she had already more than amply indulged her carnal desires for the time being. She let out a long sigh.

'Are you all right? I didn't mean to shock you. Well actually that's not true,' he amended, 'but I just wanted to get my point across.'

'I'm fine, thank you,' she answered primly, 'and it's okay, I believe you.'

Laughing, he pushed her off his lap, 'Thank the good Lord for that, now I can go and get a drink.'

During this exchange Nicolai had been silent, watching the interaction between them. If Karin had known how jealous he had felt, watching first the video of Jon touching her, then the two girls, then, finally Kurt, she would have cried with relief. As it was, his expression was impassive.

'I hope my friends' behaviour has not upset you too much this evening,' he said, breaking his silence.

Karin looked warily at him, but he seemed sincere. 'Think nothing of it, I haven't.' She hoped she sounded more convincing than she felt. She looked at her watch, wondering if the evening would wind itself up naturally or if she would have to make a positive move to leave. Nicolai reached out, steadying her with a strong hand on her arm.

'Don't go yet Karin, please. I want you to stay.'

Chapter Eleven

Walking over to the window, drawing back the heavy curtains and looking out Karin saw that the sky was pitch black. At some point, without her noticing, the evening had given way to night. She looked at her watch, it was only two o'clock but so much had happened it seemed much later and now she was feeling exhausted. She glanced around the room behind her, it seemed almost deserted. Jon and Rakel had slipped away about half an hour earlier, groping each other like crazy. She wondered why she didn't feel concerned that Jon hadn't stuck by her throughout the evening, after all they were supposed to be on a date but, she reasoned, what it boiled down to was that he didn't really mean anything to her other than a superlative cure for a hurt ego and a frustrated body.

Nicolai was also absent from the room. He and Kurt had talked about world affairs for a while until Nicolai was interrupted by a telephone call which he was taking in private in his study. Now Kurt was playing backgammon with Gloria, leaving Karin to alternately sit on her own or pace the room, nursing yet another drink and wondering how the hell she was going to get out of there and on with her life. She was already dreading the void that Rosalinde's absence would leave and, although she distrusted the man, she knew she would miss the excitement of her untimely clashes with Nicolai.

Just then the door opened and her heart missed a beat, as it always did when Nicolai made an entrance. Pausing briefly to whisper something to Kurt he strode over to the bar and poured himself a large Scotch. With a surge of hope mixed with desire she watched his eyes alight upon her. She was determined that this time, no matter what he said to her, she was going to remain calm and relaxed. He sauntered over to her and sat down a little too close for comfort. Automatically, Karin tried to put a little distance between them but the weight of his body on the soft leather pulled her towards him like a magnet. If only he wasn't so loathsome, she thought, enjoying the aroma of his masculinity after the sweet, floral perfume of the two women she'd made love with earlier.

Frantically, she searched her mind for something interesting to say. His very nearness made her feel tongue-tied, making her wish she was the sort of person who could manufacture a witty, incisive comment from thin air and drop it casually from her lips as soon as there was an untimely gap in the conversation.

'How is Rosalinde?' Damn, what an idiot, she chastised herself, even she knew that one of the least effective ways to capture a man's interest was to ask him about his wife.

'She is okay, I think. Still in Scotland of course.' Nicolai smiled, apparently not in the least concerned by the inappropriateness of her question.

His voice and demeanour gave no indication of what, if anything, had taken place in Scotland between himself and Rosalinde. For a while only the rattle of the dice and occasional murmurs of 'aha' or 'take that you bastard' from Kurt and Gloria broke the silence of the room. Karin could hear her heart beating loudly. Nicolai had not said or done anything in the least suggestive, yet she felt unbearably aroused simply by his proximity.

Perhaps it's better that he doesn't speak, she thought to herself, then he can't give me cause to hate him.

Taking a large sip of her drink to calm her thudding heart, she was suddenly overcome by a violent attack of the hiccups. Mortified, she tried holding her breath but it was no use. She had no doubt that Nicolai had noticed her predicament and she was irritated that he did nothing to help her. She thought he could at least thump her hard on the back, or offer to get her a glass of water, or something. Several minutes passed, the silence shattered every few seconds by a loud 'hic', the situation was becoming unbearable, definitely past being a joke. Just as she was beginning to despair of ever living a normal life again, Nicolai thrust his hand up between her legs and kissed her, hard. In stunned outrage she leaped to her feet and turned upon him angrily, but he was laughing at her.

'The hiccups have gone now I believe.'

He was quite right, the shock of his actions had cured her, a good half a minute passed without a single hiccup. Despite herself, she joined in the laughter, the mixture of relief and alcohol causing tears to roll down her cheeks. When she stopped to think about it, it had been very pleasant to be kissed by Nicolai.

Without making a conscious decision, she stopped laughing abruptly, looked at him with an uncharacteristically solemn expression and pulled him to her, returning his kiss with a vengeance. To her relief he didn't try to score points by rebuffing her embrace but responded with surprising tenderness. Tasting of Scotch, his tongue sought hers, his hands automatically moving down her body to gently stroke the outer swell of her breasts. She plunged her own fingers deep into his thick, dark hair, enjoying the weight of it in her hands, moving to the nape of his neck to stroke the shorter hairs that curled over his shirt collar. Over his shoulder she caught a glimpse of Kurt's expression. He did not look pleased and for some unfathomable reason Karin started to feel embarrassed until Gloria nudged him, drawing his attention back to their game.

Nicolai rose, taking Karin by the hand, 'Shall we?'

She hesitated, it was one thing to kiss him and for him to kiss her back, but did she really want more from him than that? If she was being honest with herself it was something that she had wanted for a long time, since their first meeting in fact, but now it was almost a reality she was frightened. He was not like other men, at best he made her feel slightly apprehensive and at worst . . . It would take her a long time to get over her anger at the discovery of the two-way mirror. Every part of her was shivering with trepidation.

'I won't force you, darling. I am not hard up for a woman, but I am hard. Here, feel for yourself.'

He took her hand and placed it firmly on his bulge, she could feel the strength of his erection through the thick material. It pulsed disturbingly beneath her fingers as she looked tremulously up at him. His blue eyes crinkled in a genuine smile, simultaneously dispelling her fear and fanning the flames of desire already smouldering deep within her. That was it, she had to have him. Clasping a strong arm around her waist he led her up the stairs, feeling her swaying hips brush against his thigh. With each tortuous step she shivered again, but this time with the thrill of anticipation. He led her to his bedroom, holding the door only slightly open so that she had to squeeze past his unyielding body to enter. Briefly, she glanced around, the familiarity of this room was reassuring even though her previous visits there had not been at his invitation.

Despite the prolonged, orgiastic session she'd enjoyed earlier with Rakel and Gloria, Karin could feel urgent darts of desire attacking her nerve endings. Expertly, Nicolai unhooked her corset, she stood with her back to him, hands on hips enjoying the sensation of his fingers brushing against the skin on her back, and the way he paused after undoing each hook to kiss and lick each new portion of flesh as it emerged. To make this easier he knelt down and she felt his hair brush against her shoulder-blades, his breath cool against her white-hot flesh. He was certainly very skilful and Karin soon found herself moaning and clutching her own breasts with desire as he tossed the leather garment to one side.

With maddening slowness he ran his hands up and down the length of her legs, the friction of his hands against the nylon stockings increasing her body heat. He took his time too about removing her skirt, unzipping it gradually, stopping every now and then to run his hands over her hips and across her belly, then painstakingly easing it over the curves of her hips and buttocks and inching it down her legs. Following the trail of her skirt with his tongue, he licked the insides of her thighs, behind her knees and even the arch of her insteps. When this process was complete, Karin stepped out of it and started to turn around to face him, but with one hand on her shoulder he stopped her.

'No, not yet my sweet, I have not even begun to love you properly.'

He didn't remove her stockings or panties but, by exerting the merest suggestion of pressure from his hands against her back, he urged her to bend forward slightly. Gripping the ornate iron bedstead at the foot of the bed to steady herself, she struggled for breath as he began to caress the smooth globes of her buttocks with one hand, whilst with the other he reached between her legs rubbing and massaging her tormented flesh until her panties were soaked with her own juices. She could feel her clitoris swollen and throbbing and her breasts ached for his touch. Desperate for relief, she pressed her distended nipples against the icy bedstead, almost expecting the iron to turn molten from the heat which was emanating from them.

With a relief that quickly evolved into extreme desire she felt him remove her panties. She couldn't see what he was doing to her but she could feel his expert fingers gently opening her, probing, examining. From time to time he inserted his fingers into her then withdrew them almost immediately, using her juices to massage her clitoris. It was bliss and agony and almost painfully, acutely erotic. Although her legs were trembling violently with desire, she dared to release one hand in order to massage her own breasts, kneading them and pressing them together, pinching the nipples and rubbing them frantically against the wrought-iron.

Feverish with lust and desperate to feel his cock inside her, Karin turned back to face him, dragging him with her around the side of the bed, falling backwards onto the coverlet, ripping at his clothes. Breasts heaving, her breath coming in short gasps, she fought with his clothing, finally managing to remove his jacket. Calmly and deliberately Nicolai detached her scrabbling fingers and removed his own socks and shoes. She looked pleadingly at him as he sat beside her, looking directly and intently at her, scanning her face for tell-tale signals that he was succeeding in pleasuring her. To an observer he would have appeared totally in control of the situation and, to all intents and purposes, untouched by any trace of passion for her. It was only the definite outline of his erection that gave him away to her.

'I knew you would be this beautiful,' he murmured softly as he began stroking her breasts, rubbing and moulding them in his large, capable hands, teasing the hard buds of her nipples with little tugs and pinches. His touch was not delicate like that of the two women but this did not lessen its impact on her. She was quick to recognise that the foundation of her desire for Nicolai was cerebral rather than physical. To be blunt, she fancied him like crazy and had done so for a long time. Craving contact with his skin, she tugged off his tie and undid the buttons on his shirt, easing it back from his shoulders and down his arms. His skin was covered in a fine downy hair like a peach. Good, she was repulsed by men that were too hairy. Instead of pulling him down on top of her she pushed him backwards, straddling him and leaning forward to crush her breasts against his chest.

'Oooh,' she allowed a long sigh of pleasure to escape from her lips.

Just as she reached a hand down behind her back to undo the zipper on his trousers there was a sharp rap on the door.

'It's time,' a voice hissed urgently. 'Are you there Nicolai?' It was Kurt.

Immediately, Nicolai pushed Karin to one side and leaped up from the bed, reaching for his shirt as he did so. Bewildered, Karin watched him.

'What the hell . . .' she started, but Nicolai was already half-way out of the door.

'I'll explain everything later, got to rush.'

In his haste he started to put his jacket on upside down. Realising his mistake, he stopped in the doorway, turning the jacket around as he looked at Karin apologetically.

'By the way,' he added as an afterthought, 'don't go anywhere or talk to anyone outside the house until I get back.' And, with that parting shot, he was gone.

Flabbergasted by all that had just taken place, Karin sank back against the pillows, her overwhelming disappointment and frustration only outweighed by her curiosity. For a moment she toyed with the idea of toying with herself but her galloping heart had already slowed down to a beat that was just a fraction faster than normal and her nipples had deflated like popped pink bubblegum. It was disconcerting how quickly things could revert back to the normal and mundane and she wondered if this was a foretaste of how her life would revert if she decided to take Colin back.

Bloody hell, things must be going badly when they made her think about her husband!

Dispiritedly, she got dressed yet again, struggling for some time with the corset top and wishing she had someone to help her. Downstairs, the room where they had all been was now deserted. Gloria had gone . . . somewhere, Karin presumed she had accompanied Kurt and Nicolai, whilst Jon and Rakel were still going at it hammer and tongs in the *mirror room*. Just as she reached the bottom of the staircase Rakel had started howling like a wolf, now her howls were being drowned out by the bed hammering against the wall, it was so loud and so violent that she half expected it to break through the plaster at any second. With a smile she picked up her discarded glass and raised it to the builders of the house, the durability of their work was certainly being put to the test tonight.

Sipping the tart liquid thoughtfully, she browsed through a number of magazines which had been tastefully arranged on a side table. Whether she would admit it to herself or not, she was unintentionally trying to avoid the temptation to open the drapes that disguised the two-way mirror. Eventually, she gave in, tugging at the cord until the mirror and what lay behind it were completely revealed.

The room looked totally devastated, as though it had been the victim of a violent tornado. Somehow, and she marvelled at the force Jon and Rakel must have exerted on it, the huge bed had moved; twisted slightly askew so that one corner was completely away from the wall. The few books and ornaments that had graced the side tables had been knocked over, or were strewn across the floor, even the light fitting was dangling precariously from a single wire. Despite their protracted exertions they were still going as strong as ever – Jon spreadeagled naked on the bed with Rakel astride him, riding him ferociously, her face contorted in a grimace of concentration. He, lunging upward, striving to keep pace with his Valkyrie lover. Although it was fascinating at first, Karin soon became bored and eventually she curled up on one of the leather sofas, falling immediately into a deep, dreamless sleep.

Many hours later she awoke to find the room bathed in sunlight. The first thing that caught her attention was the mirror, on the other side she could see the nude figure of Rakel, lying on the bed on her stomach fast asleep. Jon, however, was nowhere to be seen. She needed to use the bathroom. Padding up the stairs in bare feet, she paused first of all outside Nicolai's room then, feeling a little like Goldilocks in the three bears' house, she decided against going back in there and, instead, continued along the landing to Rosalinde's bedroom. As she pushed open the door she was not prepared for the shocking sight which met her eyes; the whole, beautiful room had been completely ransacked!

Karin was totally stunned. When had this happened? Why had this happened? If burglars had raided the house, how had she managed to sleep through it? Staring around in disbelief she saw that every cupboard and drawer gaped open, their contents spilling out haphazardly onto the carpet. On the dressing table were piles of papers and all Rosalinde's cosmetics had been scattered on the same surface, some of them broken, their contents congealed together in a multi-coloured, gooey mass. Picking her way carefully across the floor, Karin opened the door to the *en-suite* bathroom. It was the same story in there, with globs of talcum powder and cosmetics everywhere. Shocked, she made her way out of Rosalinde's room and back along the landing to the main bathroom.

Once inside she locked the door and sat down on the lavatory, trying to clear her head. None of her experiences lately made any sense. Wishing she had some clean clothes to put on, she washed her face thoroughly then checked the bathroom cabinet. Thankfully, there was a small jar of cold cream which she used to remove the last smears of make-up and, better yet, a selection of brand new toothbrushes. Resolutely, she scrubbed away the taste of gin and sex. She felt a little more human now but it was still not enough, quickly she peeled off her clothes and showered until she felt completely clean and clear headed. Clad only in a towel she made her way back to Rosalinde's room and borrowed a clean pair of panties, a pile of which were lying conveniently next to the door, and a luxuriously thick, white towelling bathrobe. Stuffing her own clothes into a carrier bag she wandered back downstairs.

Her arrival was greeted by the fully dressed figure of Jon who looked disgustingly fresh and awake.

'Breakfast?' He enquired, waving a frying pan under her nose.

Revolted, she shook her head. Trust him to think of food. Now she came to think about it, food and sex were the only things he seemed to care about.

As if he could read her mind he asked, 'Is Rakel with us yet?'

'No Jon, I think you wore her out.' Karin's tone was sarcastic, but Jon grinned, taking her words as a compliment.

Whistling happily, he sauntered back into the kitchen. Despite her concern at what had happened the night before, it couldn't prevent her from smiling at his arrogance. Following him into the vast, airy kitchen she sat down at a huge pine table, gratefully accepting his revised offer of a cup of rich, steaming coffee. After nursing her drink thoughtfully for a few minutes, she finally spoke out.

'Do *you* know what's going on?'

Jon kept his back to her, intent on his eggs and bacon which were spluttering away merrily on top of the stove.

'Going on?' he tried to feign innocence but sounded less convincing than a party political broadcast.

She was just about to press him further when there came the sound of a key in the front door lock, setting her coffee down so hurriedly that a small amount spilled onto the table, she rushed out into the hallway, it was Kurt. The surprise and disappointment that it wasn't Nicolai manifested itself instantly on her face.

'Oh, it's you,' she said in a small voice, somewhat ungraciously.

Unsmiling, Kurt took her arm, leading her back to the kitchen. 'Nicolai has some business to attend to, he'll be back in a couple of hours or so.'

'Kurt, tell me what's going on, please,' she looked up at him imploringly. 'I feel as though I'm caught in the middle of a game but someone forgot to tell me the rules.'

Kurt nodded, 'I understand that but I really can't say anything about the situation until Nicolai gets here.'

Easing himself wearily into the seat next to Karin, he reached across the table for the coffee pot, pouring a cup for himself and topping up her mug. Karin glanced at him. From his rumpled appearance and tired eyes she guessed he had been awake all night. At that moment Rakel wandered into the kitchen, rubbing her eyes and looking totally gorgeous despite the fact that she had just awoken after a very heavy night. Immediately, Jon left his breakfast and bounded up the stairs, returning a few moments later with an identical bathrobe to the one Karin was wearing, considerately he draped it around Rakel's naked body.

Nodding her thanks, she leaned against the door frame, not bothering to wrap the bathrobe around herself. Unselfconsciously, she sipped at the cup of coffee Kurt handed to her. The silence was deafening, the air thick with unanswered questions. Finally, Rakel spoke.

'Gloria and Nicolai, they are not here too?' They all nodded, knowing instantly what she had meant to say and too polite to correct her English.

Then it was Kurt's turn. 'I seem to recall Nicolai saying something about this place having a swimming pool – who's for a swim?'

Relieved to have something to do, they all leaped at the chance. Jon led the way across the sun dappled gardens, through the archway, to the pool. Karin had to admit it did look very inviting and immediately felt her body start to relax. After everything that had happened between them it hardly seemed appropriate to bother with swimsuits, Karin glanced at Rakel who shrugged her bathrobe off her shoulders and plunged into the water. Taking a deep breath Karin did the same, gasping as she surfaced from her dive, the iciness of the water taking her breath away. Jon and Kurt hopped around, divesting themselves of socks and trousers, before diving in quickly and swimming a few lengths.

Enjoying the tranquillity, Karin swam leisurely up

and down the pool for a few lengths, alternating between breast-stroke and a lazy crawl. As the sun rose higher in the sky Rakel announced that she was going to sunbathe. By this time Jon had returned to the house to make a pitcher of iced tea and Kurt, meanwhile, was sitting on the side of the pool apparently lost in his own thoughts, his legs dangling in the cool water. He was the only person in their party apart from Nicolai who Karin hadn't seen naked and she couldn't help surreptitiously sneaking a glance in his direction. He was certainly well built . . . in more ways than one. Floating on her back, she stared up through the glass ceiling at the deep blue sky above, pondering on what it would be like to be penetrated by a cock the size of Kurt's. His colossal member was not only as thick as one of her wrists, it was a good ten inches in length at least!

This revelation obviously hadn't gone unnoticed by Rakel, she was already stalking across the lawn, like a naked amazon, a blonde Hyppolyta in pursuit of her prey. Suddenly Karin was jolted out of her reverie by the welcome sound of Nicolai's voice, turning her head she saw his handsome figure striding across the lawn accompanied by the diminutive Gloria who was now dressed in denim shorts and a T-shirt. Both were laughing and looking extremely pleased with themselves.

Kurt looked across at Karin and smiled, 'It looks as though we'll be able to put you out of your misery at long last.

Nicolai waited until they were all fully dressed and comfortably seated in the sitting room, glasses of iced tea to hand. Standing immobile in front of the fireplace he cleared his throat.

'I feel like a solicitor about to read the will,' he joked.

Karin looked imploringly at Kurt who said, 'For God's sake Nicolai, are you going to tell them or am I?'

'No, it's okay,' Nicolai put up his hand apologetically. 'The fact is Kurt and Gloria are detectives.' His disclosure was met with stunned silence, so he continued, 'They were sent over here from the United States on a special investigation.' He paused for a minute and looked directly at Karin. If he had expected her to appear surprised he wasn't disappointed.

Finally, she found her voice, 'Go on,' she urged.

Nicolai nodded. 'For the past six months or so I've been helping them to uncover a smuggling ring.'

'What, drugs . . . coke and that?' Jon asked, with a look that told of more than a passing interest.

'No, not drugs,' Nicolai looked down at his feet then back at Karin, 'diamonds.'

He cleared his throat nervously, obviously groping around for the gentlest way to break the next piece of news. In the end he tried, unsuccessfully, to sound casual.

'By the way, Rosalinde is also a detective, posing as my wife was merely her cover.'

Karin gasped, unable to believe what he was saying. Rosalinde. Cool, refined Rosalinde, a detective and not really married to Nicolai at all. She almost laughed aloud, the whole idea was preposterous, this was real life for goodness sake, not some late night movie!

'I know it's hard to believe,' Nicolai's voice softened. 'No one would have suspected her of it, that's the whole point, that's why she was ideal.'

Kurt nodded. 'That's right, she was perfectly convincing as a rich, bored housewife who had nothing better to do but pamper herself at a beauty shop. She's been investigating the salon for months now.'

'She even feigned a love affair with one of the ringleaders,' added Gloria. Noting the questioning look on Karin's face she added, 'Do you remember Martin? You met him at your impromptu birthday party here at the house. Well he and his accomplice Julia were posing as beauticians.'

'Yes, I remember,' murmured Karin slowly, then a horrible thought dawned on her. 'But I thought Rosalinde and Martin were . . .'

'Oh, yes, the great romance,' Nicolai laughed, 'it was all part of the act I'm afraid.'

'Oh, Nicolai I can't believe that,' Karin burst out. 'Rosalinde was over the moon about falling for Martin.'

Despite the things she had been told about Rosalinde, Karin still found it hard to accept that she had been caught up in a gigantic hoax. And what of their *special* friendship, had that been a lie like everything else? All of a sudden Karin felt nauseous.

'Excuse me for a moment.'

Staggering from the room, she made her way outside and stood on the patio taking in huge gasps of air, hoping that her head would eventually clear and the tremors in her stomach subside. Presently she felt Nicolai's hand on her shoulder, gently he held her stroking her hair. When she finally stopped shaking Nicolai took her face in his hands, he spoke softly.

'Rosalinde didn't set out to be deliberately cruel, Karin, but make no mistake about it she's good at her job, a professional through and through.'

Nicolai almost sounded bitter and Karin suddenly wondered if he had enjoyed being *married* to Rosalinde.

'Nicolai I . . .' she didn't really know what to say to him, what use were mere words anyway?

Taking her by the arm he guided her back to the sitting room, resuming his position in front of the fireplace. Karin sat quietly, trying to digest everything Nicolai had said. No one else spoke, each too wrapped up in their own thoughts. Eventually, Rakel stood up.

'Nicolai darling, it is time I love and leave.'

She undulated gracefully across the room and kissed him on the cheek, then repeated her action with every one else. Kissing Karin last, she paused to whisper in her ear.

'Last night it was good yes, perhaps we do again?'

Karin sincerely doubted it but nodded anyway which seemed to satisfy Rakel. Kurt and Gloria also stood up to go, in turn they reached out to shake Karin by the hand.

'Now we've got a stack of paperwork to get through, it's time we made a start.' Kurt sounded positive but looked wistful, as though he wished he could stay and continue the party.

Under any other circumstances Karin would have probably felt the same but as it was she still felt totally wiped out by the revelations about Rosalinde. Nicolai followed the three of them to the front door, leaving Karin alone with her thoughts. She just couldn't believe it, surely it was a joke, one of those TV programmes perhaps which ended up with someone whipping off a false beard and announcing that it had all been a funny prank. The trouble was, there was no one left in the room and neither Nicolai nor Jon had beards. She looked around her, Jon had disappeared, although she hadn't noticed him leave.

At that moment Nicolai came back into the room. Walking over to Karin he sat down beside her, taking her hands between his.

'Are you all right?' His concern was genuine.

The tone of his voice was the last straw for Karin who suddenly crumpled, allowing a torrent of tears to fall unchecked. Nicolai said nothing but sat and waited patiently until she had calmed down a little. Dabbing her cheeks with the corner of his immaculate white handkerchief, he looked deep into her eyes. 'I know you are feeling shocked and a little foolish but there's no way you could have guessed what Rosalinde was up to.'

Karin sniffed, 'Do you think she liked me at all, or was our friendship just part of her game-plan too?'

Nicolai smiled, 'I thought that was bothering you. Of course she liked you, you were a good friend to her. What she does for a living had nothing to do with her relationship with you.'

Karin was still not convinced. 'I feel like such a fool, how could I have missed something big like that when it was going on under my very nose?'

Nicolai laughed, 'Don't you think there'll be a few other people asking themselves that very same question?' He reached for her hands, clasping them between his.

'Please believe me when I tell you, Karin, you've got nothing to reproach yourself for. As I said earlier, Rosalinde is a professional.'

'Which of the salon staff were involved in the smuggling ring?' Karin was interested now, keen to know all the details.

'Only the manager, I can't remember his name.'

Karin was shocked all over again, she never would have believed it possible. 'You don't mean Pierre?'

'Yes, that's him, a very cool customer, very plausible.' Nicolai got up and walked over to the drinks table.

'You look as though you could do with one of these,' he held up a brandy bottle.

Karin nodded gratefully, after last night she couldn't have faced another drop of gin but a glass of brandy was just what she needed to dull the edges of her renewed shock.

'I can't believe Pierre was involved, he was always so nice.' She reached out her hand, accepting the large brandy goblet from Nicolai. As she swirled the pungent liquid around the bowl of the glass, a terrible thought struck her.

'What about Lise, Pierre's niece who worked at the salon, surely she wasn't mixed up in it as well?'

Nicolai shook his head. Relieved she let out a long sigh, she had been starting to feel as though everything she had experienced and everyone she had met during the past few months had been part of one gigantic hoax. Without doubt, the morning's disclosures had certainly rocked her newly acquired sense of self-esteem.

'Pierre used Lise to some extent, as a cover, just like he used the salon, but we have no evidence to suggest that Lise knew what her uncle was up to.'

As though he had just come to a momentous decision, Nicolai stood up.

'You look as though you could do with some nourishment my dear, let me take you out to lunch.'

Karin's first impulse was to decline his invitation, her clothing was wildly inappropriate for lunch in a restaurant and she still felt nauseous, though whether this was due to shock, or a legacy from the night before, she wasn't sure. As always, Nicolai read her mind.

'I'll take you home first so that you can change your clothes.'

She wavered for a moment then, accepting that she didn't want to lose Nicolai just yet, she nodded. Suddenly she felt hopeful again, the day was yet young and an intimate lunch might just encourage Nicolai to finish what they had started the night before.

Chapter Twelve

As her house was not far out of town he took her to the same small Italian bistro they had lunched at the day they had first met properly, at the salon with Rosalinde. Just entering the restaurant brought a wealth of poignant memories flooding back. Despite her earlier misgivings about her ability to eat, the food was so delicious that she couldn't help tucking in with gusto. During their meal Nicolai went into more detail about the undercover operation and the almost obscenely large part he had played in helping Kurt, Gloria and Rosalinde to nail the diamond smugglers.

'Didn't you feel the slightest bit guilty about what you were doing?' asked Karin, dipping her breadstick into the anchovy relish. 'You were both very convincing as a married couple.'

'In name only.' Nicolai seemed overly keen to reassure her on that point. 'We had to be convincing Karin, the whole investigation, perhaps even people's lives were at stake.' He took a sip of wine, his expression wistful, 'I must admit that sometimes it felt good to be able to introduce Rosalinde as *my wife*; she's a very beautiful woman.'

Karin was struck by a sharp pang of envy, perhaps now that they were no longer working together

Rosalinde would feel inclined to encourage Nicolai's attraction to her? Still there were a myriad questions tumbling over themselves in her mind.

'But what about Rosalinde's distress concerning your infidelity?' Karin pressed. 'And your ehm . . .' she cleared her throat and looked down at her hands, feeling acutely embarrassed, 'your sexual preferences. According to her you were Casanova with bells on?'

Nicolai shrugged, trying to look nonchalant but failing badly.

Karin pressed on remorselessly, 'She poured out her heart to me constantly Nicolai, there was no way she could have made all that up, or faked her feelings to such an extent.'

He looked down at his plate, toying with a few strands of fettuccine, then brought his eyes up to meet hers, staring long and hard at her. 'I am no angel Karin. What can I tell you, I love women, all women, often I just cannot resist their charms.'

'But that's not good enough Nicolai.' Despite the seductiveness of his blue eyes, Karin could feel the anger against him welling up inside her again.

Smiling, Nicolai put out his hand and stroked her hair. 'Dear, sweet, naïve Karin. After all you have experienced during these past few months you have learned nothing.'

Karin shifted uncomfortably in her seat, it was true she had enjoyed some eye-opening encounters since her split with Colin. Some very large illusions had been shattered during the past few months and she now understood that it was possible to divorce sex from love, that the two things did not necessarily go hand in hand.

Nicolai leaned towards her, his voice barely a whisper.

'You don't give up easily do you Karin?'

She shook her head, a sick feeling manifested in the pit of her stomach in anticipation of what he was about to reveal. Nicolai continued in the same low voice.

'If I am to admit to you the truth, that Rosalinde and I did enjoy a sexual relationship during out time together, you must never tell a living soul, it could destroy her career.'

Karin looked visibly shocked, now that he had told her the truth she wished they could have kept up the pretence. Seeing that she was upset, Nicolai hastened to reassure her.

'There was never any romance involved, Karin, Rosalinde and I never fell in love with each other, it was just sex between two people who were thrown together for a period of time. Besides,' he added decisively, 'I don't know what love is.'

Noting the look of challenge in Karin's eyes, he put a finger to her lips, 'Don't say it Karin, and don't ever think it. You cannot change me because, basically, I don't want to be changed. I like my life as it is. Use your efforts on someone who deserves a woman like you.'

At one time she would have felt rebuffed but her newly acquired perception helped her to understand Nicolai's point of view, and to accept that it was no reflection on her personally. With that piece of unfinished business put behind them, Karin decided to settle down and enjoy the rest of her lunch. Later, over coffee, she ventured to ask another question which had been brewing at the back of her mind ever since the previous night.

'Nicolai, if I remember correctly, either you or Kurt mentioned something about Inspector Maddison last night, what was that about?'

Nicolai laughed loudly, almost spilling his drink. 'Oh, my goodness, yes, Maddison the Marquis.'

'What?' Karin looked confused.

He leaned forward, speaking in a low, confidential tone, 'According to Kurt and Gloria that is the local constabulary's nickname for him. Apparently he has a bit of a reputation for being, how shall I put it, a little on the sadistic side,' Nicolai was clearly enjoying the expression on Karin's face.

'But how did you know . . .?' Then it dawned on her, of course, how could she have been so stupid.

'I was under surveillance too, wasn't I?'

He nodded, 'Of course, you spent an extraordinary amount of time at the beauty salon. We couldn't be sure at the outset if you were involved.'

Another thought occurred to her. 'What exactly happened last night, I mean which bits were play acting and which were real?'

He looked serious, 'It was all real Karin.'

'Yes, but . . . well . . .'

'You mean where did the business with Rakel and Gloria and you come into it?'

'Yes, I suppose so,' she stared hard into the depths of her coffee cup, trying in vain not to blush.

After calling the waiter over to their table to refill their cups, Nicolai leaned back in his chair, preparing himself to satisfy her curiosity for once and for all.

'Okay, this is what happened. I went to Scotland with Rosalinde as planned, when we got there Martin was waiting and she dropped her *bombshell* about being in love with Martin and wanting a divorce from me.' He paused to take a sip of his coffee.

'Go on,' urged Karin, leaning forward.

'Naturally, I played the outraged cuckold and stormed out of the hotel. It was all going to plan, Gloria was waiting for me around the corner whilst Kurt was in another part of the hotel listening to Rosalinde's conversation with Martin. Rosalinde was wearing a wire,' he added, noting Karin's questioning look.

'As arranged, we came back to the house but I hadn't been expecting to see your car in the driveway, it nearly threw our plan out completely. Fortunately, I knew Rakel was in the country and always eager to see me, even at short notice.'

Karin sucked in her breath, my God, she thought, some things never change, the man was still as arrogant as ever. Nicolai didn't appear to notice her irritation.

'I called her hotel in town and went straight over to pick her up, then we all came back to the house. The rest you know.'

'So, all the sex and everything, that was all real?'

'Why, didn't it feel real?' he laughed as Karin blushed again.

'You know what I mean.' Then, 'Just a minute,' her brain was trying to assimilate all the unusual events of the past couple of days. At once, she remembered Rosalinde's ransacked bedroom. 'What happened in Rosalinde's room, and when did it happen?'

'As you know, Kurt, Gloria and I got a telephone call at about two o'clock. It was from Rosalinde to say that she had finally got a full confession from Martin and Julia. They came back down here by plane and, after a few hours questioning at the station, Martin admitted to having hidden his share of the diamonds in Rosalinde's room while everyone was downstairs enjoying your birthday party. Gloria and I came back here at, oh, about five a.m., and searched Rosalinde's room until we recovered the diamonds.'

'But, I didn't hear you come back.'

Nicolai put down his cup, rose and walked around the table to her, 'You were out of it darling.'

Remembering how she had fallen asleep on the sofa, Karin suddenly felt extremely tired all over again.

'Come on,' Nicolai put his hand out to her, 'let's get you to bed.'

One look at her expression made him laugh out loud, 'I'll rephrase that. Let me take you to your home so that you can go to bed, in your own bed, alone. Now is that clear enough for you?'

Karin nodded, feeling foolish. When, oh, when was she ever going to get her mind out of her panties and onto a higher plane? No sooner had she settled down in the passenger seat of Nicolai's car and he had started the engine, than she fell into a deep sleep. Before she realised it, she was home. Groggily she staggered up to her front door, groping in her handbag for her key.

'I'll have Jon return your car sometime later today,' offered Nicolai.

Karin smiled gratefully, 'Thanks Nicolai, please ask

him just to post the keys through the letterbox, I think I'm just going to sleep for the rest of the day.'

'Okay, I'll do that. Oh, by the way,' Nicolai looked faintly embarrassed and stared at his feet.

'Yes Nicolai?'

'Do you think you would be willing to see me again? Perhaps we could have dinner together in a couple of days?'

Karin reached up and kissed him gently on the lips, 'Yes please,' she murmured in his ear.

She stood on the front doorstep for a long time watching his car recede into the distance, although he had gone his aura still surrounded her and she was already feeling the first stirrings of anticipation at seeing him again. Thankfully, she had a good excuse to call him, she had forgotten to ask how and when she would be able to contact Rosalinde, something she now felt very anxious to do. For her own peace of mind, she needed to hear Rosalinde's side of things. For one thing, she wouldn't be entirely happy about seeing Nicolai again unless she could be sure that she would not be hurting her friend by doing so.

Wearily she stepped inside the house, closing the front door carefully behind her. How on earth had she managed to make her life so complicated? A few short month's ago she had been a housewife and mother, now she was involved, albeit very innocently, in a diamond smuggling ring. No wonder she felt tired.

It was about eleven o'clock the following morning when the doorbell rang, to her enormous surprise and pleasure it was Dominic, looking as cheerful and as gorgeous as ever.

'Hi, Karin,' he grinned, holding a bottle of champagne aloft. 'I was just passing and thought, "Now whose going to help me celebrate my latest sale." Then it struck me, of course, who better than the luscious, wonderful, super-sexy Karin?'

Karin laughed, 'No wonder you're such a good salesman, you managed to come out with all that and look like you meant it.'

'Karin!' He pretended to look shocked.

Stepping backwards she allowed him to squeeze past her into the narrow hallway. 'Go on through.'

It seemed strange Dominic being there in her sitting room, surrounded by her things. The only real male presence the house had known before was Colin and having Dominic there instead seemed slightly unreal. Distractedly, she guided him into the conservatory, her favourite part of the house.

'I don't think I'll be very good company today, I'm afraid.'

Trembling, she held out two glasses which he filled to the brim with the foaming liquid, a horrible thought had struck her: at this stage it would probably be too risky to confide in Dominic about Rosalinde and all that had happened recently. Taking a sip of champagne Dominic leaned back in his chair, looking totally relaxed in the unfamiliar surroundings. She was struck by how different he and Nicolai were; whereas Dominic was easy going and relaxed, Nicolai was withdrawn and mysterious. Damn Nicolai, she suddenly felt angry, he always seemed to infiltrate her thoughts these days. Even when she was with another man.

'What's up?' Dominic's friendly tone cut through her black mood.

He patted his knee invitingly, 'Come, sit on my knee little girl and tell Uncle Dominic all about it.'

Laughing, she shook her head, choosing to sit opposite him instead but close enough so that their knees touched. She couldn't tell Dominic the real reason so she improvised.

'I've got husband troubles.' Noting the way Dominic immediately looked around in alarm she laughed, 'Don't panic, perhaps I should have said ex-husband.'

'Phew, Karin,' Dominic wiped imaginary beads of sweat from his brow, 'you could give a man a heart attack you know.'

'Yes, I know,' Karin smirked, grateful that Dominic had a superb talent for making her feel glad to be a woman.

Dominic immediately understood, 'You can say that again.' Appraising her thoughtfully, he added, 'You're looking good Karin, are you sure you don't want to sit on my knee?'

She was very tempted but all the events that had taken place during the past couple of days were causing havoc with her emotions. Improvising wildly, she explained to Dominic that her ex-husband was causing her some problems. She didn't feel very convincing but he was nodding, for once looking extremely serious.

'I know what you're going through, my wife and I spit up two years ago and the wounds are only just starting to heal now.'

Karin was surprised, he seemed so happy go lucky all the time that she never suspected there was a more sober, wiser side to this man. She realised that despite her new-found experience she still had a lot to learn, especially the lesson that would teach her to regard men as people first and sex machines second, or even third. Sympathetically, she put out her hand, touching Dominic gently on the thigh. It was not meant as a sexual gesture but Dominic immediately grabbed her wrist and placed her hand over his crotch.

'Dominic, please,' she felt slightly irritated, 'I was trying to demonstrate a little compassion.'

Dominic grinned, mischievously, 'I know Karin but I can get that sort of understanding from my mother.'

'You're incorrigible Dominic, d'you know that?' She looked squarely at him, laughter in her eyes.

He decided right there and then that she was beautiful and was about to tell her so when they were interrupted by the sound of the telephone ringing. Karin jumped up to answer it but Dominic stopped her.

'That'll be Karl looking for me. Tell him I've already left and am on my way back, will you?'

Minutes later Karin returned, grinning broadly, 'You were right it was Karl but he wasn't fooled, he said that he knows you're still here and to get your arse back pronto.' She laughed, 'He's a hard taskmaster isn't he?'

Dominic nodded wearily, then a grin spread over his face, 'Sod Karl, let me take you out to lunch Karin, then perhaps we could go out to a club tonight or something?'

'I'd like that Dominic, very much.'

'Great, I'll ring Karl and square it with him,' he stood up and followed her eyes as she glanced in the direction of the telephone.

'By the way,' said Karin as he picked up the receiver, 'who did you just sell one of your cars to? If it was someone local I might know the lucky ba . . . so and so,' she amended hastily.

'He's not that local but you are good friends with his wife and you met him at Silverstone, he placed the order while he was there. Nicolai Andreas?'

'Of course, I remember,' Karin smiled shakily at Dominic.

It was strange, but despite everything that had happened between them the mere mention of his name still made her quiver with excitement. Thankfully, Dominic appeared not to notice and was soon otherwise engaged, trying to convince Karl that he could manage without him for the day.

'I'll go and get changed.'

She was speaking to herself, Dominic did not look up as Karin left the room and made her way upstairs thoughtfully – for a few moments she had managed to forget all about Rosalinde and Nicolai, now it all came flooding back into her mind.

Dominic led her to the passenger side of a black Cobra. Immediately her mind conjured up an image of Nicolai behind the wheel of his new car, she had to admit the style of car suited him perfectly.

As they pulled away from the kerb Karin smiled up at Dominic's handsome, smiling profile, 'Where are we going?'

Without taking his eyes off the road Dominic put out a hand and squeezed her thigh, 'Trust me, I know this great little place, it's not far from here.'

He smiled an open, easy smile that started her stomach quivering. My God, she thought, amazed at herself, after all I've been through lately I'm still as horny as hell? She smiled back in what she hoped was a slightly seductive manner, filled with the promise of delights yet to come. The sexual tension was now evident between them and it was with a slight feeling of regret that Dominic pulled into a side street and parked the car. He leaned over her, ostensibly to help her with her seat-belt. His nearness felt incredibly arousing and she inhaled deeply, enjoying the familiarity of his scent in her nostrils.

He murmured softly in her ear, 'We're here.'

Karin looked around, her anticipation turning to dread, of all the restaurants that swelled the city streets the one he chose had to be none other than the same bistro where she and Nicolai had dined. She should have known things were running too smoothly.

'Dominic,' she hesitated, fervently hoping he wouldn't make the situation any worse, 'do you think we could go somewhere else to eat?'

His suprise was obvious, 'But this is a great place Karin, I can really recommend it.'

Not interested in her arguments, he was already halfway out of the car. She sighed, if she stuck to her guns they would probably end up having an argument. The best thing she could do, she reasoned, would be to eat and run, literally. There was no way she could sit comfortably with Dominic and make small talk while the spectre of Nicolai hung over them. Taking a deep breath she opened the car door and joined him on the pavement. Once inside the restaurant she felt less apprehensive, the waiter seated them at a table upstairs where it was more spacious and less romantic – she and Nicolai had always sat downstairs where it was more intimate – making it seem as though they were in a completely different place.

The only vaguely awkward moment was when the waiter approached them and, turning to Karin, said how nice it was to see her there again so soon. Dominic looked a little surprised but didn't say anything. Annoyed with herself, she wondered why she was so apprehensive, she had every right to go there with another man if she wanted. The problem was, Nicolai wasn't just any man, he was, well . . . he was Nicolai. Oh, no, there was Nicolai!

She didn't want to believe her own eyes but it was true, he had obviously come upstairs to use the men's lavatory. She tried in vain to hide behind her menu.

'Karin, darling, how lovely to see you again,' the voice was unmistakable.

Looking up slowly she blushed, 'Oh, Nicolai what a pleasant surprise.' She knew full well that her innocent act convinced neither of the men.

Dominic spoke, 'It's nice to see you again Mr Andreas.'

His tone was calm and friendly but Karin knew him well enough to detect a distinct edge of annoyance. Never having known Dominic to be in anything less than high spirits she prayed that he wouldn't turn all macho and cause a scene. The two men chatted for a while and tried to include her in their conversation but she kept her eyes cast downwards hardly daring to look at either of them.

'I didn't realise you and Mr Andreas were also old friends,' Dominic's voice sounded strangely stuffy as he extended a hand reluctantly towards Nicolai who was proffering his own to signal his departure.

The two men shook hands briefly, then Nicolai turned to Karin, his seductive eyes forcing her to look up at him. 'I am dining with Rakel, she is going back to Sweden tomorrow, perhaps you would like to stop by our table and say goodbye.'

Karin nodded, not trusting herself to speak. Whereas Dominic had earlier caused small sparks of desire to ignite within her, Nicolai instantly turned her insides into a raging inferno.

Nicolai smiled, satisfied and, after giving Dominic a

curt nod, turned on his heel and weaved his way confidently through the tightly packed tables to the staircase. She followed Nicolai's retreating figure with her eyes until he had completely disappeared down the staircase then turned her attention back to the menu, hoping that by concentrating on the choice of dishes she could stop her heart from hammering so hard in her chest. The waiter appeared once again and took their orders, a distinctly chilly atmosphere had settled over their table and she shivered, holding her breath in anticipation of the comment that Dominic was bound to make sooner or later. It came as soon as the waiter was out of earshot.

'One of your other boyfriends I presume?'

'Hardly, Dominic, his wife is a very good friend of mine.'

She hoped she sounded cool and collected but the very mention of Rosalinde only served to remind her that she no longer knew whether she and the older woman were still friends and that they still had a lot of unfinished business to deal with. She glanced at Dominic, surprisingly he seemed to have accepted her reply at face value and was now scanning the room. Watching his eyes alight on each customer, taking in every detail of their appearance, reminded her of a game she used to play in her mind whenever she went out socially, fantasising about other people's lives, what they were called, where they lived, even trying to guess what food or drink they would order. Obviously Dominic had played the same game as they both started to speak at the same time.

'Have you ever wondered . . .?'

They laughed, the camaraderie breaking the ice between them once again. Karin couldn't help wondering if their relationship would always be like this from now on, two steps forward and one step back, they carried around so much hurt and mistrust from their previous relationships that she wondered if they could ever overcome it. Thankfully, the remainder of their meal was relaxed, enjoyable even. Dominic complimented her on her deep tan and new hairstyle which prompted her to tell him about the beauty salon.

She found it distinctly awkward having to watch what she said to him, there were so many details she had to skirt around. He, in turn, told her what he and Karl had been getting up to, how their business was faring and so forth.

'It sounds as though you've got a great thing going together.'

She was pleased for Dominic but also a little sad for herself, feeling suddenly that everything she thought she could expect from the immediate future had been wiped out in one fell swoop. Feeling suddenly very tired, she pushed back her chair and rose from her seat. 'Do you mind if we skip dessert and coffee?'

'No, not if you want to, are you all right?' Dominic looked genuinely concerned.

'Yes, just a little exhausted with the heat that's all.'

Then she suddenly remembered Rakel. 'Would you excuse me while I just pop downstairs and say goodbye to my friend Rakel, I could meet you down there in a few minutes.'

Without waiting for his answer, she dodged quickly through the tables, almost running down the stairs. As she reached the bottom of the staircase she spotted Rakel's blonde head. She was laughing at something, Nicolai's hand resting on her bare arm. A surge of jealousy coursed through Karin's veins, she wished fervently that she enjoyed the same intimacy with Nicolai that Rakel obviously took for granted. Planting a smile firmly on her lips, she made her way to their table. As soon as she saw her, Rakel beamed, her whole face lighting up.

'Karin, Nicolai told me you was come here but I didn't believe.'

'I'm sorry to hear you're going back to Sweden tomorrow.'

Despite her envy, Karin felt genuinely regretful that she probably wouldn't see Rakel again. She felt Nicolai's eyes upon her but didn't trust herself to return his gaze.

Rakel stood up. 'Please excuse, I must the loo be using.' Then she turned to Karin, 'Will you come with me Karin, I would like to have talk to you in secret?'

Rakel smile apologetically at Nicolai, who merely nodded.

'Don't mind me, girls, three's company and all that.'

Karin swallowed hard, she hoped talking was all Rakel wanted to do, she didn't feel in the mood for a lesbian scene in the middle of the restaurant, although, she thought with a giggle, it would certainly be an eye opener for Dominic who still thought of her as being very naïve. Nodding to Nicolai, Karin followed Rakel through the restaurant noting how all the other men in the place seemed hypnotised, their eyes locked firmly on Rakel's taut buttocks as she undulated around the tables. Once inside the lavatory, Rakel locked herself inside one cubicle and Karin in the other. A few seconds later they both emerged, automatically turned to the basins and began washing their hands. Rakel caught Karin's eyes in the mirror.

'He like you, you know.'

Karin didn't trust herself to speak, instead she concentrated a little too hard on scrubbing her spotless fingernails.

Rakel continued. 'Nicolai, he told me he wishes there was not the friendship between you and Rosalinde, then you would not be worrying she is hurt by you and Nicolai having sex.' It was a long sentence for Rakel and she broke off, a look of concentration on her face as she went over her knowledge of English grammar in her head. 'That was not good English, no?'

Karin was contrite, she had just let Rakel struggle on without even having the decency to reply. The truth was though, she was shocked and excited by what Rakel had just told her, obviously the girl still believed that there was something going on between Nicolai and Rosalinde. The possibility that perhaps Rakel was right was something that Karin was not prepared to consider right now. Like Rakel, she chose her words carefully.

'I like Nicolai too but, well, I would feel disloyal to Rosalinde, do you know what I mean?'

Rakel nodded, 'She is your friend, you don't want to hurt her. I understand but she and Nicolai they just have sex, it's not a, a . . . big deal to either of them.'

Just then they were interrupted by a waitress as she popped her head around the door.

'There are two gentlemen out here who are wondering if you two have drowned.'

Karin and Rakel both laughed, 'Please tell them we'll be right out.'

Karin turned back to Rakel, 'Thanks Rakel, I know what I must do now.'

Rakel smiled back, 'Write to me, let me be knowing what happens. Nicolai, he has my address in Sweden.'

She reached forward, clasping Karin to her in a hug. Karin returned the embrace, there were no sexual overtones, it felt comforting, they had a genuine understanding based on mutual experience and friendship, anything else that had occurred between them was relegated firmly to the past. Arm in arm they went back into the restaurant, enjoying the different expressions on the faces of the two men as they each saw something different in the two women walking towards them.

Chapter Thirteen

For a split second Karin couldn't remember which man she was with. Automatically focusing her attention upon Nicolai as she re-entered the main body of the restaurant then remembering, almost with a jolt of disappointment, that the man who stood beside him was in fact her escort for the day. Quickly, she switched her smile to Dominic instead.

She needn't have worried, his gaze bypassed her completely, totally encompassing the devastating figure of Rakel. Finally, Karin had to nudge him on the arm to gain his attention.

'Dominic, I'd like you meet a very good friend of mine, Rakel um . . .' she suddenly realised that she didn't even know the Swedish woman's surname.

'Andersson,' Rakel filled in for her, extending her hand graciously towards Dominic.

He grasped it, open mouthed, like a drowning man. Karin was amazed by his reaction, he was usually so sure of himself, so laid back, yet it was the second time that day she'd seen him lose his cool completely. She decided this new, more human side of him was very endearing. Nicolai had remained silent during this exchange, his face impassive. Now he spoke.

'I think we should be going Rakel.'

Seemingly reluctant, Rakel let go of Dominic's hand then, turning to Karin, she embraced her again.

'Do not be a stranger Karin, we are friends forever, yes?'

Karin nodded, feeling tears welling up inside her, she swallowed hard, wondering if she could trust herself to speak but Rakel was already half-way out of the door, beaming happily and waving goodbye. Nicolai did not smile as they left and Karin couldn't help wondering if what Rakel had told her was entirely true, or if she had simply misunderstood Nicolai's true feelings. Well, it was too late to worry about it now, they were gone and she still had Dominic and the rest of the day and evening to look forward to.

The poignant end to their meal had left her feeling jittery. As she arrived home Karin walked straight into the sitting room and poured herself a large gin and tonic. Dominic followed her warily, obviously still a little confused about the relationship between Karin and the people they had met in the restaurant. The atmosphere had certainly been highly charged but he wasn't sure whether he should press her for an explanation. Karin sat down heavily on the sofa and waved her hand dismissively at the array of bottles.

'Help yourself.'

He wavered, 'I shouldn't really, I'm driving remember?'

Karin glanced at him indifferently, 'Please yourself,' then realising with a pang that she was behaving very unfairly to the person who least deserved such treatment, allowed her face to soften into a smile for the first time in hours.

'We could always find something else to do instead.' She hoped she sounded provocative and was rewarded by the expression on Dominic's face.

He poured himself a glass of plain tonic water and sat down next to her, 'I really enjoy your company Karin, I just want you to know that.'

'Mmm, sorry, what did you say?' She was back to thinking about Nicolai again.

He stroked her arm lightly, trying to regain her attention, 'Your friend Rakel seemed very nice.'

Even in her distracted state Karin could recognise a gross understatement when she heard one. She threw back her head and laughed. 'Don't even think about it, she eats men like you for breakfast.'

She blushed as she experienced a sudden flashback to Rakel *eating* her. She wondered how Dominic would react if she told him about her experiences with Rakel and Gloria. To the best of her knowledge the idea of two or more women making it together was most men's favourite fantasy.

'I can understand why Nicolai Andreas would feel tempted by her, although his wife is gorgeous too.'

'His wife! Oh you mean Rosalinde?' Karin had forgotten that Dominic didn't know that the Andreas' marriage was a hoax.

Dominic looked a little confused, 'Of course. Why, does he have a harem then?'

'In his dreams,' Karin muttered under her breath. Then aloud she said, 'Why don't we go upstairs and make ourselves more comfortable, Dominic?'

As usual, Dominic didn't need to be asked twice although Karin felt slightly guilty, as though she was using him in some way. Half-way up the stairs she thought, 'What the hell, Dominic is a good lover and at least with him there are no third, or even fourth parties to come between us; no secrets or lies surrounding our relationship. And there was still the fact that she enjoyed sex with Dominic. In truth she was feeling more than a little frustrated, particularly so since her most recent unconsummated encounter with Nicolai and the memories evoked by her contact with Rakel. Nor had she been able to foget her first encounter with Nicolai in the ladies lavoratory at the bistro. Just remembering the sensation of his urgent hands upon her burning flesh turned her legs to jelly.

As she lay on the bed, kissing Dominic passionately, their clothes a distant memory, she became guiltily aware that on this occasion she *was* using him and in the worst way possible, as a substitute for the *real thing* – Nicolai. This she knew now beyond a shadow of a doubt. The sparks of desire igniting within her were not being lit by his touch but by the recollection of another man, another time. Everything that had happened to her during that special evening at Nicolai's house now seemed remote, a series of disjointed incidents which had no bearing on her current life. At one time she had firmly believed that she and Nicolai were destined to come together eventually, to be joined in a magical union of minds and bodies. Laying there, in the arms of a different lover, she felt an overwhelming sadness that it was merely hope that kept her feelings for Nicolai alive, not reality.

Forcing her mind back to the present she concentrated on putting on a good performance for Dominic, going through the motions in mindless cordiality. Stroking his erection, making the right noises as he rubbed her clitoris and probed her vagina. Soon it would all be over and they would get dressed and go out somewhere, she pretending to enjoy herself, desperate to be able to forget everything at least for a few hours. With renewed optimism she manoeuvred herself around so that she could suck Dominic's penis.

Encouraged by the first stirrings of genuine enjoyment since they'd started making love that afternoon, she clamped her lips firmly around the smooth head of his cock, taking in as much of him as she possibly could, whilst at the same time massaging his testicles with feverish hands. In some ways, his touch upon her body felt comforting rather than mind-blowingly exciting, although that in itself was arousing as far as she was concerned. Although they had only known each other for a little over a week, Dominic and she had made love a number of times and, being a quick and very willing learner, it was getting to the stage where he knew her body better than any other man, even her ex-husband, and therefore knew how best to please her.

It was exciting to realise that if she could reach this stage so quickly with a man, the possibilities for her future sexual enjoyment were as numerous as she chose to make them. Dominic had come to know one side of her but there were already others, both men and women, who had opened up other parts of her body and soul. Doubtless there would be different lovers in the future, divergent personalities who could help her expand the various facets of her inner self. Once again she felt liberated by her own thoughts, encouraged that every day she learned something new about herself and the people around her. Now it was time to stop thinking and start enjoying what she was doing and the person she was doing it with.

Relaxing instantly, Karin allowed herself to be carried away on a wave of pleasure, her thoughts nothing more than an occasional dip into her memory banks to retrieve useful fragments of fantasy and experience to heighten the sensations that were assailing her limply acquiescent body. Her swollen, pulsating vulva was reaping the benefits of Dominic's gratitude for an explosive orgasm, brought about entirely by Karin's expertise at sucking his cock. Unhesitatingly, he buried his head between her legs, teasing her mercilessly with his tongue and lips, demonstrating an expertise that had not been honed upon *her* pliant flesh.

Briefly, she wondered how many women he had actually bedded and then an image so clear and detailed that it seemed almost real flashed through her fevered mind. She was back in the mirror room but this time it was Dominic, not Jon, who lay prostrate under Rakel's pounding hips.

'Aaahh, oohhh, oh my God!' She exploded suddenly with an orgasm so intense she almost blacked out.

With barely concealed satisfaction, Dominic raised his head and grinned smugly. A feeble smile flickered across Karin's face, 'Take me Dominic, do it now.'

He didn't need to be asked twice, already firm again he plunged his penis deep inside her, making her wince as the tip nudged against her cervix. She had forgotten how generously endowed her lover was. Summoning up a burst of energy, she rolled him over onto his back, her vagina still maintaining a firm grip on his erection. Triumphantly, she sat astride him, this was also something new to their standard love-making routine. Gently she raised and lowered herself, making sure that he did not penetrate her too deeply by grasping the bottom of his shaft in one hand.

Staring deep into his eyes and, noting how a look of surprise and undisguised pleasure had overtaken his determined expression, she deliberately rubbed her breasts with her free hand, licking her lips as she tugged at each nipple in turn and rolled them between her thumb and forefinger. Without taking her eyes from his face she raised her hand to her mouth, flicked out her tongue and lapped against each finger, making sure each was well coated with saliva before thrusting them between her legs, stroking them up and down between her swollen labia. Deliberately, she moved her hips, delighting in his changing expressions and the erogenous feeling of power that this position evoked in her.

Her excitement was building fast, every drop of blood, every ounce of kinetic energy had gathered within the narrow framework of her pelvis forming a powerhouse of tumultuous motion. Writhing, grinding, rocking, impaled on a throbbing shaft of volcanic ecstasy, she rode his immobilised cock in a frenzy of wild abandon. She didn't notice when or how he came; at that moment he was irrevelant to her as long as his erection lasted. There was nothing cosy or familiar about this act, it was not love-making, she was using him as a sex instrument, a convenient means to achieve physical gratification. Perhaps one day in the future she would come to the conclusion that there would never be anything particularly cerebral between them and that would signify the end of their relationship for once and for all. But for now he had a cock, a tongue, a pair of hands and that was sufficient, it was all she needed from him.

Rendered insensible by the violence of their orgasms they lay side by side; together, yet apart. Eventually they fell asleep that way, neither having the energy nor the inclination to attempt to make smalltalk.

When Karin awoke, an hour or so later, she felt more like her old self. She smiled contentedly at Dominic's still sleeping form, admiring the beauty of his lightly tanned body as he lay on his stomach, naked except for the crisp, white cotton sheet which covered the lower part of his slightly splayed legs. Without pausing to think about what she was doing she picked up the telephone and dialled Rosalinde's number. Madge answered, Mr Andreas was away on business, no she didn't know for how long. Mrs Andreas was not coming back to the house, she was sorry but she didn't wish to discuss her employers on the telephone. Karin thanked her and rang off. Damn, she should never have done that, now everything that had happened was fresh in her mind again.

For another hour she sat sipping a fresh drink, contemplating Dominic as he slept. She wanted to confide in him but didn't know how he would react to her story, particularly the part where they had all watched the video film of herself with Jon, or her session with Rakel and Gloria. Nor was she sure if it was ethical to tell anyone about the diamond smuggling while the perpetrators were still awaiting trial. In the end, although she was longing to unburden herself, she decided it was best to say nothing for the time being.

All her cares were pushed to the deepest recesses of her mind as, later that evening, she and Dominic sat side by side, nursing drinks as they watched groups of young teenagers bump and grind their way around the postage-stamp sized space the night-club owners laughingly called a dance-floor.

'I feel old,' groaned Dominic, as a young lad about the same age as Karin's son, Chris, back-flipped past their table.

Karin laughed, 'You feel okay to me.'

Removing her hand from his crotch, with a look of mock disdain Dominic said, 'You only want me for my body, I'm just a cheap plaything to you.'

Nodding cheekily, Karin replaced her hand, allowing it to rest lightly, possessively on his bulge. No one could see, it was much too dark in the club. She thought about the remainder of the night that was yet to come. No doubt Dominic would take her home and they would make passionate love until the dawn broke. She sighed, contented, it was a wonderful existence but it couldn't go on forever, her children were due home the following week.

Determined not to waste any more time when she could be at home in bed with Dominic, she reached down beside her for her handbag.

'Take me home please, Dominic, before I fall asleep on you.'

Despite all that she had experienced recently she still didn't feel confident enough to tell Dominic outright that she wanted to go home and have sex with him.

Dominic immediately leaped to his feet, his expression aghast, 'Don't you dare woman, I need you . . . Now!'

Thinking he was joking, as usual, Karin started to laugh then screamed with horror as he picked her up and flung her over his shoulder. To the amusement of the other revellers he carried her through the club, looking for all the world like a modern-day Tarzan with his Jane. Once they were outside on the pavement, Karin began beating him on the back with her fists.

'For God's sake put me down Dominic, people are looking.'

Indeed, several people had stopped to stare at them and it didn't help that there was a taxi rank outside the club. Several of the drivers' heads appeared through their cab windows, cheering loudly.

'Go on my son, give her one for me!'

Red as a beetroot, Karin buried her face in his jacket,

he obviously had no intention of putting her down just yet. With a determined, 'Right', he tightened his grip on her and started walking purposefully down the street. Where on earth were they going? They rounded a corner and then another until they found themselves at the rear of the night-club. The alleyway was narrow, dark and totally deserted. As he set her down gently, her stiletto-clad feet struggling to balance on the uneven cobblestones, Karin caught the glint in Dominic's eye.

'Oh no, Dominic you can't be serious, not here?' She felt horrified yet at the same time extremely aroused: someone could come across them at any minute.

Dominic tore at her blouse, exposing her breasts to the cool night air. A sharp breeze tugged at her nipples like icy fingers. Feeling weak at the knees, she fumbled with the zipper on his trousers. It was stiff and her hands were trembling with lust.

'Here, let me.' Dominic released the zipper allowing his pulsating cock to leap into her waiting hands.

Massaging it rhythmically, she felt it throb and grow releasing a small spurt of semen. In one swift movement, Dominic pulled down her tights and panties. Kicking off her shoes as he did so Karin allowed him to drag them off her legs. Hiking up her skirt, she exposed her body to him, feeling the cold, unyielding roughness of the wall against her naked buttocks. It was a little awkward but he managed to lift her up, raising her until her vagina was directly over his rock hard penis. With a wriggle and a downward thrust she enveloped him, allowing him to thrust into her as her bottom grazed the hard brick.

It was the most wonderful, exhilarating experience and she felt liberated by it. Heedless of the possibility that a complete stranger could round the corner at any moment she allowed herself to enjoy the moment, to take things as they came. Gripping Dominic by his hair she rubbed her breasts against his face, feeling the stubble on his chin graze her sensitive skin with delicious harshness. A chilly breeze swirled around her exposed skin, drying her juices immediately on contact and caressing her burning vulva, it was a welcome relief, the places where their bodies came into contact were warm, tropically moist with perspiration and desire.

They came simultaneously; he with a few shallow thrusts followed by a protracted groan; she with a fiery intensity that sapped her strength leaving her legs weak and shaking. Sated, they leaned against the wall, waiting for their energy to return and their hearts and breathing to slow down to a normal rate. The sound of footsteps in the not too remote distance prompted them into a flurry of enforced activity, Dominic hastily zipping his fly whilst Karin retrieved her tights and panties, stuffing them into her handbag. Grabbing her by the hand Dominic pulled her to him, and kissed her deeply until the interloper passed them by.

Laughing until tears ran down their faces they rounded the corner to the high street. Karin flatly refused to brazen out her return in the face of knowing winks and nods from the taxi drivers. Instead, she stood on the pavement shivering until Dominic pulled up alongside her, this time in a dark green Cobra. Snuggling into the welcoming softness of the leather passenger seat, she smiled to herself, life was good, very good and, if she did but know it, it would get even better.

Karin was in the bath when the doorbell rang early the following morning, she heard Dominic's feet on the stairs and then voices in the hallway. In no time Dominic was standing in front of her, his face like thunder.

'It's your friend's husband, Nicolai Andreas.'

Trembling violently Karin stepped out of the bath, pulling her bathrobe around her shivering body and knotting it securely. Dominic was still hovering by the door, an unfathomable expression on his face.

'Tell him I'll be down in a minute,' she whispered urgently. 'Show him into the sitting room and offer him a cup of tea or something. Please,' she added as an afterthought.

'Okay,' Dominic's tone was surly.

After a few seconds Karin could hear Dominic's usual cheerful tones, interspersed with Nicolai's voice, deep, dark and as smooth as silk. They were talking about Cobras, Dominic's other favourite subject. She leaned against the wall, trying in vain to steady her nerves, it had been less than twenty-four hours since their last meeting, yet it felt like years. She had intended to try calling him again as soon as Dominic had left. Apart from anything else she was anxious to speak to Rosalinde, to hear her side of the story. Taking a deep breath she opened the door to the sitting room. Pausing for a moment in the doorway she couldn't help admiring his physique, even standing with his back to her as he was now she still found him incredibly attractive. Her heart hammering against her ribs, she cleared her throat.

'Nicolai, what a pleasant suprise.'

Her breath caught as he turned to her, as always his seductive expression instantly reminding her what it meant to be a woman. Her legs felt weak with renewed desire. Carefully, she sat down in the nearest armchair, drawing her bathrobe tighter around herself. Despite the thick terry-cotton, she felt as though Nicolai's eyes had stripped her naked.

'You look lovely as ever, Karin.'

His voice was like silk, caressing her in an all too familiar way. Karin shrugged, trying to appear nonchalant, particularly as Dominic was regarding the pair of them with an unfathomable expression.

'What brings you here Nicolai?'

'I'll come straight to the point,' he sat down opposite her, leaning forward intently as he spoke.

'Rosalinde has asked to see you.'

At his words, all the breath left her body. At last! She had begun to think that her *friend* no longer wanted anything to do with her. Unable to find her voice, Karin concentrated on stirring the tea that Dominic had made. With a supreme effort she turned casually to face Nicolai, her eyes instantly drowning in his.

'Milk and sugar?'

Smiling, he accepted her offer of both, taking the opportunity to cast his eyes into the deep vee of her neckline as she bent forward to pour first the milk and then the tea. Glancing at him, she immediately looked down, blushing hard. Some things never change, she thought to herself, overcome by an intense feeling of relief mixed with desire. She formed her words carefully.

'How is Rosalinde, what happened to her?'

'She's okay, at the moment she's putting the finishing touches to her case against the smugglers.'

'So the trial hasn't started yet. When do you think it will take place?'

Nicolai sighed, stirring his tea slowly, 'Who can tell, the wheels of justice grind slowly Karin.'

He paused, sipping the strong brew, then continued, 'She's already given evidence at a sort of pre-trial and bail was refused, since then she's been staying at a hotel near Winchester where the actual trial will take place.'

There was a lull in the conversation and Dominic cleared his throat. Karin started in surprise, she had forgotten that he was there. She glanced at him but he was staring out of the window, apparently ignoring her conversation with Nicolai. No doubt he would have a lot of questions for her as soon as Nicolai left. Oh well, it would be a relief to finally get everything out in the open. After a few minutes, during which she and Nicolai sipped their tea in silence, she plucked up the courage to ask the big question that had been plaguing her ever since she had found out about Rosalinde and the diamond smuggling.

'Nicolai, tell me honestly, will I have to testify in court?'

With a huge sigh of relief she watched as he shook his head, 'I don't think that's likely. All the witnesses have already been questioned, if you haven't heard anything by now I doubt if you'll be called to give evidence.'

He looked at his watch, 'Nevertheless, we should perhaps go over your version of events just in case. Could you manage lunch?'

Her heart leaped, then sank again almost as quickly, – she had forgotten about Dominic.

'We haven't . . . no,' she emphasised the *we* but Dominic turned to face her, shaking his head.

'Don't bother to include me in your plans, I have to get back to the workshop or Karl will send out tracker dogs or something.'

To Karin's intense relief his tone was light, perhaps Nicolai had said something to reassure him before she entered the room. Nicolai stood up and held out his hand to Dominic.

'It was nice to meet you again and, by the way, the car is going like a dream.'

Dominic smiled a genuine smile and shook Nicolai's hand enthusiastically, a positive remark about one of his cars was the best compliment he could receive.

'I'm really pleased you said that, but,' he added, 'if you ever need any advice or anything please don't hesitate to call either myself or Karl.' He withdrew a business card from his wallet and handed it to Nicolai. Then he turned to Karin and brushed her cheek with his lips.

'I have to go now but I'll ring you soon. You were fantastic last night by the way.'

Karin blushed hotly, noticing the way Nicolai glanced at her, intrigued. Desperate to put some distance between herself and Nicolai, she made for the doorway.

'I'll see you out, Dominic.'

Nicolai was talking to someone on his mobile telephone when she returned. With a satisfied smile he concluded the conversation and looked across at her as she entered the room.

'I just spoke to Madge, she's going to rustle up one of her delicious lunches for us. Today we dine *Chez* Andreas.'

Happiness welled up in her, as did the certainty that now Nicolai was back in her life things would soon start to look up. She left Nicolai to make a few business calls, while she scampered up the stairs to her room to get dressed.

At Karin's insistence she followed Nicolai in her own car. The route was achingly familiar and, quite naturally, she found herself remembering her previous visits to the house and recalling odd fragments of the long conversations she and Rosalinde had enjoyed. It seemed strange to be going there as Nicolai's guest and even stranger to know that Rosalinde would not be waiting for her when she arrived. As she pulled into the long driveway her gaze took in the the full, impressive length of the house with its towering, ivy-clad walls, as though she were seeing it again for the very first time.

'Oh Nicolai, I'd forgotten how fantastic this house is.'

Without waiting for his invitation she walked through the open front door into the vast hallway. Nicolai smiled as he watched her, Karin noticed his look and began to apologise but he stopped her, pressing his fingers to her lips.

'It's okay Karin, you've probably spent more time at this house in the past couple of weeks than I have.' Then he added, 'I'd forgotten how fantastic you are.'

Briefly he brushed his lips against hers then, before she had time to respond either way, took her by the hand and led her into the dining room where the long, polished table was set for lunch. With a slight pang Karin noticed that there were not two but three place-settings convivially arranged at one end. Nicolai noticed her expression but offered no explanation, preferring instead to concentrate on opening a bottle of champagne. Smiling, Karin accepted a glass of the effervescent liquid, then walked over to the window, looking thoughtfully out across the well-tended lawns. So much had happened there, so much had passed between them, perhaps it was too late to go back, too late for her and Nicolai?

As if he could read her mind, Nicolai asked her, 'Are you looking forward to seeing Rosalinde again after all that has happened?'

Nervously twisting the stem of the delicate tulip-shaped glass between her fingers, Karin glanced down at her hands. 'I honestly don't know.' She looked at Nicolai imploringly, 'Do you think things could ever be the same between us, I can't help wondering if Rosalinde would have been so friendly towards me if she hadn't had an ulterior motive?'

'Of course she would Karin, she really liked . . . likes you,' Nicolai spoke softly.

'Have you . . . have you been down to see her yourself?'

She couldn't help wondering whether the strange relationship between Rosalinde and Nicolai would also continue now they were no longer forced to be together. He looked embarrassed.

'Yes, I have.' He put up a hand to silence her, 'I know, I was determined that I wouldn't but what can I say? I'm a weak man.'

Karin laughed then, 'Oh come off it Nicolai, anyway, I'm glad you didn't just drop her after all you've been through together.'

He smiled back, the tension between them thankfully broken. Suddenly remembering the third place setting Karin said. 'By the way, are you expecting another guest?'

As if in answer to her question someone rang the bell at the front door and a few seconds later Madge ushered a short, balding gentleman into the room.

Chapter Fourteen

There was something vaguely familiar about the visitor that Karin couldn't quite put her finger upon. Unnerved by the way the man looked her up and down, Karin turned away from him and stared pointedly at Nicolai until he took the hint.

'Karin, I'd like you to meet Rosalinde's immediate superior and the officer in charge of the diamond smuggling investigation, Chief Superintendent Ramsey.'

Again, the name rang a bell in the dim recesses of her memory but she still couldn't recall when and where they had met before until he actually spoke, his voice surprisingly loud and deep for such a nondescript looking person.

'The young lady and I have already met, a dinner party at my home, do you recall my dear?'

Of course, it all came back to her now, Inspector Maddison had taken her there and spent all evening with his hands up her dress, albeit very discreetly. She blushed at the memory, amazed at the way her stomach instantly tightened and embarrassed at the rush of moisture which soaked the crotch of her panties. Finding it difficult to speak she shook the Chief Superintendent's proffered hand and nodded with an expression on her face that she hoped would pass for a polite smile.

'I'm sorry, I didn't recognise you without your clothes on, I mean your uniform . . .' she blushed wildly and groped around for something sensible to say but the Chief Superintendent put up a hand to silence her.

'Believe me, you are not the first person who has ever said that to me and I daresay you won't be the last.'

He didn't smile as he spoke but his voice was softer, less authoritarian and at least it seemed her *faux pas* had broken the ice somewhat. Nicolai poured a drink for the 'super', as he insisted they both call him, and then suggested that they all sat down and enjoyed their lunch. The conversation was, not unnaturally, mainly centred on the diamond smuggling investigation and the forthcoming trial. Nicolai mentioned that Karin hadn't actually been issued with a summons to testify in court. The super frowned.

'You are bound to receive some notification soon, I have no doubt you will be called to attend the trial although whether you will actually be called to give evidence is debatable.'

Karin suppressed a groan, her children were due to return home in the next week or so and she didn't really want to be put in the position of asking Colin if he could look after both of them. When the super left the room to use the bathroom she broached the subject of Rosalinde again.

'Whatever happens, I would like to see Rosalinde very much. How quickly do you think you could arrange it?'

'I'm not sure, it may take a couple of days but, rest assured, I will call you as soon as I have any news.'

There was one major question at the forefront of her mind and she couldn't put off asking him any longer. 'I don't suppose . . .?'

She didn't really like asking him but the prospect of visiting an unfamiliar area alone, and in such difficult circumstances, bothered her more than she cared to admit, even to herself. Reading her mind, Nicolai nodded.

'Of course I will go with you, if that is what you wish.'

When the chief superintendent returned he made it

quite clear that he had private business to discuss with Nicolai and that Karin was an unwelcome intruder. Quick to take the hint she made her excuses and, regretfully, prepared to leave despite her longing to stay in Nicolai's presence. On the drive home she hugged the knowledge that Nicolai would soon be calling her about visiting Rosalinde around herself like a comforting blanket, she couldn't bear the prospect of not seeing him again. Despite the fact that she had only just left him she already felt her body yearning to be near him once again.

As it turned out Karin didn't have to wait all that long before she saw Nicolai again. As she stood on her front doorstep, juggling the bags of shopping that she'd bought on the way home to cheer herself up, an elderly neighbour came bustling up her garden path, she bore an ominous looking envelope.

'Oh, I'm so glad I've caught you at long last,' the woman held out the envelope, 'the postman delivered this to me by mistake over a week ago, I knew it must be important because I had to sign for it.'

Karin fought hard to quell the mixed feelings of annoyance and panic that welled up inside her. Forcing her lips into a smile she thanked her neighbour and accepted the belated communication. Of course it was the thing she most dreaded, a summons. She looked at the date – she was due to appear in court less than a week's time! Without further hesitation she went inside and called Nicolai.

He arrived to collect her the day before the trial, as usual looking every bit as sleek and expensive as the car he drove. He had promised her that he would make an open ended booking for them at a hotel near the court and, bearing this in mind, she had packed with extreme care, making sure that she included plenty of seductive underwear. He hadn't actually mentioned whether he would reserve a double room for them, or two singles, but either way she was determined that this time she would not let him get away.

It was another blisteringly hot day and, conscious of the fact that they would be travelling for some distance and in a convertible, she had deliberately chosen to wear as little clothing as possible, making sure she covered her whole body liberally with protective sun lotion. Consequently, she literally slid into the passenger seat, every curve enhanced by the sheen left by the barrier cream. Her appearance didn't go unnoticed by Nicolai, a sharp intake of breath indicating his true feelings although he said nothing other than a curt, 'hello'.

Satisfied for now by his reaction Karin merely smiled. If he wanted to continue to play games with her then she was quite prepared to fight dirty. With a careless wriggle she allowed her legs to part slightly, her wrap-over skirt automatically falling open to reveal the full length of her glistening, lightly tanned legs. Nicolai pretended not to notice but, after they had driven a few miles further he allowed his left hand to rest lightly on her thigh. Without taking his eyes off the road ahead, his fingers tormented her trembling flesh, first stroking then kneading until all her senses were concentrated on that single, intoxicated portion of her body.

After a couple of hours driving this way, Nicolai pulled into a garage.

'I need to use the lavatory and make some phone calls,' he explained.

They walked across the wide expanse of forecourt to the service station, the pair of them automatically parting to avail themselves of the separate facilities. As soon as she had locked herself inside the ladies lavatory, Karin removed her bra and panties and tucked them discretely into the side pocket of her tote bag. As she stepped outside a light breeze stirred the hem of her skirt, threatening to lift it and expose her naked sex to any passerby. The very thought gave her such a thrill that she almost came on the spot. Almost immediately, the breeze died away and, on trembling legs, she made her way back to the comparative safety of Nicolai's car.

Nicolai hadn't yet returned, she could see him some

distance away talking on his mobile telephone. Karin looked around her. Parked some way from the actual service station yet quite a distance from the road, the car was relatively secluded. Desperate for some relief from the sexual tension Nicolai's caresses had created, she surreptitiously slipped a hand between her legs. Thanks to the coating of sun lotion, her fingers slid easily between her labia and over her clitoris. Unsure of how much time she had available to her, Karin rubbed frantically, her unusual situation providing all the outside stimulus she needed to rapidly achieve a satisfying orgasm.

She opened her eyes to find Nicolai staring at her, an unfathomable expression on his face. Acutely embarrassed but determined not to give him the satisfaction of knowing the way she felt, Karin nonchalantly removed her hand and tucked her skirt around her legs demurely before giving him a satisfied smile. 'All finished?'

'I could ask you the same,' Nicolai glanced down at her lap and then looked straight at her face which, despite her determination to the contrary, was beginning to turn very pink.

Without saying another word he walked around to the driver's side of the car and climbed in beside her. As soon as they were out on the open road he again took his left hand off the steering wheel, although this time he placed it firmly between her legs, his expert fingers insinuating themselves between her labia and deep into the moist recesses of her vagina.

The whole situation seemed to her so highly erotic that she might die from the sheer pleasure of it. There she was, speeding along the open highway in highly charged luxury, her hair streaming out behind her, her nostrils filled with the seductive aromas of expensive leather and her own arousal, her legs parted as wide as the dimensions of the Cobra would allow and the gorgeous, seductive Nicolai beside her, his hand creating sexual havoc with the most sensitive parts of her body. It was too much for any woman to bear. With an explosive force that she felt could have so easily ripped her apart, she came, her wild screams carried away on the slipstream.

They drove straight to the court where they literally bumped into Rosalinde just as she was leaving. 'You look like shit darling.'

Karin laughed, weak with relief that Rosalinde had not changed in the slightest. She glanced down at herself, her scant clothes crumpled and stained with perspiration and probably other unmentionable secretions. Rosalinde was taking her by the arm.

'My hotel is just around the corner, we'll be more comfortable talking there.' She looked at Nicolai, who for once looked uncertain. 'Would you like to accompany us, you're quite welcome although I must admit girl's talk is not quite so much fun when there's a man around.'

Rosalinde glanced at Karin who nodded her agreement. Nicolai took the hint.

'I have some important calls to make,' he looked directly at Karin, 'our hotel is The Grand, it's a few miles from here but I daresay any taxi driver would know of it. I'll expect you when I see you shall I?'

Karin couldn't tell if he was annoyed, or simply embarrassed to be in the company of herself and Rosalinde now that she knew the truth about them. Whatever Nicolai's feelings, she was dying to talk to Rosalinde and couldn't wait until they were alone.

'Don't worry about me Nicolai, I'll find it,' said Karin.

He gave each of them a curt peck on the cheek, then turned on his heel and walked back up the street towards the car-park. Both women eyed him thoughtfully for a little while then Rosalinde turned to Karin and grabbed her arm again, simultaneously flagging down a taxi, explaining that she'd been on her feet all day and couldn't face even a short walk.

Much to Karin's relief, the camaraderie between them was as strong as ever. Rosalinde briefly explained her part in the investigation, although Karin knew most of the details by now. The big question that remained unanswered as far as she was concerned was did Rosalinde still want to continue a relationship with Nicolai, and if so, what kind of relationship? Finally there was a suitable lull in the conversation and, her heart hammering in her chest, Karin decided to take the bull by the horns.

'What about you and Nicolai?'

Rosalinde shrugged, 'What about Nicolai and I? You know we're not really married, I don't have any claim to him.' She stared hard at Karin. 'If you're asking me for my permission to sleep with him, or my blessing, then please, feel free.'

Aghast at her incisiveness, Karin stared at her. Then, with a sinking feeling that quickly turned to one of gratitude she understood that Rosalinde had hit the nail squarely on the head, as usual. Even so, Rosalinde and Nicolai had enjoyed a relationship of sorts.

'Nicolai said, well he intimated that . . .' Karin groped around for the right words, blushing and stammering badly, it was only where Nicolai was concerned that she felt so gauche, damn him.

Smiling indulgently, Rosalinde cut across her embarrassment yet again. 'Nicolai said we'd slept together, right?'

Karin nodded, looking down at her hands. Rosalinde paused, choosing her words carefully so that she didn't hurt her friend any more than she had to.

'It's true, we had sex quite a few times and,' she stopped and drew in her breath, wondering if she should continue with what she was about to say, but Karin pressed her.

'Go on.'

'Well,' Rosalinde tossed back her long dark hair and looked Karin squarely in the eye, 'I enjoyed it Karin, I won't deny it and if Nicolai wanted me again I would go to him, but . . .' She noticed the way Karin's lower lip wobbled but carried on without pausing for breath. 'But, I would not want to exclude other men from my life and certainly wouldn't expect Nicolai to be faithful to me.

Apart from any other reason it's just not in his nature – he is not a one woman man,' she added pointedly.

'I wouldn't even count on him being a one woman at a time man,' quipped Karin, managing a small, crooked smile, despite herself.

Her feeble attempt to humour broke the ice between them and suddenly the two women found themselves laughing hysterically until tears rolled down their cheeks. As soon as she could catch her breath, Rosalinde ordered some food and wine from room service and for the rest of the evening she and Karin ate, drank and compared notes on Nicolai. At first they were still a little hesitant with each other, Rosalinde holding back a few details for fear of hurting Karin but as time wore on, their tongues loosened by alcohol and a renewed closeness, she opened up. Similarly, Karin revealed everything that had happened so far: from the first meeting with Nicolai in the café, to Nicolai's disclosure about the video tape, her attempt to retrieve it and her experience with Rakel and Gloria.

Rosalinde seemed particularly intrigued about this particular episode. 'I'm impressed Karin, I thought I was a woman of the world but you are way ahead of me there.' They were laying on their stomachs on the thickly carpeted floor and now Rosalinde edged forward, cupping her chin in her hands, a keen expression on her face.

Karin looked at her askance, 'Aren't you going to ask me?'

'Ask you what?'

'What it was like of course.'

'No, I'm not the slightest bit interested.'

Rosalinde had already proved herself to be a good liar, for the best of reasons, but there was no way she could fool Karin this time.

It was impossible for Karin to explain the difference between making love to a man and making love to a woman, or two women for that matter. In reality she supposed that, just as every man was different in bed, so was every woman. Nevertheless, Rosalinde wouldn't let her off that lightly and pressed her for all the physical details. As Karin spoke she couldn't help wondering if Rosalinde wanted to sleep with her. Despite the fact that she was a very beautiful woman, there was no way she could think of Rosalinde in a sexual way, they were good friends and that was as far as she wanted their relationship to go. She glanced at the older woman but fortunately she was looking at her watch.

'My God,' gasped Rosalinde, 'do you realise it's past three o'clock, I have to be in court again first thing in the morning?'

They both scrambled to their feet, Karin looking around for her shoes and her bag whilst Rosalinde called the reception desk to order a taxi for her and book an alarm call for herself in a few hours time.

By the time Karin arrived at her own hotel she found Nicolai had indeed booked them separate rooms and had retired hours ago. With a slight feeling of regret she let herself into her empty room and climbed wearily into bed alone.

If Nicolai had been annoyed or disappointed that she had not returned earlier to their hotel he showed no sign of it the following morning, greeting her arrival in the dining room with an easy smile.

'We have a couple of hours to kill before we're due in court,' he told her, 'so if you want a leisurely breakfast you are in luck.'

In truth the last thing she felt like doing was eating, a dreadful combination of nervousness at being alone in a hotel with Nicolai and the prospect of appearing in court, not to mention the copious amount of wine she had imbibed the previous evening, conspired to make her feel more than a little queasy. Nevertheless, after forcing down a slice of toast and several cups of strong coffee she felt much better and decided to while away the time browsing in the hotel's many boutiques.

When Karin announed her intention, Nicolai ordered a fresh pot of coffee and then settled down on one of the comfortable sofas which the hotel had strategically arranged in small, intimate groups, throughout the vast lobby. He picked up a newspaper.

'Shopping is not really interesting for me, I'll wait here until you get back.'

Karin browsed around the hotel shops, totally absorbed in the variety of the merchandise on offer, although many of the items were totally impractical and very expensive. Eventually she decided to treat herself to a small compact containing a selection of eye-shadows, lipsticks and blushers, a set of make-up brushes and a roomy cosmetics bag to put them all in. After paying for her purchases she wandered into another boutique to look at the underwear on display. She was just admiring a pure silk camisole with matching panties in a deep violet colour when she sensed someone standing behind her. It was Nicolai of course. As usual, he made her feel gauche and extremely guilty, although she'd done nothing at all to be embarrassed about.

Blushing furiously she turned to him. 'Is it time to leave already?'

'Mmm.'

Nicolai seemed distracted, he fingered the garments in such an intimate way that Karin almost felt as though he were caressing her. Instantly, she imagined herself putting them on for his benefit and then Nicolai removing them again. She felt weak at the thought and put out a hand to steady herself, her fingers coming into contact with the rich textile of Nicolai's suit. Gently he led her from the boutique.

'I think you should have eaten something a little more substantial.'

Karin shook her head. 'I'm okay, it's probably just nerves or the heat or something.'

Apparently satisfied at her explanation, Nicolai walked over to the reception desk to hand in their room keys and speak briefly to the receptionist. Karin eyed the girl's reaction to Nicolai with interest. Wherever he went, women of all types and all ages seemed to fall under his spell, and she was no exception. As he returned to her side Karin impulsively turned and, standing on tiptoe, gave him a long, lingering kiss on the lips. He tasted of richly roasted coffee and smelled deliciously of expensive aftershave, probably Calvin Klein, Karin thought to herself absently as she revelled in the closeness of his body. Reluctantly, she moved away from him and bent to pick up her bag. Quickly stowing her purchases away in its copious interior she followed Nicolai to the car-park.

Almost from the moment they arrived at the courthouse Nicolai disappeared, only reappearing when it was time for lunch. They dined at a local pub, Rosalinde joining them half-way through the main course.

'How's it going?' Karin asked between mouthfuls of prawn salad.

Rosalinde shrugged, 'So, so. I think it's going to drag on for a few more days though, the defence seem to have enough character witnesses lined up to cast a remake of *Ben Hur*.'

They all laughed loudly, attracting a waitress to their table who simultaneously took Rosalinde's order whilst casting longing glances at Nicolai. Karin noticed immediately and moved a little closer to him, her thigh grazing his in a gesture of possessiveness. Nicolai didn't seem to notice either overture, concentrating instead on his plate of cold roast beef, but Rosalinde caught Karin's eye and winked.

'I can't really tell you too much,' she continued as soon as the waitress had left. 'Either one of you may have to go in and testify yet and I wouldn't want them to get off because I've been indiscrete. The less you know, the less chance you have of saying something you shouldn't.'

Despite Rosalinde's warning, neither Karin nor Nicolai were called into the courtroom although they couldn't leave until the judge called a halt for the day. As they walked back to the car together, Karin couldn't help feeling pleased that they would have to return to the court again the following day, that meant she and Nicolai would be together for at least another twenty-four hours. Despite the warmth of the late afternoon she shivered slightly at the prospect of the forthcoming evening, perhaps now she and Nicolai would finally be able to come together, in every possible meaning of the phrase.

Karin could not remember exactly how their argument had started but by the time they reached Nicolai's car she was determined never to speak to him again. She recalled mentioning that she admired Rosalinde's dedication to her career and how she, herself would like to spend the future doing something a little more cerebrally challenging, not to mention financially rewarding, with the remainder of her life. In response Nicolai had delivered a flippant remark to the effect that women should content themselves to striving for perfection in the kitchen and the bedroom. Despite his arrogance, Karin knew very well it was a totally uncharacteristic remark for him to make and probably designed to provoke her, yet her nerves were so strung out that she totally over-reacted.

'You pig,' she spat, 'you total, utter, complete, loathsome pig!'

'Why, whatever is the matter Karin, did I say something to upset you?' there was a distinct trace of laughter in his voice but Karin wasn't joining in.

She shook her head, not trusting herself to even look at him let alone speak. In irritated response he flung open the car door, hardly bothering to wait until she had got herself settled into the passenger seat before slamming it shut. With exaggerated patience, she opened the door again and removed her seat-belt which had become trapped and, her heart in her mouth, she gripped her hands together in her lap as he gunned the powerful vehicle down the straight lengths of road, braking violently at each sharp bend.

At this rate I won't live long enough to have to make

a career decision, she thought ruefully to herself, almost smiling at the irony despite her annoyance.

'Nicolai slow down, please,' she entreated wearily.

'Not until you tell me what's going on with you, I was joking that was all.'

His tone was as fierce as his driving technique. Then, looking at her pinched expression, his voice softened and he eased his foot from the accelerator. They were still driving fast but at least he was now driving safely.

'You sounded to me as though you meant every word,' she wasn't going to let him off that easily, if there was one thing she detested it was chauvinsim. Colin had operated every double standard that had ever been invented, which no doubt was the reason why she reacted so badly to Nicolai's remark.

Apparently not wishing to dignify Karin's claim by responding any further, Nicolai stared straight ahead, concentrating on his driving, and they spent the rest of the journey locked in silent combat. Finally, Nicolai spoke.

'I really did not mean what I said Karin.'

'Mmm,' she wanted desperately to believe him, to laugh it off and put everything right between them again but something indefinable was stopping her. It was as though she was compelled to push their relationship to the limit even though her longing for Nicolai was all-encompassing, almost a physical pain. Nicolai spoke again but this time he miscalculated badly, believing that her non-committal response signified an end to hostilities.

'Once alone in my room we can see how well you perform, then perhaps I'll ask the manager of the hotel to put you to work in the kitchens, we'll soon find out how you measure up in the perfect woman stakes.'

'Right,' Karin screamed, 'that's it, stop the car Nicolai I don't want to spend another minute with you.'

It was a potentially powerful gesture, totally ruined by the fact that they had just pulled up in front of the hotel. Doubly annoyed by this, Karin opened the passenger door before he had a chance to stop completely and half tripped out of the car. Angrily, she stalked up the steps to the hotel, completely oblivious to Nicolai's expression. She expected that he was creased up with laughter, whereas, if she had bothered to look back, she would have seen that he was completely baffled.

She retrieved her room key from reception, then, without waiting for Nicolai, took the lift straight to the third floor, her door was right next to the double doors and she unlocked it quickly, closing it behind her in relief. She desperately needed to put some space between her and Nicolai before she burned her bridges completely. It was true, she was angry, desperately so, but at the same time she knew she was being unnecessarily hard on Nicolai. Nevertheless, she was shocked at his flippancy, it had been totally unwarranted and she despised him for it.

Buoyed by her renewed feelings of loathing for Nicolai Andreas, she reached for the telephone, pausing only to reach inside her handbag for the souvenir pen which bore the telephone number of Dominic's workshop. Her call was answered on the fourth ring.

'AC Coachworks, Karl speaking.'

He sounded so normal and so friendly that Karin had difficulty finding her voice, feeling extremely close to tears.

'Hi Karl,' she tried to sound bright, 'is Dominic around?'

He recognised her voice immediately, 'Oh, hi Karin. No I'm sorry he isn't, is it important?'

'Yes,' Karin wanted to say, 'help me I'm drowning.' Instead she said, 'Will he be long, can you ask him to call me back?'

'Only if you don't mind waiting a week,' Karl's voice was regretful, then he added, 'he's at a motor fair in Germany, no doubt he's fondling a *Fräulein* as we speak.' He laughed, then, when Karin didn't respond, realised that he had said the wrong thing. 'I'm sorry Karin, I wasn't thinking.'

'No, that's okay, Karl, Dominic's a free agent he can see and feel whoever he wants,' she hoped she sounded more convincing than she felt.

'Can I give him a message?' Karl sounded relieved.

'No, don't worry, I'll call him at home next week sometime,' she sounded positive but, in reality, the following week seemed an awfully long way off.

'Okay, take care of yourself Karin, we'll have to all go out together for a drink sometime,' Karl added as an afterthought.

She agreed, although she didn't think it very likely. From time to time Karl had hinted that he would like to re-enact their threesome but she wasn't keen to repeat the experience, preferring her regular one-on-one sessions with Dominic. She replaced the receiver thoughtfully, there was Dominic half-way across Europe, footloose and fancy free, having a great time. And there was she, holed up in the depths of the English countryside with someone she couldn't even bear to look at. There was no doubt about it, she and Dominic were good friends and great lovers but that was it, there would never be anything more to their relationship and, in all honesty, she wouldn't want it any other way.

Eventually, having accepted that thanks to the court case she couldn't just pack her bags and go home, she drifted off into a deep, dreamless, restorative sleep that left her feeling fresh and full of hope for the future. Glancing at her watch, she was surprised to see it was barely six-thirty and even more surprised to discover that she felt ravenous. Her first reaction was to reach for the telephone, intending to call room service but something stopped her. There was no reason why she shouldn't go down to the dining room alone, she wasn't obliged to dine with Nicolai. She didn't owe him anything and he wasn't duty-bound to her, there was absolutely nothing to stop them parting amicably and for good. Resolutely, she pushed away all lustful thoughts and traces of regret, deciding that some things just were not meant to be.

As she walked across the room to the *en-suite* bathroom, she noticed a package on the dressing table. It was a shallow, white box, tied with gold ribbon. There was a card attached, with trembling fingers she ripped open the envelope and stared at the words on the gold-edged card.

'Please wear these for me tonight.'

The card was unsigned but she assumed that the gift was from Nicolai. Tentatively she undid the ribbon and lifted the lid from the box. Nestled inside layer upon layer of tissue paper was the violet silk camisole set that she had been admiring in the hotel's lingerie boutique. Obviously, Nicolai had arranged for its purchase and delivery to her room before they left for the court. She shivered, it suddenly seemed like such a long time ago. Of course there was no way she could accept his gift. Regretfully, she tucked the fine garments back into the tissue paper and replaced the lid on the box, she would take it down to the reception desk and ask the hotel to return it.

She looked at her watch a second time, almost seven, time to get a move on. Thankfully, her bathroom shower boasted a powerful spray and she lathered her body over and over again. Refreshed, she wandered back into the bedroom and the first thing that caught her eye was the gift box. Oh, what the hell, she decided, she would write out a cheque to Nicolai refunding him for the underwear, that way it would be a gift to herself instead. Excitedly, she opened the box once more.

A small shiver of anticipation coursed through her body as the smooth silk of the panties slid up her legs, instantly moulding themselves around her curves like a lover's caress. Next she slipped the camisole over her head, her nipples reacting instantly to the cool silk as it wafted lightly over them. She paused to admire her reflection in the mirror. There was no doubt, the garments looked stunning on her. So much so that it seemed almost a crime to cover them with outer clothing.

She had brought two dresses with her: one, a classic

little black dress, quite stylish but totally un-sexy, the other a rich burgundy wine colour, short, strappy, more suited to a night-club than a hotel dining room. She wavered for just a moment, her 'what the hell' attitude continuing to lead her astray. Quickly she pulled on the burgundy coloured dress, smoothing it over her hips and buttocks, turning this way and that in front of the mirror. Just for a change, she pinned up her hair in a loose top-knot and added a pair of dangly, gold earrings and a thin, gold bracelet. Finally, satisfied with her appearance, she slicked on a final coat of lipstick, checked the contents of her clutch bag and picked up her room key.

She was almost out of the door when she remembered something. Going to her other handbag she took out her cheque-book and pen, wrote out a cheque and sealed it, noteless, in one of the envelopes supplied by the hotel. On the front she simply wrote, N. Andreas. Ignoring the lift, she glided down the staircase, enjoying the looks of admiration she received from some of the other guests, men and women alike. At the reception desk she handed over the envelope and was just enquiring about a table for one in the dining room when she felt Nicolai's hot breath on her neck.

'Is that for me?'

Without waiting for her answer, he reached around her and took possession of the envelope. Opening it quickly he let the cheque flutter onto the reception desk. He smoothed it out and raised an eyebrow quizzically.

'What's this for, services un-rendered?'

Blatantly ignoring his sarcasm, she turned to him, a false smile stuck firmly to her lips. 'It's for the underwear actually, I wish to keep it but not as a gift from you.'

'Fine.' He turned to the receptionist, treating her to one of his most seductive smiles, 'Do you have any tables free for dinner?'

Karin experienced a brief stab of jealousy as the girl almost wilted under his gaze.

'Would that be a table for two, sir?' She looked equally enviously at Karin.

'One,' Karin interjected quickly, 'I shall be dining alone.'

She couldn't trust herself to look at Nicolai, although his voice sounded perfectly calm and unconcerned when he spoke.

'The lady is quite right, we would each like a table for one, unless . . .' he allowed his finger to trail down the receptionist's neck and throat, stopping just short of the swell of her breasts. She and Karin both gasped simultaneously but not with the same provocation.

'I'm sorry, sir,' the receptionist simpered, 'I just came on duty I'm afraid, my shift doesn't finish until three o'clock.'

'Perhaps I shall still be awake at three,' Nicolai murmured suggestively.

Karin coughed and Nicolai immediately looked sideways at her.

'Perhaps you could kindly stop harassing the hotel staff long enough for me to get my table,' she said, with as much dignity as she could muster.

The receptionist was immediately apologetic, in a flutter of seating plans and booking forms she allocated a table to Karin and one to Nicolai. Fortunately, as far as Karin was concerned, they were quite a distance apart. The receptionist hit the bell on the counter with the palm of her hand, the sharp 'ping' summoned a bell-boy.

'Please show these guests to tables twelve and eighteen,' she ordered.

Karin thought her officious tone was doubtless meant to impress Nicolai, if so she would not be disappointed by his nod and smile of *gratitude*. God, he makes me sick, she thought for the umpteenth time since she first met him. All eyes turned to look at them as they entered the dining room, indeed they made a stunning couple – if only they had been a couple. Nicolai, tall, dark, distinguished and evidently wealthy. She, a curvaceous, attractive blonde, who was clearly 'happy in her own skin'. A couple of waiters immediately came up to them, relieving the bell-boy of his charges. One of them, the most attractive man in the room according to Karin's brief recce, took complete charge of her, guiding her by the elbow to her table, making sure she was seated comfortably, and so forth. As he left her perusing the extensive menu, she couldn't help smiling secretively. To hell with Nicolai, perhaps an uncomplicated one-night stand with a good-looking waiter would turn out to be the perfect antidote to her complex love life.

Chapter Fifteen

Glancing across the room at Nicolai's table it gave her great satisfaction to note that he was glowering, although he had no claims on her and she had no interest in him. At least that was supposed to be the situation. A few minutes later the waiter returned to take her order for an aperitif, he was more than simply good-looking she decided, watching him weave his way confidently through the tables, with his wavy blond hair and golden tan he was downright gorgeous. And quite the opposite of Nicolai, although she didn't care to admit to herself that the reason for her sudden attraction to the waiter was somehow tied to her anger with her erstwhile companion. After some deliberation she chose a medium priced bottle of white wine.

'An excellent choice, madam,' the waiter sounded sincere but Karin was not fooled, certain he must say the same thing to all his lady diners.

As he poured the wine his sleeve brushed against her breast, immediately she blushed feeling the hateful glow spread quickly over her cheeks, throat and chest. She fanned herself with her napkin. The waiter was quick to notice.

'Are you too warm, madam, would you prefer a table by the window?'

'No, really, I'm okay.'

She cleared her throat, praying hard for the blush to subside. It wasn't only the top half of her that was on fire, as soon as he had touched her a small glow had started up in the pit of her stomach. Shifting slightly in her seat, she crossed her legs, enjoying the way he appraised her.

'I think I'll have the salmon to start and then the chicken with the . . .' she consulted the menu once again, 'with the lemon sauce, and some asparagus.'

Satisfied with her choice, she closed the menu and handed it back to him. On the other side of the room Nicolai was making his selection, she glanced at him then looked away staring instead at a couple, probably well into their sixties, holding hands and generally acting like a couple of teenagers on a first date. Karin envied them, wondering if they had married young, or if it was their second, or even third time around. Wistfully, she let her eyes drift across all the tables, everywhere she looked were couples, the only two people in the entire dining room who were on their own were herself and Nicolai.

The waiter caught her eye as she was looking around and, assuming that she wanted something else, made his way quickly to her table. He stood, looking at her expectantly, pencil poised over pad.

'Is there something else you require, madam?'

She was about to say no when a thought occurred to her. 'Are you very busy at the moment?'

He shook his head, 'Things don't usually liven up in here before eight-thirty.'

She indicated the chair beside her, 'Could you, I mean, would you like to sit down and just talk to me for a little while?'

His hesitation led her to the conclusion that she had made a big mistake.

'It's okay, I just felt in need of some company that's all.'

He glanced around, everyone was busy eating and

talking, the other waiters were all standing idle by the serving area. As though reaching a momentous snap decision he sat down, his voice a whisper even though they could not be overheard.

'I'm not supposed to fraternise with the guests, even one as gorgeous as you,' he ran his eyes appreciatively over her body, then he added, 'but perhaps you would join me for a drink later, I get off at ten.'

She nodded, 'I'd like that, shall we meet in the bar?'

'No, not here, or I could find myself out of a job.' He thought for a moment, 'There's a little club I go to in town, Quartz, do you know it?'

'No, I don't come from here, remember,' she smiled and took a sip of her wine.

He pretended to slap himself for his stupidity, 'Forgive me, I'm an idiot.'

Karin laughed, 'If you tell me where it is, I'll find it.'

He glanced quickly around again, one of the other waiters was gesturing to him.

'Look, I've got to go,' he stood up hastily, 'just grab a cab and tell the driver the name, they all know it, I'll see you in there at ten-thirty, okay?'

'Okay,' she laughed, eyeing the other waiter who was now mouthing frantically. 'Now go before you get the sack.'

After that exchange the dining room began to fill up rather quickly, barely leaving him time to serve her meal let alone indulge in any further conversation. She had just finished dessert when Nicolai approached her table and sat down uninvited.

'Trying to seduce the hotel staff now are we?'

His tone was sarcastic, tinged with anger and something else that Karin couldn't define, she immediately leaped to her own defence.

'He didn't need any encouragement.'

Like the waiter, Nicolai appraised her entire body with a single sweeping glance. 'That does not surprise me.'

She ignored the compliment, focusing instead on his action. Whereas the waiter's appraisal had been pleasantly flattering, Nicolai's inspired an instant inferno in the pit of her stomach. Not wishing to acknowledge her reaction as anything but overwhelming anger at his cheek, she turned on him.

'You don't own me Nicolai, and anyway, you started it by chatting up the receptionist,' she finished lamely.

Much to her increased annoyance he started to laugh. 'I do believe you are jealous, Karin darling.'

He put out his hand and patted her condescendingly on the knee. She leaped at his touch as though his hand had transmitted a shock; certainly the atmosphere between them was electric. They were interrupted by the arrival of the waiter, who glared threateningly at Nicolai.

'Is this gentleman disturbing you, madam,' he asked solicitously, glaring once again at an amused Nicolai.

Blushing, Karin shook her head, 'No it's all right,' she looked straight at him, steadfastly ignoring her uninvited guest. 'Please bring me the bill.'

Nicolai sighed and stood up, 'I hope you know what you are doing,' was all he said.

It wasn't difficult to find the club. The waiter had been right, as soon as she said the name 'Quartz' the taxi driver nodded and pulled away from the front of the hotel. Although she had assumed the hotel was deep in the middle of the countryside, it only took ten minutes for the taxi to reach the town centre. After driving for a few minutes around some back streets, the driver stopped outside a small building sandwiched between the rear of a department store and a factory. At first glance the club appeared deserted, tentatively she pulled the door handle and was immediately taken aback by the bright lights and the noise coming from the interior.

A doorman dressed in a tuxedo waved her past him, pointing her in the direction of a steep staircase. Below her feet the floor shook to the 'boom, boom' rhythm of the music and her nostrils were assauled by the acrid smell of cigarette smoke, cannabis and other substances that were beyond the realm of her experience.

Cautiously picking her way down the staircase, her eyes gradually became accustomed to the strange lighting. Below her people were dancing, crushed together yet moving in unison as though riding the crests of many waves. To her right was a long bar lit with pink and green neon lights. As soon as she reached the bottom of the stairs she headed in that direction, grateful that there was a stool free for her to sit on. She ordered a gin and tonic then started to survey the crowd, occasionally glancing towards the staircase to spot her *date* when he arrived.

With a feeling of trepidation she realised that not only was she in a strange place, surrounded by strange people but she was waiting to meet someone with whom she hadn't even exchanged names. Suddenly she felt home-sick, or to be more precise, she found herself longing for Nicolai. She was just about to turn tail and run when she noticed her waiter had arrived. Standing at the top of the staircase he looked around for a few seconds before his eyes alighted on her. Her heart began to hammer in her chest as he smiled and waved. Feebly, she waved back and within seconds he was at her side, ordering a drink for himself and asking her if she would like another. She shook her head, the last thing she wanted was to get drunk and lose control of the situation. Ignoring her pro-tests, he passed her glass to the barman then asked her, in a necessarily loud voice, if she would like to dance.

He took her hand to help her down from the high bar-stool, keeping a firm grip on her as they wended their way through the crowded dance floor until they found a few square inches they could make their own. Abruptly, the frantic music changed to a slow ballad and he automatically enfolded her in his arms. Whisper-ing into her hair, he asked her name. She moved her head back, looking into his face.

'Karin, with an "eye en", what's yours?'

She felt like a teenager as he replied that his name was Barry and proceeded to run through the ritual gamut of questions: where do you live? are you single? have you any children? She sensed he was impressed when she said her son was almost seventeen.

'You hardly look old enough to be a mum at all, let alone have a son that old.'

She grinned to herself, it was an old line but she didn't think she would ever tire of hearing it.

'What about you?' she asked him.

He said he was thirty-three, divorced, no kids and planned to open his own restaurant one day in the not too distant future. 'I've learned all I need to know, now it's just a question of getting the financing together,' he looked at her thoughtfully. 'I don't suppose you would consider backing me?'

Karin laughed, 'If you wanted a rich divorcee then you're barking up the wrong tree, I haven't got two pennies to rub together.'

He shrugged, 'Never mind it was worth a try, want another drink?'

A table had become vacant next to the dance floor, Barry guided her over to it.

'Sit down and I'll get our drinks from the bar.'

She peered at her watch, it was eleven-thirty. Glancing around she noticed a distinct change in the clientele, the younger contingent seemed to have left, making way for an older, more distinguished collection of pin-stripe suited businessmen and just a few, much younger women. Obviously paid escorts, thought Karin. The music changed too, now it was less disco, more Motown. Several of the men swayed laconically around the dance floor, dutifully groping their bored looking partners, no doubt so they could convince themselves the following day that they had enjoyed a great evening.

She looked at Barry and then nodded in the direction of the dance floor. 'I hope, come the morning, they think it was worth the expense.'

She was surprised by Barry's reaction to her innocent comment. 'Why wouldn't they, those girls know what they're doing and so do their punters,' his face was deadly serious.

She put up her hand in mock self defence, 'Okay, Barry, I didn't mean anything by it.'

Nervously, she sipped her drink and for the second time that evening wished she was at home, or back at the hotel with Nicolai. Better the devil you know, she mused to herself. She took another sip of her drink. Despite the heavy meal she had enjoyed at the hotel the alcohol was beginning to affect her, she felt a little woozy and didn't protest when Barry put his arm around her waist, his thumb just grazing the underside of her breast. Without warning the atmosphere inside the club changed again, the lights becoming much dimmer and the music fading away almost to nothingness. As though at some unseen command, the people who were dancing returned to their seats and anyone who could moved to a table closer to the dance floor.

At that point the lights went out completely, through the pitch-black came the sound of heavy rock music then, to Karin's surprise, a spotlight shone down on the dance floor, picking out the figure of a muscular black girl wearing a minute bikini. For several minutes she posed and flexed her muscles, squeezing and releasing her buttocks within inches of Karin and Barry. To Karin's shocked surprise Barry reached out and tucked a five pound note in the cleft between the girl's buttocks and, as she worked her way around the perimeter of the dance floor, several other men followed suit.

The music changed abruptly and with it came a change of performer, or rather an addition. A young red-haired girl, barely older than Natalie, Karin thought to herself in dismay, also began to bump and grind her way around the floor. She was wearing a white corset, stockings and suspenders. Her small breasts jutting out from the lacy quarter cups as though they were being served to the audience on two plates, the white skin translucent under the harsh glare of the spotlight. At the top of her thighs a neatly trimmed triangle of pubic hair was clearly visible. Despite her automatically programmed feelings of repulsion, Karin felt herself becoming warm.

She started to rise to her feet but Barry stopped her, pulling her back down onto the seat with slightly more force than was necessary.

'Where do you think you're off to?'

Karin swallowed hard, 'I need to use the bathroom.'

'Oh,' he seemed satisfied with her explanation, 'straight past the bar, first door on the right, you can't miss it.'

She nodded her thanks and wove her way unsteadily through the tightly packed tables, trying her best to avoid the groping fingers of the audience. Once inside the lavatory, she leaned gratefully against the basin, letting the cold water run over her wrists in an effort to sober herself up. She had to get out of the club but the only way out was past the dance floor and up the stairs, Barry would be bound to see her leaving. Hastily, she dried her hands and, with trembling fingers applied a fresh coat of lipstick. Picking up her bag she made a decision, she was leaving now and if Barry didn't like it, well, that was too bad, he could stay in this sleazy place all night for all she cared.

Suddenly, an image of Nicolai flashed through her mind; oh how he would laugh if he saw the predicament she had got herself into now. Except, deep down, she knew he wouldn't laugh, he would be worried about her, concerned for her safety. With a flash of insight she realised that, although not exactly innocent, Nicolai had more morals than many other men and, for the second time that evening, she craved the comfort of his presence.

Opening the door tentatively, she was immediately assailed by the noise and the smoke and the smell of the place. As she neared the dance floor she saw the two girls, black skin entwined with white, having sex in front of the leering faces of about forty men. Crude taunts and jibes emanated from their foul mouths. Disgusted, Karin made for the stairs, trying hard not to look anywhere other than straight ahead. Just as her hand touched the banister she felt Barry's breath scald her neck as he whispered harshly in her ear.

'What the hell do you think you're doing?'

Although shaking with fear she turned on him angrily. 'I know exactly what I'm doing, I'm leaving.'

'That's what you think,' he grabbed roughly at her arm but she shook him off.

In a fit of blind fury she swung around and jabbed her knee firmly in his groin. With a yell he bent over double, automatically releasing his grip on her. Without pausing for thought, Karin ran up the staircase, flung open the door and dashed out into the street. Fortunately, a row of taxis were waiting to be hired. She gave the name of her hotel to the driver of the taxi nearest to her and climbed in gratefully but, before she had chance to shut the door Barry was forcing his way inside the cab. She was in no position to fight him and hoped that he wouldn't try to attack her in the cab. She needn't have worried, on the drive home his charming self returned and he apologised for assuming that she would appreciate the sort of 'entertainment' the club had to offer.

Fighting against an instinctive reaction to apologise for her own behaviour in return she stared out of the window, preferring to ignore him rather than listen to his pathetic excuses. At the hotel he insisted on paying for the taxi and, after a moment's consideration, she decided to let him, stalking up the steps to the hotel entrance without a backward glance. He caught up with her in the lobby.

'Shall we continue our evening in your room?' he murmured suggestively.

'I don't think so, no,' Karin answered frostily, glaring at him with undisguised contempt. 'I'm pretty sure that you and I have nothing in common.'

His friendly façade wavered, 'Don't mess with me Karin,' he warned, taking a threatening step towards her.

She looked around her frantically, the lobby was deserted, even the receptionist was nowhere to be seen. Trying to sound braver than she felt she groped in her handbag for her room key, gratefully her fingers closed around the plastic tag.

'I'm going now,' she stated as firmly as she could.

He blocked her path, 'Correction, we're going now.'

'Correction, you're not going anywhere, the lady is with me.'

Nicolai had appeared from nowhere and now had his arm protectively around Karin's shoulders, her body sagged against his, limp with relief. Before Barry had the opportunity to respond, Nicolai ushered Karin toward the lifts, leaving the waiter staring after them open-mouthed. As soon as the lift door closed, she turned to Nicolai.

'Thank you for that,' she looked down at the floor, choosing her words carefully. 'I also owe you an apology.' He started to interject but she put up her hand to stop him, 'No, really, ever since you made that wise-crack this afternoon I've treated you like dirt and I'm sorry, please forgive me.'

She looked up at his handsome profile, tears pricking her eyelashes. The lift reached their floor with a 'ping' and the door opened. Nicolai guided her out into the hallway and took her key from her. Silently, she followed him until they stood outside her room, he unlocked the door and waited for her to enter. With her heart hammering like a pneumatic drill, her legs like jelly and her mouth as dry as the Sahara desert, she whispered to him almost shyly.

'Would you like to come in?'

'I thought you would never ask,' Nicolai laughed. Scooping her up in his arms he carried her, kicking and laughing over the threshold, dumping her unceremoniously onto the bed. They stopped laughing simultaneously, holding one another's gaze. A silent vow of understanding passed from one to the other, a thousand words unspoken but nothing left unsaid. Wordlessly, she held out her arms to him and he came to her, filling the void within her in a way none of her other lovers had managed to achieve.

Their bodies melted into each other, fitting together in perfect harmony like the parts of a Chinese puzzle. For a long time they merely held each other and kissed, drinking in the taste of one another, luxuriating in the knowledge that, for them, time stood still. There was no need to rush, no temptation to grasp at what lay there for the taking. Night would turn to day, yet the round of pleasure needn't end, only when they had finally had their fill of each other would the scythe of time rend them asunder.

Never had she felt so hot, or so cold, the portions of bare skin reacting to each breath cast upon it with goose-flesh, and a series of shivers running down her spine. Beneath the thin, silky layers of her clothing it was another story, her flesh was fiery, swollen with the heat of passion, her scalding blood coursing through her veins like molten lava, bringing a flush of desire to the fleshy, most sensitive parts of her febrile body.

His hands were the catalyst, manipulating her body with tenderness and strength, introducing her, minute upon minute, to exquisite new sensations, his caresses a symphony of pleasure. Eagerly she opened herself to him, holding nothing back. She had waited a long time for this moment. Upon occasion they had teased each other with the promise of sensual experiences yet to come and aroused one another physically, each pursuing the other with dishonourable intentions, now the time for playing games was past.

His pleasure in her was evident. Like a starving man he seized upon each new portion of her body as it became exposed to him, groaning as he kissed and licked her tormented flesh. She in turn writhed under him, quickly surrendering all attempts to stimulate him as his caresses forced her to submerge beneath the weight of ecstacy. As his fingers sought to penetrate her pulsating flesh, she felt herself drowning, her eyes misting over in a haze of passion.

Finally, he stripped her dress completely from her body revealing the silk underwear beneath. A shiver of anticipation ran through her as he feasted his eyes on her trembling form. The brief garments now clung damply to the curves of her perspiration soaked body, her swollen, elongated nipples outlined prominently through the thin material. He sucked in his breath.

'I knew this would suit you,' Nicolai ran his hands slowly over her breasts and stomach, his voice hoarse with passion.

'Nicolai, about the cheque . . .' Karin wanted to make things completely right between them but he silenced her, pressing his middle finger to her lips. Her clitoris throbbed violently, she could smell herself on him.

'It doesn't matter.'

She opened her mouth slightly. Closing her lips around his finger she sucked hard. He never took his eyes from hers. Reaching downward she undid the belt on his trousers and his fly, immediately her hands were filled with the pulsating energy of his cock. Smiling, she released his finger, sliding down the bed to take his other part of him between her lips. She delighted in his penis, like a young child with lollipop, licking and sucking, teasing the tip then running her tongue down the whole length of his shaft.

Purposefully, she manoeuvred herself around so that her pussy was positioned directly over his face. Briefly, she stopped sucking him, holding her breath until she felt the touch of his fingers between her legs, moving the material of her panties to one side. With immense relief she felt the warmth of his breath on her vagina and the soft wetness of his tongue as it lapped against her clitoris. Overcoming a selfish urge to relinquish her own manipulations of him so that she might concentrate fully on the sensations created by his tongue, she returned to his cock with a vengeance, squeezing his testicles hard and massaging the sensitive area between his scrotum and anus.

After a few seconds he moved his hips violently, his penis fell from her mouth with a 'plop'. She giggled momentarily, her laughter soon turning to moans as she felt an orgasm building within her. Kneading her buttocks with both hands, he continued to lick and suck at her tormented flesh. At first she supported herself on her hands, then gradually gave in to the sensations, sinking downward until her head rested on his knees. Cupping her breasts in her own hands she rubbed the silky material across her swollen nipples, desperate for release of some kind.

When it happened it was neither slowly nor gently but in a torrent, a searing jolt of ecstasy which seemed to rip her apart. Before her climax had a chance to subside she was hit by another bolt of pleasure, and another, it was as though his tongue had found a magic button and he just kept on pressing it. In a frenzy of pleasure she begged him to stop, just for a second of respite, just until she could regain the gift of breathing. But he showed no mercy. Quickly, he pushed her away from him, onto the bed, pulling down her panties and tossing them away in a single, swift execution. Frantically she struggled with the camisole, wrenching it from her body as though it were a bone-crushing serpent.

The blissful sensation of cool air upon her raging skin was all too brief. Soon she was burning up, aching for the satisfaction that only his touch upon her body could bring about. Desperately, she thrust her hips at him, urging him to touch her, take her, eat her, penetrate her, do whatever he wanted to her only, please God, let it be now. He didn't disappoint her, rising up between her trembling legs like a mightly colossus, his cock tantalisingly erect, red and swollen with unrequited passion. He smiled a knowing smile before plunging deep within her, lighting the touch-paper at the very core of her being.

With a scream of pleasure she rose to meet him on the second thrust, throwing her whole body upward and forward, so that she finished the movement in his arms, her painfully swollen breasts seeking solace against his chest. Tearing at his shirt, she pressed the feverish orbs against his naked skin, forcing his hands between them until his expert fingers were crushing her nipples.

Too many forces were at work here now, sensation

heaped upon sensation in a frenzy of disorder. How could she move? How could she not move? She was impaled upon him but it was still not enough. Desperately she thrust her own hand between her legs, furiously rubbing her throbbing vulva. She needed more of him. Writhing and grinding her hips against his she splayed her legs as far apart as they would go. Look at me damn you, she wanted to scream, see yourself, down there between my legs, and tell me how I look to you?

She may have spoken these words aloud, or it might just have been another manifestation of their unspoken understanding but he looked at her, really looked at her. Somehow managing to convey his thoughts in a wordless lyric, expressing the totality of their emotion. At once she felt beautiful, voluptuous, like the most desirable woman on earth and this was what finally shook her to the core.

When morning broke they were surprised to find that they had slept at all. Seemingly, their passion had endured for hours, well past the night until the first traces of dawn's early light pierced the monotony of the ink-black sky. She felt happy, blissfully so, lying there in Nicolai's arms, their legs entwined amongst rumpled sheets. For no apparent reason she suddenly felt sad. Nicolai looked at her, concerned by her pinched expression.

'Everything okay?' he murmured into her hair, seizing the opportunity to inhale the glorious scent of her as he did so.

Karin nodded, then with jolt of surprise she felt a dam burst inside her, it had been a long time in coming. Silently, Nicolai gathered her into his arms and held her there, stroking her hair, waiting for the sobs which wracked her body to subside. Wise as always, Nicolai spoke to her gently but in a matter of fact way.

'This is our first time, not our last, there are no need for tears, Karin.'

She nodded, groping at the side of her for the box of tissues. Patiently, Nicolai handed one to her.

'I know that, well ...' she amended, 'I *hoped* this wouldn't be our only time.' She blew her nose, desperate to find the right words, the last thing she wanted was for Nicolai to feel trapped by her. Sitting up straight on the bed she crossed her legs, yoga-style and looked at him, a serious expression on her face.

'I don't want you to think that I think I have any claims on you. I like you Nicolai, I like you a lot but I don't think I'm in love with you and I certainly don't feel I could pin you down to a serious relationship. Anyway,' she added honestly, 'I've got one or two men friends already and I enjoy sex with them almost as much as I enjoy it with you.'

She took a deep breath, hoping desperately that she hadn't misread the situation and jumped in with both feet. But Nicolai was smiling, looking genuinely relieved.

'I am glad Karin, I didn't want to risk hurting your feelings but I am not the type of man to be faithful, or answerable to anyone else. I would like it if we could be friends, perhaps get together occasionally for a meal and things.'

'I'll certainly look forward to the *things*,' Karin laughed, 'and if we managed to find some time to eat as well then that will be a bonus.'

He held out his arms to her and she snuggled up against him. It had been a strange summer, a time of good and bad experiences and certainly a period of personal growth. In a nutshell she had managed to *find* her true self. She glanced at Nicolai's profile, he really was a handsome man and, under other circumstances, perhaps they could have been soul mates, as it was she would happily settle for being good friends and sometime-lovers.

Smiling down at her he asked her if she was hungry, she nodded eagerly, jumping on him and nibbling his earlobe.

'Do you think you could manage to extend your stay by a few more days once the trial's over?' he said.

'Yes, why did you have something in mind?'
'How does another seventy-two hours of my body grab you?'
'Nicolai, you can grab me anytime you like.'
'Can I hold you to that?'
'Only if you hold me to you first.'
'Okay.'
'Fan . . . tastic!'

NO LADY
Saskia Hope

30 year-old Kate dumps her boyfriend, walks out of her job and sets off in search of sexual adventure. Set against the rugged terrain of the Pyrenees, the love-making is as rough as the landscape. Only a sense of danger can satisfy her longing for erotic encounters beyond the boundaries of ordinary experience.

ISBN 0 352 32857 6

WEB OF DESIRE
Sophie Danson

High-flying executive Marcie is gradually drawn away from the normality of her married life. Strange messages begin to appear on her computer, summoning her to sinister and fetishistic sexual liaisons with strangers whose identity remains secret. She's given glimpses of the world of The Omega Network, where her every desire is known and fulfilled.

ISBN 0 352 32856 8

BLUE HOTEL
Cherri Pickford

Hotelier Ramon can't understand why best-selling author Floy Pennington has come to stay at his quiet hotel in the rural idyll of the English countryside. Her exhibitionist tendencies are driving him crazy, as are her increasingly wanton encounters with the hotel's other guests.

ISBN 0 352 32858 4

CASSANDRA'S CONFLICT
Fredrica Alleyn

Behind the respectable facade of a house in present-day Hampstead lies a world of decadent indulgence and darkly bizarre eroticism. The sternly attractive Baron and his beautiful but cruel wife are playing games with the young Cassandra, employed as a nanny in their sumptuous household. Games where only the Baron knows the rules, and where there can only be one winner.

ISBN 0 352 32859 2

THE CAPTIVE FLESH

Cleo Cordell

Marietta and Claudine, French aristocrats saved from pirates, learn their invitation to stay at the opulent Algerian mansion of their rescuer, Kasim, requires something in return; their complete surrender to the ecstasy of pleasure in pain. Kasim's decadent orgies also require the services of the handsome blonde slave, Gabriel – perfect in his male beauty. Together in their slavery, they savour delights at the depths of shame.

ISBN 0 352 32872 X

PLEASURE HUNT

Sophie Danson

Sexual adventurer Olympia Deschamps is determined to become a member of the Legion D'Amour – the most exclusive society of French libertines who pride themselves on their capacity for limitless erotic pleasure. Set in Paris – Europe's most romantic city – Olympia's sense of unbridled hedonism finds release in an extraordinary variety of libidinous challenges.

ISBN 0 352 32880 0

ODALISQUE

Fleur Reynolds

A tale of family intrigue and depravity set against the glittering backdrop of the designer set. Auralie and Jeanine are cousins, both young, glamorous and wealthy. Catering to the business classes with their design consultancy and exclusive hotel, this facade of respectability conceals a reality of bitter rivalry and unnatural love.

ISBN 0 352 32887 8

OUTLAW LOVER

Saskia Hope

Fee Cambridge lives in an upper level deluxe pleasuredome of technologically advanced comfort. The pirates live in the harsh outer reaches of the decaying 21st century city where lawlessness abounds in a sexual underworld. Bored with her predictable husband and pampered lifestyle, Fee ventures into the wild side of town, finding an urban outlaw who becomes her lover. Leading a double life of piracy and privilege, will her taste for adventure get her too deep into danger?

ISBN 0 352 32909 2

AVALON NIGHTS

Sophie Danson

On a stormy night in Camelot, a shape-shifting sorceress weaves a potent spell. Enthralled by her magical powers, each knight of the Round Table – King Arthur included – must tell the tale of his most lustful conquest. Virtuous knights, brave and true, recount before the gathering ribald deeds more befitting licentious knaves. Before the evening is done, the sorceress must complete a mystic quest for the grail of ultimate pleasure.

ISBN 0 352 32910 6

THE SENSES BEJEWELLED

Cleo Cordell

Willing captives Marietta and Claudine are settling into an opulent life at Kasim's harem. But 18th century Algeria can be a hostile place. When the women are kidnapped by Kasim's sworn enemy, they face indignities that will test the boundaries of erotic experience. Marietta is reunited with her slave lover Gabriel, whose heart she previously broke. Will Kasim win back his cherished concubines? This is the sequel to *The Captive Flesh*.

ISBN 0 352 32904 1

GEMINI HEAT

Portia Da Costa

As the metropolis sizzles in freak early summer temperatures, twin sisters Deana and Delia find themselves cooking up a heatwave of their own. Jackson de Guile, master of power dynamics and wealthy connoisseur of fine things, draws them both into a web of luxuriously decadent debauchery. Sooner or later, one of them has to make a life-changing decision.

ISBN 0 352 32912 2

VIRTUOSO

Katrina Vincenzi

Mika and Serena, darlings of classical music's jet-set, inhabit a world of secluded passion. The reason? Since Mika's tragic accident which put a stop to his meteoric rise to fame as a solo violinist, he cannot face the world, and together they lead a decadent, reclusive existence. But Serena is determined to change things. The potent force of her ravenous sensuality cannot be ignored, as she rekindles Mika's zest for love and life through unexpected means. But together they share a dark secret.

ISBN 0 352 32912 2

MOON OF DESIRE
Sophie Danson

When Soraya Chilton is posted to the ancient and mysterious city of Ragzburg on a mission for the Foreign Office, strange things begin to happen to her. Wild, sexual urges overwhelm her at the coming of each full moon. Will her boyfriend, Anton, be her saviour – or her victim? What price will she have to pay to lift the curse of unquenchable lust that courses through her veins?

ISBN 0 352 32911 4

FIONA'S FATE
Fredrica Alleyn

When Fiona Sheldon is kidnapped by the infamous Trimarchi brothers, along with her friend Bethany, she finds herself acting in ways her husband Duncan would be shocked by. For it is he who owes the brothers money and is more concerned to free his voluptuous mistress than his shy and quiet wife. Alessandro Trimarchi makes full use of this opportunity to discover the true extent of Fiona's suppressed, but powerful, sexuality.

ISBN 0 352 32913 0

HANDMAIDEN OF PALMYRA
Fleur Reynolds

3rd century Palmyra: a lush oasis in the Syrian desert. The beautiful and fiercely independent Samoya takes her place in the temple of Antioch as an apprentice priestess. Decadent bachelor Prince Alif has other plans for her and sends his scheming sister to bring her to his Bacchanalian wedding feast. Embarking on a journey across the desert, Samoya encounters Marcus, the battle-hardened centurion who will unearth the core of her desires and change the course of her destiny.

ISBN 0 352 32919 X

OUTLAW FANTASY
Saskia Hope

For Fee Cambridge, playing with fire had become a full time job. Helping her pirate lover to escape his lawless lifestyle had its rewards as well as its drawbacks. On the outer reaches of the 21st century metropolis the Amazenes are on the prowl; fierce warrior women who have some unfinished business with Fee's lover. Will she be able to stop him straying back to the wrong side of the tracks? This is the sequel to *Outlaw Lover*.

ISBN 0 352 32920 3

Three special, longer length Black Lace summer sizzlers published in June 1994.

THE SILKEN CAGE
Sophie Danson

When University lecturer, Maria Treharne, inherits her aunt's mansion in Cornwall, she finds herself the subject of strange and unexpected attention. Her new dwelling resides on much-prized land; sacred, some would say. Anthony Pendorran has waited a long time for the mistress to arrive at Brackwater Tor. Now she's here, his lust can be quenched as their longing for each other has a hunger beyond the realm of the physical. Using the craft of goddess worship and sexual magnetism, Maria finds allies and foes in this savage and beautiful landscape.

ISBN 0 352 32928 9

RIVER OF SECRETS
Saskia Hope & Georgia Angelis

When intrepid female reporter Sydney Johnson takes over someone else's assignment up the Amazon river, the planned exploration seems straightforward enough. But the crew's photographer seems to be keeping some very shady company and the handsome botanist is proving to be a distraction with a difference. Sydney soon realises this mission to find a lost Inca city has a hidden agenda. Everyone is behaving so strangely, so sexually, and the tropical humidity is reaching fever pitch as if a mysterious force is working its magic over the expedition. Echoing with primeval sounds, the jungle holds both dangers and delights for Sydney in this Indiana Jones-esque story of lust and adventure.

ISBN 0 352 32925 4

VELVET CLAWS
Cleo Cordell

It's the 19th century; a time of exploration and discovery and young, spirited Gwendoline Farnshawe is determined not to be left behind in the parlour when the handsome and celebrated anthropologist, Jonathan Kimberton, is planning his latest expedition to Africa. Rebelling against Victorian society's expectation of a young woman and lured by the mystery and exotic climate of this exciting continent, Gwendoline sets sail with her entourage bound for a land of unknown pleasures.

ISBN 0 352 32926 2

WE NEED YOUR HELP . . .
to plan the future of women's erotic fiction –

– and no stamp required!

Yours are the only opinions that matter.

Black Lace is the first series of books devoted to erotic fiction by women for women.

We intend to keep providing the best-written, sexiest books you can buy. And we'd appreciate your help and valued opinion of the books so far. Tell us what you want to read.

THE BLACK LACE QUESTIONNAIRE

SECTION ONE: ABOUT YOU

1.1 Sex (*we presume you are female, but so as not to discriminate*)
Are you?

Male	☐
Female	☐

1.2 Age

under 21	☐	21–30	☐
31–40	☐	41–50	☐
51–60	☐	over 60	☐

1.3 At what age did you leave full-time education?

still in education	☐	16 or younger	☐
17–19	☐	20 or older	☐

1.4 Occupation ______________________________

1.5 Annual household income

under £10,000	☐	£10–£20,000	☐
£20–£30,000	☐	£30–£40,000	☐
over £40,000	☐		

1.6 We are perfectly happy for you to remain anonymous; but if you would like to receive information on other publications available, please insert your name and address

____

____

____

____

SECTION TWO: ABOUT BUYING BLACK LACE BOOKS

2.1 How did you acquire this copy of *Summer of Enlightenment*?

I bought it myself	☐	My partner bought it	☐
I borrowed/found it	☐		

2.2 How did you find out about Black Lace books?

- I saw them in a shop ☐
- I saw them advertised in a magazine ☐
- I saw the London Underground posters ☐
- I read about them in ______________________
- Other ______________________

2.3 Please tick the following statements you agree with:

- I would be less embarrassed about buying Black Lace books if the cover pictures were less explicit ☐
- I think that in general the pictures on Black Lace books are about right ☐
- I think Black Lace cover pictures should be as explicit as possible ☐

2.4 Would you read a Black Lace book in a public place – on a train for instance?

Yes	☐	No	☐

SECTION THREE: ABOUT THIS BLACK LACE BOOK

3.1 Do you think the sex content in this book is:

Too much	☐	About right	☐
Not enough	☐		

3.2 Do you think the writing style in this book is:

Too unreal/escapist	☐	About right	☐
Too down to earth	☐		

3.3 Do you think the story in this book is:

Too complicated	☐	About right	☐
Too boring/simple	☐		

3.4 Do you think the cover of this book is:

Too explicit	☐	About right	☐
Not explicit enough	☐		

Here's a space for any other comments:

SECTION FOUR: ABOUT OTHER BLACK LACE BOOKS

4.1 How many Black Lace books have you read? ☐

4.2 If more than one, which one did you prefer?

___

4.3 Why?

SECTION FIVE: ABOUT YOUR IDEAL EROTIC NOVEL

We want to publish the books you want to read – so this is your chance to tell us exactly what your ideal erotic novel would be like.

5.1 Using a scale of 1 to 5 (1 = no interest at all, 5 = your ideal), please rate the following possible settings for an erotic novel:

- Medieval/barbarian/sword 'n' sorcery ☐
- Renaissance/Elizabethan/Restoration ☐
- Victorian/Edwardian ☐
- 1920s & 1930s – the Jazz Age ☐
- Present day ☐
- Future/Science Fiction ☐

5.2 Using the same scale of 1 to 5, please rate the following themes you may find in an erotic novel:

- Submissive male/dominant female ☐
- Submissive female/dominant male ☐
- Lesbianism ☐
- Bondage/fetishism ☐
- Romantic love ☐
- Experimental sex e.g. anal/watersports/sex toys ☐
- Gay male sex ☐
- Group sex ☐

Using the same scale of 1 to 5, please rate the following styles in which an erotic novel could be written:

- Realistic, down to earth, set in real life ☐
- Escapist fantasy, but just about believable ☐
- Completely unreal, impressionistic, dreamlike ☐

5.3 Would you prefer your ideal erotic novel to be written from the viewpoint of the main male characters or the main female characters?

- Male ☐ Female ☐
- Both ☐

5.4 What would your ideal Black Lace heroine be like? Tick as many as you like:

Dominant	☐	Glamorous	☐
Extroverted	☐	Contemporary	☐
Independent	☐	Bisexual	☐
Adventurous	☐	Naive	☐
Intellectual	☐	Introverted	☐
Professional	☐	Kinky	☐
Submissive	☐	Anything else?	☐
Ordinary	☐	______________	

5.5 What would your ideal male lead character be like? Again, tick as many as you like:

Rugged	☐		
Athletic	☐	Caring	☐
Sophisticated	☐	Cruel	☐
Retiring	☐	Debonair	☐
Outdoor-type	☐	Naive	☐
Executive-type	☐	Intellectual	☐
Ordinary	☐	Professional	☐
Kinky	☐	Romantic	☐
Hunky	☐		
Sexually dominant	☐	Anything else?	☐
Sexually submissive	☐	______________	

5.6 Is there one particular setting or subject matter that your ideal erotic novel would contain?

____

SECTION SIX: LAST WORDS

6.1 What do you like best about Black Lace books?

____

6.2 What do you most dislike about Black Lace books?

____

6.3 In what way, if any, would you like to change Black Lace covers?

____

6.4 Here's a space for any other comments:

____

____

____

____

Thank you for completing this questionnaire. Now tear it out of the book – carefully! – put it in an envelope and send it to:

Black Lace
FREEPOST
London
W10 5BR

No stamp is required if you are resident in the U.K.